BENEATH
THE WAVES

What Reviewers Say About Ali Vali's Work

Balance of Forces: Toujours Ici

"A stunning addition to the vampire legend, *Balance of Forces: Toujour Ici*, is one that stands apart from the rest."—*Bibliophilic Book Blog*

Carly's Sound

"Vali paints vivid pictures with her words—*Carly's Sound* is a great romance, with some wonderfully hot sex."—*Midwest Book Review*

"It's no surprise that passion is indeed possible a second time around"—*Q Syndicate*

The Devil Inside

"Vali's fluid writing style quickly puts the reader at ease, which makes the story and its characters equally easy to get to know and care about. When you find yourself talking out loud to the characters in a book, you know the work is polished and professional, as well as entertaining."—*Family and Friends Magazine*

"Not only is *The Devil Inside* a ripping mystery, it's also an intimate character study."—*L-Word Literature*

"*The Devil Inside* is the first of what promises to be a very exciting series. …While telling an exciting story that grips the reader, Vali has also fully fleshed out her heroes and villains. *The Devil Inside* is that rarity: a fascinating crime novel which includes a tender love story and leaves the reader with a cliffhanger ending."—*MegaScene*

Visit us at www.boldstrokesbooks.com

By the Author

Carly's Sound

Second Season

Calling the Dead

Blue Skies

Love Match

The Dragon Tree Legacy

The Romance Vote

Girls with Guns

Beneath the Waves

Forces Series

Balance of Forces: Toujours Ici

Battle of Forces: Sera Toujours

The Cain Casey Saga

The Devil Inside

The Devil Unleashed

Deal with the Devil

The Devil Be Damned

The Devil's Orchard

BENEATH THE WAVES

by
Ali Vali

2016

BENEATH THE WAVES
© 2016 By Ali Vali. All Rights Reserved.

ISBN 13: 978-1-62639-609-8

This Trade Paperback Original Is Published By
Bold Strokes Books, Inc.
P.O. Box 249
Valley Falls, NY 12185

First Edition: May 2016

Credits
Editor: Shelley Thrasher
Production Design: Susan Ramundo
Cover Design By Sheri (graphicartist2020@hotmail.com)

Acknowledgments

Thank you first to Radclyffe for your support, advice, and for giving me such a wonderful home with BSB. You, Sandy, and the rest of the team have been supportive and continue to make the process not only fun but flawless.

There are things from my childhood that left an impression that are hard to forget. All those adventure books that fired my imagination made me an avid reader, but the ones that I really loved were any book about Atlantis and the Bermuda Triangle. That there could be a place under the water hidden from us, or a place that held secrets that could make ships disappear without a trace to me were page turners. That's where this book was born all those years ago, so thank you to Radclyffe for allowing me to finally add my tale to those from my childhood.

Thank you to Shelley Thrasher for again making the editing process a great learning experience. Losing about a third of the book because of a bad flash drive a week before my deadline was the type of excitement I don't ever want to repeat, so thanks, Shelley, for making a stressful situation less painful. Your patience, teachings and assistance are always appreciated, but your friendship is what I treasure most.

Thank you to the BSB team who all work so hard to bring every book to print, you guys are the best in the business. Thank you, Sheri, for always finding the right cover for every book, to the other authors who are always there to offer encouragement, and to my beta reader. How lucky I am to have Connie Ward offer her input and humor from the beginning of every book, so thank you for keeping me on track.

Thanks to *you*, the reader. Your support at events and your wonderful emails have meant so much to me. Everything I write is always done with you in mind.

Thirty-one years seems like a long time, but it's gone by in a flash. The loss of my dad this past year was difficult, but C was there to hold my hand not only through the hard times, but through our great adventures. If life is a canvas, mine is full of bright colors and a collage of happy times because of you. The good thing is there is still plenty of painting left to do, so thank you for loving me and making me laugh no matter what. You're my best friend, and I love you. *Verdad!*

Dedication

For C
A lifetime is not enough

And

For my niece and nephew
You make me proud in every way

CHAPTER ONE

"Gods, let me not screw this up," Kai Merlin said as she stood naked staring out into the dark waters outside the glass wall in her room, gripping and relaxing her hands. In the distance she could see the patrol vessels that hovered close by, but still far away enough to ensure privacy.

She was at the eve of the day she'd both looked forward to and dreaded. Leaving the safety of home and her parents made her nervous, though not enough to put it off. She wasn't the first to do this, but she was different, no matter her parents' efforts to raise her with as normal a childhood as they could. Despite that fact, she was under the microscope of a nation.

"One of these days you'll make the front page, if you keep this up," her mother Galen said as she came into view in the reflection, holding up a robe for her.

"Don't give me that," she said as she turned around so Galen could tie the robe closed. "Your consort tells me you're seldom clothed once your day is done, and since you're the one who taught me the wonders of skinny-dipping, I believe her."

"Your mom talks too much."

"And my mama loves her anyway," Kai said as she kissed her mama's forehead before leading her to the sofa behind them. "Will you miss me as much as I will you guys?"

"Don't make me cry since I promised your mom I wouldn't embarrass you by blubbering through this whole thing tomorrow. And yes, terribly, if that was a serious question." Galen rested her head on her shoulder, something Kai remembered doing when she was younger and didn't top her birthmother by nine inches. "I'm your mother and I miss you when you're gone thirty minutes, so this should be pure torture."

"Will I hurt your feelings if I admit how excited I am, even if I'll miss you?"

"I'd be disappointed if you weren't," Galen said as she took her hand.

"So would I," Hadley, her second mother, said from behind them. "We love you, and not a day will go by that we aren't here if you need us, but it's time for you to start down your path."

"You promise to keep this one out of trouble?" she said as she tapped Galen's forehead.

"I'm sure that if the stories of the sirens were true, all of them would look like your mother."

"I might keep my clothes on tonight if you're comparing me to some sea monsters," Galen said, shaking her finger at Hadley.

"They lured unsuspecting seafarers because they were as beautiful as you," Hadley said as she ran her fingers through Galen's light-blond hair.

"Listen well, tadpole," Galen said as she laughed. "This one can talk her way out of anything."

"Well, almost anything. The seafarers didn't realize they were in danger until it was too late," Hadley said, laughing as she threw the bag she'd carried in at Kai. "By the time I woke up from that love stupor you put me in, I was forever wrapped around your little finger."

"Such a complainer you are," Galen said as she accepted Hadley's kiss. "And I had to do everything I could to make sure all those pretty girls that were after you crashed and burned on the rocks."

"You two are going to keep me blushing until I'm ninety," she said when Hadley bent and kissed Galen again.

"You've got more to worry about than that." Hadley ran her hand over Kai's head. "Are you ready?"

She nodded and moved to a chair so her mothers could sit together. "I've planned for months and have been involved in every stage of implementation, so if I forgot anything, it was a committee oversight," she said and smiled. "Is this for me or your siren there?"

"A gift from your mama and me," Hadley said as she pointed to the present. "We want you to look good, but let's go over one more thing before you open it."

"I've already promised to be good."

"You seldom are, so listen," Galen said with a wink. "Tomorrow after the ceremony we'd like to talk to you about something that has to do with your mission."

"What is it?"

"Your mama said tomorrow." Hadley put her hand up to keep her from bugging them anymore.

"You're seriously going to leave me hanging so I won't be able to sleep tonight?" She glanced from Hadley to Galen.

"Open that and it'll ease the pain," Hadley said.

Inside was a new uniform with the insignias of team leader and academy graduate. Once her mission was done, she hoped her uniform would resemble her mother Hadley's and the sleeves would be covered with the history of the missions she'd completed all over the world. For someone who'd married well, her mom had never taken the easy road, and she and her mama had always been proud of her for that.

"You have fulfilled my greatest wish from the day your mama placed you in my arms, and we couldn't be prouder of the woman you've become. The gods gifted us with only one child, and now I know why. No other could've been more perfect for us than you, Kai, and your mother and I love you," Hadley said as she stood up and helped Galen to her feet. "Our future's in good hands."

Kai hugged Hadley first and then comforted a crying Galen, who seemed unable to get any words out. "I might be an only child, but maybe that's a good thing. It would've been hell sharing you two more than I have to already. Thank you for the gift and for everything else."

"Try to get some sleep, since the eyes of the nation will be on you tomorrow," Hadley said as she put her arms around Galen.

"No pressure, Mom, thanks."

"You'll do great." Galen placed her hand on her cheek. "After tomorrow every single and available citizen will want you as much as they do this one." She pointed back to Hadley.

"That's a burden I'm willing to carry," she said, making them all laugh.

❖

"Jesus...Vivien."

Vivien Palmer heard hers and God's name called out sharply, which broke her out of her daydreams. Every man around the large conference table was staring and frowning at her except for her brother Frankie. His smile probably wasn't because of her inattentiveness, but because, like her, he figured the board members present thought she was having a blonde moment. No one except Frankie and her thought these things were less than riveting, so she almost felt the restraint it took Frankie not to laugh.

"I'm sorry, what was the question?" she asked her father, Winston Palmer, who happened to be the guy with the biggest frown.

"What's the estimate for Triton?" he repeated, his lips barely moving because of his clenched teeth.

They stared at each other until her father rolled his eyes and sat, obviously not in the mood to push her in front of an audience waving as if to give her the floor. She wrapped her hand around the carved shell at her throat and prayed for the patience it took her to make it through these board of directors meetings her father insisted she attend. Given a choice, she would've traded the confinement of the teak walls, big leather chairs, and the testosterone-tinged air for digging a ditch in a hurricane.

This was a command performance, though, since she was the most experienced member of upper management on the only subject on the agenda. Triton was the newest production platform in the Palmer Oil Production and Exploration Company's fleet, and it had been her responsibility from the drafting table all the way through the construction and implementation phases. This actually was the first full day she'd put in at the office in months, and if she had her way, it'd be the last for a while.

"The crew's sleeping-quarter modules will ship in about a week, so expect them in place twenty days after that. Everything else looks good for the startup date we're shooting for, but we can't relax yet.

We've passed every test OSHA has thought to throw at us, but we expected that after the Deep Water Horizon disaster. Permitting has become a nightmare, so we can't afford any slipups if we want to expand operations in the outer shelf with the leases we just acquired."

"We have a solid safety record," one of the board members said. "That should count for something, damn it."

"Whatever any of us did before Horizon doesn't matter to the inspectors. Everyone in the Gulf of Mexico has to prove themselves all over again, especially in deep water," she said as Frankie winked at her after clicking through the pictures she'd provided for her presentation. "None of the inspectors wants to be the one explaining how something happened again to CNN and every other news outlet in the world while gruesome pictures of birds play in the background."

"Those news-hound sons of bitches kept showing the same damn birds," another board member said.

"We padded our absolute goal date with a forty-day cushion, and we're well below that, so I wouldn't worry too much about it," Frankie said, as if that fact would calm everyone down. "Vivien always exceeds expectations, and I don't see her coming up short this time."

Frankie, or Franklin Winston Palmer V, as the board referred to him, wore a suit and tie, but Vivien knew the twin to her shell rested at the base of his throat. It was one of the many things they had in common, along with being the two sole heirs to Palmer Oil. Their father was taking his turn at the helm, but their fate as far as he was concerned was to run the company and grow it like every generation of Palmers before them, whether they wanted to or not. On most days she leaned toward the "or not" part of the equation, since her father didn't tolerate any deviation from his carefully plotted plan well.

"Franklin's right. We'll be fine, and they'll back off," Winston said as he stood again. "They know better than anyone how hungry the world is for oil, and Triton's sitting on a shitload of it. If they fail us on anything just to be petty and set us back, there'll be hell to pay."

Her father wasn't allowed near inspectors for a reason, but that didn't stop him from delivering that particular lecture whenever he could when she was within earshot, since she was the one responsible for making them happy with their facilities. To show weakness toward any asshole with a clipboard representing the state or the federal government was tantamount to treason in Winston's worldview.

"The world *is* hungry for oil, but it scares women and children when they see it floating on the surface in big globs because some corporate douche bag wanted to cut corners," she said sweetly, and this time Frankie did laugh.

The vein bulging on her father's forehead made her stop talking, but she did straighten to her full five feet two inches to show she wasn't backing down. She was often described, no matter that it gave her heartburn, as short, cute, and blond, but no roughneck in the Gulf dared fuck with her more than once. She'd earned both the respect and reputation she'd received one confrontation at a time.

"Perhaps we'll invite an expert on manners to our next meeting to discuss what is and isn't appropriate language at board meetings," her father said as most of his cronies nodded. "The floor's open for discussion now that Vivien *is* finished." That was his warning for her to keep her mouth shut, but so did everyone else, so they adjourned earlier than Vivien thought.

"In my office," Winston said before attending to the men who'd lingered.

"You know," Frankie whispered when he rolled his wheelchair next to her, "calling him and these other douche bags out isn't your finest hour."

"A reality check never hurt anyone."

"Uh-huh," he said, and took her hand. "You have some time before you have to report to the principal's office?"

"For you, always."

CHAPTER TWO

Galen sat on her throne and gazed down at Kai, then sighed because their separation would come when this gathering concluded. How had time flown by so fast? However, Kai needed to begin the quest everyone made when they'd come of age. She'd be gone for months, and Galen would see Kai's face only on a screen. Her partner Hadley sat next to her with her hand over hers, undoubtedly having the same thoughts about their daughter, but she looked justifiably proud.

Every child in their realm started school in their third year, and until they were twelve, they learned all their lessons in the classroom. Everyone studied history to better understand what direction their future should take, and all citizens were free to choose what they would dedicate themselves to. Everyone but Kai, and only she and Hadley understood the weight of the expectations of all those people on your head.

Hadley had taken the same approach to parenting her parents had, once Kai learned to walk. That had been a special time for Hadley, and more important than the lessons on how not only to defend herself and the realm was teaching Kai the strategies it would take to do it well.

All those hours with Hadley had given Kai not only a solid foundation but a quick wit that Galen had come to love. Even as a toddler Kai had been fiercely independent, but in the training arena she'd listened and taken all Hadley's instructions seriously. For that reason Hadley had allowed Kai to accompany some of their squads out on patrol from the time she was ten.

Those opportunities had given Kai's independent streak the chance to lead her into trouble at times, but never because of bad intent. Hadley and the other trainers had done a good job of reining Kai in without being harsh, since neither of them could reprimand their daughter for a trait she'd inherited from both of them.

Stubborn determination was as big a part of who Kai was as her broad shoulders, dark hair, and eyes as green as the water on clear days. Though she shared many of their traits, her looks were all Hadley, and Galen had rejoiced in that fact from her birth. Hadley had captured her heart completely from almost their first meeting, and eventually some other lucky soul would experience the same joy with Kai.

"Enough sappy thoughts, my love," she heard Hadley whisper. "Don't keep the tadpole waiting."

She pinched the top of Hadley's hand before smiling at Kai. "What quest have you chosen, team-leader Merlin?"

Kai came closer and dropped to her knees as a sign of respect. She now wore the suit of a warrior, the one they'd gifted her with, but with one small distinction. The triton symbol lying at the center of her throat was gold instead of silver, marking her as royalty. The suit's navy material was thin but protected her from blades, bullets, and a multitude of other threats as well as regulated body temperature in all depths. Like Hadley, Kai looked strong and regal in it.

"Your majesties, I'm headed to the Gulf of Mexico and the waters that drain into it. That part of our world is sick, and it's our responsibility to try to heal it before it's too late."

"It's never too late, child," Oba Rhode said from her position three steps down from the thrones. "History teaches us this, but you've chosen well."

The high priestess and shaman of their realm had chosen the name Oba for the river goddess when she'd taken her vows. She was young, compared to her predecessor, but none of the others had complained when Galen chose her. Oba had a gift rarely seen with their people, and she had greatly helped both her and Hadley since she'd been given the water orb, one of the most treasured relics in their kingdom.

The priestess assigned to the first settlers had brought the orb from their homeland, and only the queen and the high priestess touched it.

It granted the guardian the power to see the future, even if the woman wasn't talented in that area. In Oba, though, the orb had found a true master, who could combine its power with hers so the future became as real and accurate as the present in cases the orb pronounced necessary.

"Thank you," Kai said and nodded slightly in Oba's direction. "I'll do everything in my power to make you proud," she said to her mothers.

"Who'll go with you?" Hadley asked.

"Talia Hessen and Isla Sander have accepted my invitation." Both women, who had watched over Kai for years, stepped closer and dropped to their knees. Their triton spears shone as brightly as Kai's. Each warrior eventually received a silver one that was a replica of the golden triton that belonged to the queen. "While we're on land, Ivan and Ram will guard the outpost we finished last month."

Kai glanced up to the two great whites swimming lazily above the dome where they were gathered. She'd raised the two sharks from infancy, and they shared a spirit bond that allowed them to swim wherever she did. Even at the current depth, they were both fine. No matter where she went, Ivan and Ram would follow and gladly give their lives to keep her safe.

"Rise," Galen said as she and Hadley stood. "As your queen I wish you calm seas and success, but as your mother I pray for your safety. Remember well all your lessons, and never stray too far from the water," Galen said for only Hadley and Kai to hear.

"I won't, Highness, and I promise to be good." Kai smiled up at them, then winked as she climbed up to join them. Only the high council and important guests were present in the throne room, but the proceedings were being broadcast throughout the realm. Usually graduations from their military and science academy were large affairs presided over by her mother Hadley, but like in every important moment of her life, everyone wanted to share her accomplishments. At times she longed for the anonymity of a large crowd.

"Sisters, I vow to protect the realm, the water, and our queen and her consort until my final day." She placed her hand on the golden triton and welcomed the power that coursed through her. This phenomenon occurred only when the rightful heirs to the throne held the ancient object.

"May the gods watch over you," Galen said.

Kai's hand began to glow, and she raised it toward the water above them. "And you, my Queen." The stream of light from her hand went through the glass and lit the ocean around them as it streaked to the surface. The cameras followed it so everyone could see the lightning bolt Kai had produced, proving to their subjects that the next in line would be even more powerful than her mother.

"Long prosper Atlantis," Kai yelled when she lowered her hand and took Galen's as every citizen in attendance and beyond echoed her cry.

❖

Frankie's corner office was a duplicate of Vivien's, though his displayed the treasures she'd found over the years. While she detested spending time in the Palmer Building in downtown New Orleans, Frankie thrived there, especially when it came to the contract negotiations that garnered them the new business that kept her on the water. The Gulf of Mexico's new frontier in oil exploration at the moment was over the outer shelf, and that's where she spent most of her time.

New floating platforms working in sixty-five to twelve thousand feet of water had finally tapped into a reserve, which, by conservative estimates, contained over three hundred years of crude. The water out there was deep blue, and she loved it enough to volunteer for every job that gave her the opportunity to get wet.

Everyone else in the company took one of the seaplanes in their fleet when forced to go, but she always went out in her own boat. The smell of salt and the wind in her hair gave her the freeing experience she'd had as a child when she spent her summers on her grandparents' beach. But as much as she liked being on the water, diving under it was her passion. To her, the depths were like life: they'd give up their secrets a little at a time, but only if you were willing to look.

Frankie had gladly taken the office part of the deal since water terrified him. A birth defect had stolen the use of his legs, and his wheelchair, to him, was the anchor that'd kill him if he ever fell overboard. She'd never been able to convince him otherwise.

Frankie stripped off his tie and shut his door. "You look good."

"Thank you, and thanks for covering for me last week." Her quick trip to the spot off Miami's coast hadn't been successful, but she'd had to chance it after her research into the symbols on their shells had led her to another map. None of them ever provided anything that would satisfy all her questions, but she'd chased down every lead she found. The day she got lazy would be the one on which she'd find the map that would point her to the treasure trove she knew was out there. Nothing she looked for, though, had to do with jewels and gold.

"Did you find anything?"

"Bad weather and high seas. It was weird since the sky was blue two minutes before I geared up. I've seen squalls come up, but this one was ridiculous." She lay on the couch in his office and held his hand when he rolled next to her. "Triton will keep me busy for the rest of the summer, so maybe in the fall I'll give it another shot. If we plan far enough ahead, you can come with me."

"A resort in Miami sounds good, but forget me getting on a boat with you." He laughed and squeezed her fingers. "I know this is a stupid question since you're searching whenever you can, but do you ever think about her?"

Vivien didn't need to ask who "she" was. The pain from what had happened in their childhood had healed but had left a scar that made the incident impossible to forget. Neither of them had been prone to childhood pranks or wild stories, but no one, especially their parents, had believed them.

Frankie had been the only one she'd had back then who didn't think she was completely insane. He'd seen the same thing, and no one had been able to make him change his story, not even after the forced therapy sessions they'd both been subjected to.

"I shouldn't, after all the hell we've been through, but I do—all the time. It's like an old news reel that plays in my mind even when I want to forget sometimes."

June 1994

"Throw it, sister, and you'll get a treasure." Five-year-old Frankie mangled the pronunciation of the word treasure, but his older sister Vivien understood him perfectly.

The prized sea shell she'd found would be a great addition to her collection, but she'd toss it back because Frankie had asked. He'd taken to heart the old fairy tale their mother told every time they visited their grandparents at their beach house in Key Largo, Florida. Ever since he was old enough to understand, he'd caused her to lose a number of great finds.

"If the sea gives you a treasure, throw it back," their mother Cornelia said every night as she tucked them into her old bedroom on the third floor with its two walls of windows overlooking the water. "It'll give you something even more precious in return."

"This one's really pretty, Frankie." The small conch shell was golden with dark-brown spots and pink around the edges. "Maybe it's the reward for all the other ones we threw back."

"No," Franklin said, and slammed his hands on his wheelchair. "Throw it, Mom said."

She studied it one last time, then lifted it to her ear to hear the shell's memory of the ocean. Frankie smiled when she held it to his ear as well before she hurled it as hard as she could. Her lost treasure sailed past the breaking surf, and she figured it was lost forever. Right before it hit the water, though, a hand broke the surface and caught it.

Both of them stared as the shell moved closer, but whoever held it didn't raise their head above the water until they reached the part of the beach where the waves broke. The girl who emerged appeared slightly older than Vivien's ten years, and she'd never seen a suit like the one the girl wore. Her navy-blue, almost short wetsuit, with an intricate design at the chest, appeared to fit like a second skin.

"Is something wrong with it?" the stranger asked as she held up the small shell between her thumb and index finger. "Little guy didn't make it, but keeping this honors his memory."

"Sorry, I didn't know you were out there," Vivien said. Why was this great swimmer making clicking noises with her tongue? As different and interesting as this girl seemed, she couldn't help but concentrate on the two large fins that appeared offshore, not that far out. Whatever species of sharks they belonged to had to be massive. She might've not been that old, but she'd never seen anything like them during her visits.

"So…why'd you throw it back?"

"My mom said so," Franklin said, appearing frustrated that he couldn't move closer. "We'll get a better treasure if we do."

"I've never heard that one, but maybe she's right." The girl closed her fist over the shell and waved before running back into the waves.

"Wait!" Vivien yelled, panicked because of the two circling sharks still close by. "Come back, you'll get hurt."

She moved into the water but only to her ankles, afraid to go any farther. The fins were gone, but so was the stranger, and she hoped something horrific hadn't happened to her. Whoever it was hadn't surfaced anywhere yet, so she turned and ran for the house.

"Wait for me, Frankie. I'm going for help. Keep your eyes on the water and see if you spot her."

The coast guard slowly patrolled from their pier in both directions for a few hours after their call but didn't find anything. They'd come to make sure, but no one believed Vivien's story even though Frankie vouched for her. Her parents hadn't severely punished them, but she could tell they weren't pleased. Frankie was still too young to blame, so most of her father's displeasure had landed on her shoulders.

"Anyone who sends the coast guard on wild-goose chases because of a fish story sometimes gets into big trouble," their father had said as they went to bed that night. "Do anything like that again and I promise you'll be sorry." Their mother had skipped storytime as she followed their father out. And they'd had to stay inside for the next three days.

"We weren't lying, sister," Frankie whispered into the darkness.

She could hear the waves crashing outside, the surf stirred up by the summer storm raging about a mile out. Thinking about someone she didn't know being killed that way made her sad and angry that no one had taken her seriously. Maybe the girl's parents were searching for her and would never know what happened—ever. Like those lost kids on milk cartons at the grocery, they'd be looking forever and never find a sign of her.

"I know, Frankie. We tried so it's not our fault." She wiped the tears from her cheeks with the edge of her sheet but tried to keep her voice steady.

"You think she's okay?"

"Yeah," she said, to protect Frankie from nightmares. "That's why they didn't find her. She swam far away with our shell for good luck."

She closed her eyes and tried to remember everything about the stranger. What the girl had said made the encounter seem important. "Little guy didn't make it, but keeping this will honor his memory." Holding the girl's image would honor her memory if she hadn't made it.

She could still see the small conch shell around the girl's neck. It was carved with something, but she'd been too far away to see what it was. She went to sleep, where a night of scary images waited for her.

❖

It had been an instant of Vivien's life, five minutes tops, and when compared to how old she was now, it was a flash, but she couldn't forget the girl in the surf. When she'd seen her rise from the water, she'd thought, "I've finally found you." But she'd been ten. Ten years of age wasn't old enough to make such profound statements, but damn if the memory hadn't stuck.

"You know what's weird?" Frankie said and sighed. "That was the only time I've ever known for sure what it was to run. I looked at her and that's what I felt." Frankie tapped his legs and laughed, as if at the absurdity of what he was saying, and she admired him for never allowing his fate to kill his spirit.

"That's not weird, and I'm glad it's one of the only things you remember about all that."

"No. I remember all the grilling and tests to make sure we both weren't crazy. I left that part out so I don't have to dwell on the fact our parents thought we were dropping lines of coke at such a tender age." His legs were small and frail compared to the rest of him, and they'd prevented him from trying to find someone to share his life with. "I'm not whining about the stumps," he said and slapped above his knee, "but the joy of a memory I shouldn't have made me want to keep it safe."

"I'm not giving up," she said and kissed his hand. "There was never anything on the news, and no one ever reported her missing, so I know she's still out there."

"You know she is because Mom never admitted to these," he said, and tapped at the base of his throat where his shell sat. The leather that held them in place had grown with them and had never worn through the years they'd worn them. It was another impossibility they chose to ignore, but nothing would ever make them give the shells up.

"Speaking of, are you going tomorrow tonight?"

"Mom said it was a command performance, so I'll save you from Steve's advances," Frankie said after a short laugh.

Steve Hawksworth was the son of one of their newest board members and had set his sights on Vivien a few years before, to the delight of their parents. He was handsome, ambitious, and charming. The combination had swayed her father, but unfortunately for Steve, her father was already married. She'd dated Steve a few times to keep the peace, but he excited her about as much as having the flu.

"Christ, why can't we have a regular family meal without all the crap?"

"Because your ovaries are shriveling as we speak, and you're nowhere close to getting pregnant. The kid would have fantastic hair though." She stuck her tongue out at him, but she was already dreading the event. "Don't even go there," Frankie said shaking his finger at her.

"What?" She needed to do a better job of hiding her emotions, especially from Frankie. It was as if they could read each other's thoughts as clearly as if they'd spoken them out loud.

Their father also liked to harp on their responsibility to have more Palmers so a family member would always be at the helm of the business. That lecture was becoming more commonplace since both she and Frankie weren't anywhere near fulfilling that part of the bargain. No matter how stifling Vivien's life was at times, she at least had Franklin to commiserate with.

Business came first, though, so their parents hadn't become unbearable about their grandchild-less state. The Palmer children performed their respective duties well and had grown their production in the Gulf by double digits in a few short years. Her father was correct: the world was hungry for oil, and they were responsible not only for finding it but also pumping it out of the ground, no matter where it was. That'd been the main theme of Winston's education, a childhood lesson that was still ongoing.

"You're going through your pre-dread routine, and I don't plan to get stuck talking to Steve all night, consoling him because you're not there."

"I said I was going, and I'll be the one consoling Steve because I'm not interested in anything beyond the occasional dinner and movie when absolutely no one else I know or have seen briefly, like my mailman, is available. You'd think he'd have caught on by now."

"Don't be so oblivious." Frankie tugged her into a sitting position. "You're a classic beauty, and everyone around you, including pesky Steve, has noticed. If you weren't my sister, I'd make a move," he said as a joke.

"That girl in accounting thinks you're cute." She smiled even though she knew he believed he'd be a burden to anyone in a romantic relationship. "Why don't you invite her to dinner tonight? If she survives that, you'll know she's good dating material."

"You know that's not going to happen."

"Frankie." She stood and moved behind him so she could put her arms around him. "Your legs are defective, not your dick."

"I love it when you're crude, but she's an employee. We have rules against that. If you'd read your employee handbook you'd know these things."

"If not her, then somebody. I'm not the only one expected to produce heirs."

"When I find someone with hair as great as Steve's, I'll think about it."

"You do that, you shit," she said, and kissed his cheek. "Come on. I'll treat you to lunch."

CHAPTER THREE

Kai stood next to her parents smiling and shaking hands after the ceremony was over, but the exercise was getting boring. She wanted to leave by midday, but she wanted to make a few stops before she left that were more important than this. Before her thoughts became any more negative, her mom Hadley slapped her gently on the back of the head, warning her to plaster her smile back on and pay attention.

"Congratulations, Princess," one of the last dignitaries said as she held Kai's hand sandwiched between her own. "You've done well, and we were all impressed at how hard you strove to finish first in every category of study. Anyone who believes you were given an easier road toward graduation is sadly mistaken. Like your mothers, you truly can work anyone into the sand when you set your mind to it."

"I appreciate your kindness, ma'am. No matter what, I'll always have my critics, but it's nice to know I have someone who believes in me besides these guys." She pointed to her mothers.

"Oh, I'm sure you have more than enough admirers," the last in line said and winked, making her and her parents laugh.

"Thank you all, and please enjoy the lunch the staff prepared. I'll join you as soon as I visit the temple."

Hadley hugged her before she could escape so she could whisper in her ear. "Make sure your *prayers* don't take too long. Your mother and I'd like to talk to you privately before you leave."

"Yes, ma'am," she said, her ears burning. It truly sucked at times when your parents could literally read your mind.

The main temple stood in the center of the city, but Oba lived in the small one within the palace walls and spent a majority of her time there in case the queen needed her counsel. Kai's mother, Galen, had just appointed Oba to her post as high priestess when Kai started her required religious education, and because of her future responsibilities to the realm, Oba had become her private instructor.

In those few years, with the queen's blessing, Oba had expanded the formal gardens and worked in more water features fed by the ocean overhead. She'd explained she was more in tune with the goddess in her natural element of water.

Kai entered the grounds and noticed the silence, which meant Oba was alone and waiting for her in their favorite spot. Oba was studying a large stack of photos as she flipped through them slowly. "These things are becoming a menace." Oba held up one of the pictures Kai had taken of the super oil platforms in the Gulf while she had been building the outpost her team would use in the coming months.

"Take a deep breath and look around you," she said as she lay back, put her hands behind her head, and enjoyed the sun on her face.

Oba's garden was full of healthy flowers and edible plants, thanks to the technology they'd discovered when they'd had to go deeper to keep the realm safe and secret from the world at large. The reflectors that hovered over the water replicated the sunlight through the receptors outfitted throughout the kingdom below. Even though their home was vast, thriving, and constantly growing, they undertook each phase carefully so nature and habitat coexisted peacefully under the domes of glass that kept the Atlantic out.

"My mother always says we can all survive in the world if we treat each other with respect."

"I don't see much respect for the world around them here," Oba said as she pointed to the huge structure over the water.

"The world would be a better place if they found more efficient ways to live, but my mothers keep telling me they're still a long way off. All we can do is plant seeds and hope they grow alongside their industry." She rolled to her side, took the picture from Oba, and dropped it behind her. "You can complain all you want once I'm gone, but right now I don't have too much time."

"I should say a prayer for you and send you on your way then," Oba said as she clasped Kai's hand to help her get on her feet.

"You could, but you're not that cruel, and I'll be gone for a long time," she said as she helped Oba take off her robes and slide into their favorite pool. Oba dipped her head back but kept her eyes on her as she stripped off her uniform to join her.

"You are such a perfect balance of your mothers," Oba said as she wrapped her legs around Kai's waist when she entered the pool.

"I'd rather not talk about my mothers right now." She slid her hands down to cup Oba's ass and bring her closer.

"Tell me again why you picked someplace so far away."

"I want to try to teach both the people who build the platforms and the fishermen in that area that they can live in the same waters if they practice some of that respect my mother loves to talk about."

"What else are you going for?" Oba stretched out, and Kai heard the slight sucking sound when the gills at the back of her ears opened.

"That's all." She skimmed her fingers along Oba's abdomen to her breast. "Everything I need to find, I've found here."

"We've already had this talk, Highness. A bond between the throne and the temple is forbidden," Oba said, but didn't move away from her touch.

"Even if it's something I want." She squeezed Oba's nipple and grew wet when it puckered. "It can't be because you don't care."

"I do care," Oba said as her hips dipped below the water's surface. "You are taboo, but I can't resist. It's something I must master while you're gone. If I don't, I'll be of no use to you when you ascend to your mother's throne."

They both sank to the bottom, and Oba seemed to forget her words as she spread her legs for her. The water was salty, but she could still distinguish Oba's taste on her tongue when she wrapped her lips around her clitoris and sucked her in hard. They didn't need a grand buildup since they both wanted this.

Oba's hips bucked, and her feet floated up and landed on her back as if she were desperate for her touch. No matter how many times they shared themselves like this, Kai relished the feel of her.

Every bit of time she'd had to spend to persuade Oba to accept this aspect of their relationship had been worth it.

"Do you want me, Princess?" Kai could hear Oba's question in her mind. The shell at her throat made it possible.

"Leaving will be easier if I go with your taste on my lips." She sucked harder and slipped her fingers in. The way Oba opened up to her made her give in to everything Oba wanted, which was rougher than she usually was with anyone else.

"Harder," Oba demanded as she spread her legs wider and pulled on her hair. Kai slammed her fingers in, not worried that she'd hurt her friend and lover who'd awoken true passion and lust in her. She would certainly miss her time with Oba when she left.

"Worry about the things you can't control when they happen." Oba's voice filled her head. "On life's journey, concentrate on happiness when you experience it since it's sometimes fleeting."

She felt Oba's sex squeeze her fingers so she flattened her tongue and held her fingers still. Oba's hips moved as if she was claiming her pleasure on her own terms, and when her orgasm was done, Kai knew the same peace Oba experienced since they were still linked.

They surfaced together, and she drifted as she held Oba above her. She'd never had sex with Oba on a bed, always giving in to Oba's preference of the water. It was a reminder to both of them of their origins and who they were as a nation.

Their ancestors had come from another galaxy and had thrived for ages near the expanses of water that had lured them to Earth from their home light-years away. Earth had been a young planet then, with pristine oceans and land, so they'd made their homes for once on the shores. The group that had made the journey was led by the youngest daughter of the king, Princess Nessa, and very few men had chosen to follow.

The still unproven female warriors they'd trained had readily volunteered, and they'd been the first of many Atlantean women who'd built the kingdom they populated now. The males had eventually died off, but along with willing female warriors, they'd welcomed some of the brightest young scientists of their time. That generation had initiated the research that had allowed them to procreate without males in their population.

After a few decades they'd come to appreciate the sisterhood of their world and had shared their views and secrets with very few civilizations that had risen in Earth's history. The Amazons had been some of their greatest students, but as the world became a more volatile place, they'd returned to their origins. They'd transferred their libraries, advances, and treasures to the depths of the Atlantic Ocean and had prospered as they kept a watchful eye on humans.

They'd left some of their advances standing, such as the Egyptian pyramids and the Inca and Aztec towns and temples, just not the secrets of how they'd come to be. The pyramid shapes found in both ancient civilizations had been a homage to their home planet and the great temples they'd erected to the water gods.

It wasn't until now that some humans had chosen to finally explore the final frontier left on Earth, so they'd become more vigilant in keeping their secrets. Like on their own planet, man oftentimes destroyed what they didn't understand. Plato had written about their legend, but his story centered on the destruction of their world and had made many curious to find the remnants of their kingdom. To further throw people off their scent, they'd come up with the oddities of the Bermuda Triangle.

The vortexes some said they'd experienced, along with the freak storms, electrical fields, and other unexplainable things, were just the byproducts of the technology it took to survive northeast of the Puerto Rican Trench, the deepest part of the Atlantic. Few devices on Earth could reach the depths, and despite their size, even those had never come anywhere near them.

"Come, and I'll give you your going-away present," Oba said as she stepped out of the pool. Her quarters were located near the temple, and Kai had been inside them only for the lessons she'd started as a teenager.

The bedroom was lit with candles and the crystals they'd developed to transmit power, and Oba's bed was sprinkled with flowers. "I know you like the water so we can go back out," she said when she saw Oba's thoughtfulness.

"Kai, your thoughts and your desires are easy for me to hear when we're together." Oba sat on the bed and motioned her closer. "It's my wish to make you happy before you go."

"You don't need to worry or be sad. I'll be back before you get a chance to miss me."

Oba took her hand and kissed the tip of each finger. "Your mothers and I will always worry when you're away from us, and I want you to swear you'll be careful. I've seen…never mind."

"You can't stop now after that kind of lead-in. Tell me," she said, wanting to hear Oba's vision, if that's what it had been.

"You don't need my views to cloud your coming days."

"Your views always have insight, so please don't hold back just because we don't have time to talk about it for hours. Really, I want to know because it will help me prepare for the unexpected."

"You'll leave soon, and the quest you picked will bring you both happiness and disappointment."

"I know I can't change the world, but a lot of people along that coastline depend on the water, and it's got nothing to do with oil. I doubt any of them will be hostile, so I can handle some disappointment."

"The fishermen will accept you, but the companies that want to expand exploration will not—even if I wasn't a seer with the power of the water orb, I know that to be true. You can't expose who you are, even if you're tempted. You do and they'll either lock you away for madness or drop a bomb on this part of the ocean to try to destroy us."

She lay back and laughed. "I'm not crazy or stupid, so take your own advice about things you can't control and when to worry about them. I'd never betray my mothers or the rest of you."

The surface of the mattress dipped when Oba moved closer on her knees. "Would that be true if it was for the love of a woman?" She put her hands on Oba's back when she lay over her. "Or if I or your mothers asked?"

"I love my mothers, you, and the rest of our sisters more than life, but not even for them. Our world and our survival are worth more than the desires of one person. I've been raised to rule one day, and that was always and will continue to be the most important of the lessons I've learned." She kissed Oba on the forehead and smiled. "Do you seriously think a human woman exists that I'd fall in love with? That'd be an exercise in futility, and I very seldom set myself on useless enterprises."

"Take care of yourself then, and I'll keep you in my thoughts."

She put her fingers under Oba's chin so she'd make eye contact. "What's this weird conversation about?"

"The water orb has never failed me when it comes to certain possibilities, and I've never lied to you so I'll share my visions, but only if you want. If you wish to leave with no preconceptions of what could happen, I'll abide by that request."

"Tell me," she said, since Oba's demeanor was making her curiosity peak.

"You'll find someone who'll want you to turn away from us because she can't let go of the life she has. She's not who you first perceive her to be, but too many things tie her to the land." Oba closed her eyes as she spoke and appeared sad. "Love might seem like enough, Kai, but if you never return to us, a vital part of you will die. With time the missing piece will infect the rest of your life until all you'll know is misery."

"Are you sure all that'll come to be?"

"The orb at times gives us the possibilities, but this one feels so real it's driving me mad, though I can't know for sure."

"Why not?"

"To see the future as clearly as the past and the present would kill the part of every high priestess's soul that contains her faith. Like you and your endless questions that spring from your inquisitive mind, I need my faith in the gods and in our people, so at times the orb shows only paths that might be taken."

"But you have the gift of sight."

"My gift melded with the orb so that it belongs to it more than me, and my dreams now spring more from it than whatever source they came from before. That's why I was somewhat reluctant to tell you. What I saw could only be a dream that won't come close to becoming reality."

"It's always good to have warnings when heading off into the unfamiliar."

"Please know that I want you to be happy and in love, but we need you to rule once your mother's time is done. A challenge by anyone unworthy will lead us into chaos, and then all those stories you found so funny because of their absurdity might come true. We could end up destroying ourselves and this world if someone concerned only with power and revenge leads us."

"I found them funny because they could never happen, and not to complain, but you're killing my mood." She wished she'd had more time to put Oba at ease, but she had to go.

"You deserved the truth before you left."

"Did you tell my mothers all this?" She hated to leave, but her time was up, so she helped Oba get up and allowed her to help her dress.

"Yes, but the decision to change your mind is yours. They both agreed. It's not too late to choose something and somewhere else."

"Share a little of the faith they have in me," she said as she kissed Oba's lips. "And when I come back you'll owe me an afternoon in here."

"That's a promise I'll be glad to keep," Oba said and kissed her again.

CHAPTER FOUR

Have you given up thinking before you speak?" Winston asked when Vivien came to his office and dropped into one of the chairs facing his massive desk.

Its twin was in her father's study at home, so this reminded her of all those long talks they'd had when the nuns sent her home with a note filled with her latest infractions. The furniture was supposed to set the positions of power, but the ornate desks always reminded her of the gap between her and her father. She often wondered if he saw it the same way and, if he did, why he never came from behind the behemoth to sit beside her.

"Maybe I'm aggravated since you cut my vacation short," she said as she crossed her legs and studied the material of her skirt. "I've been at this project for over three years, so a week wasn't an unreasonable request."

"So you decided the best way to point that out was to call me and the rest of the board douche bags?"

"I said corporate types who cut corners, so if you thought I meant you or anyone in particular, you need to review our safety and protocol procedures again." She smiled at him, surprised when his expression softened and he smiled back.

"You'd have driven anyone else to drink by now," he said as she stood and walked around to lean on the front of the desk. "Do you think you could keep your colorful commentary down to a minimum from now on? I agree with you when it comes to some of those guys, but they're hard enough to deal with on a good day. Having you poke them with those sharp words of yours makes my life miserable."

"What was today all about?" she asked, having to crane her neck to look up at him.

"It's time for you to come in from the field, so meetings like that'll become more commonplace. Since that's the next logical step, I figured you and the board should get used to each other."

"Are you even interested in what I have to say or think about that?"

"I'm your father. Of course I do," he said as he crossed his arms across his chest. "I'm also the head of this company so I've got to consider that as well."

She dropped both feet to the floor and sighed. "I've given you everything you wanted, and like your friend said in there, that's got to count for something. I want to finish this project, and when I do, I'd love to talk to you about what comes next."

"We'll see, and before you stab me in the eye with a pencil, I'll take your wishes into consideration. Contrary to everything you and Franklin think about me, I love you both, and it's not my job to make you totally miserable."

"Thanks, Dad, and I love you too."

"Don't forget about dinner. Your mother's looking forward to seeing you."

"This isn't another excuse to push Steven on me, is it?"

Her father tried to hide his grimace by putting his hand over his mouth. "She invited the Hawksworth family, yes, but I'm sure you can handle it."

"Sure I can, but then will you threaten me with a manners expert?"

He laughed and opened his arms to her. "Good job on this, kiddo. I'm damn proud of you."

"Maybe if I can deliver a couple more like Triton I can retire," she said, and hearing the words made her think she meant them.

"Deliver a few more like that, and we'll expect you to take over the world."

She laughed because she knew he meant that as well. "We all have a dream, Dad, but don't hold your breath on that one. If someone granted me a wish to do whatever I wanted, I'd rather rule the sea."

"I'm sure that job is taken."

"Then my wish is to meet her one day."

"Her?" her father asked, dragging out the word. "How do you know it's not a man?"

"Call it a hunch," she said as she waved good-bye over her shoulder. She had a day of peace before her mother tried to make progress on her whacked-out fantasy of marrying her off.

Hadley stood at the portal where her ship was docked and ready to board, so Kai picked up her pace. It was time to put everything Oba had said to the back of her mind and concentrate on the trip ahead. After all the planning and preparation, she was eager to head out on the vessel she'd designed herself, with plenty of input from her mother Hadley.

The ship was as fast and maneuverable as any in their fleet underwater, but when they reached their destination it could surface as a sailboat. The mast and everything else tucked away in compartments located throughout the ship, but anyone not part of her team would never be able to tell it wasn't anything more than a regular sailing craft.

"I guess I'm taking way too long as far as they're concerned," Kai said, pointing to Ram and Ivan as they beat the glass with their tail fins as if anxious to get going.

"Be careful, and call your mother," Hadley said when they embraced. "She'll be a wreck as it is, so hearing from you every once in a while will help."

"Oba's already put the fear of the gods into me with her prophecies, so don't worry. I'll stay clear of the navy and other dangerous things out there."

"The US Navy isn't your problem," Hadley said as they watched Galen coming to join them. "It's the conspiracy theorists out there that'll have a fit if they find a good-looking kid with gills."

"Here's everything you'll need." Galen handed over a leather folio with their identification papers inside. "You're overqualified for the job they'll expect, but it'll give you better insight into their world."

"I'll do my best, and I'll be long gone before it becomes too mundane." She placed the folio in her bag and joined her mama on the wide berth. "Really, my whole purpose is to get them to adopt new safety measures so, if the unthinkable happens again, maybe there won't be as much damage. Up to now they've been like children playing with dangerous explosive devices without adult supervision."

"Try not to have too many preconceptions or let the experiences of others color your judgment. You haven't had much exposure to anyone like this outside the realm, so experiencing something first-hand will give you a new perspective. Humans have evolved from the time our people first arrived here, but one thing about them remains constant. They're compassionate and resourceful. Try to erase whatever expectations you have, or the coming months will be a waste of your time." Galen took her hand and leaned over to kiss her cheek.

"What's your opinion of the humans?"

"The simplest answer I can give you is they aren't all good, but the majority of them are. You need to get to know them, because the knowledge of who you're dealing with will help you become an effective ruler. My mother told me once that unless you care about the entirety of our home, you'll never be a good leader, and I've found that to be true."

She put her arm around her mama's shoulders and squeezed her closer. "Thanks for the advice, and no matter what I'm doing, I'll try always to make you and Mom proud of me. That means I'll never be too old for advice. At least that's what Gran told me," she said of Galen's mother.

"I'd fuss but she's a smart old bird." Galen stood and sat on the arm of Hadley's chair and took a deep breath. "As for being proud of you, we always have been. You are what's best of both of us. We strived from your birth to always lead you in the right direction, and you've never disappointed us."

"That's not to say you haven't pushed the limits at times," Hadley said with a smile. "Your choice of service is your own, but once you'd made up your mind, your mother and I decided to add to your duties."

"I'm not going to like this, am I?" Her parents had never been really harsh, but when they were this calm and united about something, they'd usually found an interesting solution to a problem. The only thing she had no clue about was what this particular problem was.

"Any warrior who serves your mother has one responsibility above all others. You want to remind her what that is?" Hadley asked.

"To follow orders unless the lives of my unit are in danger and there's a better solution," she said, repeating the first line of the academy's military text.

"Have you always done that? Or better yet, do you remember a time when you decided to ignore that rule?" Hadley asked, her smile widening with each word.

"Come on, Mom. I was twelve and you cut me some slack."

"It wasn't slack, tadpole," Hadley said as Galen nodded. "We decided to put off punishment for your impromptu visit, so you'd realize what happens when you act rashly."

"We know you tried to make things right," Galen said in her usual gentle tone. "But it's time to fix what you broke."

"How?" she asked, remembering how scared she'd been when Talia had reported back to her mom what she'd done because of a stupid whim. But once she'd made the mistake she'd tried her best to fix it.

June 1994

"Kai, you know the rules," Talia said as they crept up to the house where the two children Kai had talked to lived. "Your mothers are going to take this out on Isla and me because *we* do know better."

"They got in trouble because of me today. I shouldn't have talked to them, but I figured it'd be harmless if I pretended to be just another kid on vacation. Now I feel bad for what happened."

Kai stopped at the bottom of the steps and looked at the man who watched a baseball game on television, a beer next to him. He seemed absorbed even though the game was scoreless, so she climbed to the room where the children slept. She'd brought back the shell the girl had thrown, as well as one for her brother. She'd had them strung with the same braided leather she used, but it wasn't until she was in the room that she decided on her last step.

"This is your great treasure for throwing this back," she said as she placed the shell in the girl's slack hand. Her corn-silk hair lay spread across the pillow, and Kai found her pretty. "Be well."

She placed the other carved shell in the boy's hand, then stood between them and rubbed her hands together. The words were an ancient language, and as she spoke them softly her hands began to glow and small tendrils of light spread from her to each of the shells. When she was done, the same carvings that adorned her shell were carved into the gifts she'd left, and the lines glowed for a second longer before the golden dust fell into their hands. If they chose to wear them, they'd find the link they shared that she'd seen that afternoon on the beach would grow with age and experience. It'd also give her insight into their world and lives.

It was time to go home and face her own troubles with her parents, but this had been worth it to her. She left as quietly as she had come in and ran with Talia back to the beach. The cool water against her face was refreshing when she dove into the surf, but her thoughts went back to the children she'd met.

"Maybe I'll see you again," she thought as she swam away. "But for now it's forbidden."

"You in a way changed the course those children would've taken in life, but that wasn't a completely terrible thing. What we'd like you to do, though, is try to fix the damage that still lingers from that day," Galen said.

"How am I supposed to do that? I don't even know who they are. Besides, I'm heading to a completely different place."

"Finding them won't be hard," Hadley said, a little louder than necessary, as if to stop her whining. "The fixing we'll leave up to you."

"We're confident you'll think of something," Galen added as she stood up.

"Your mama isn't as blunt as she needs to be sometimes, so in case you missed it, thinking of something is an order. Understood?" Hadley asked as she too rose to her feet.

"Yes, ma'am," she said putting her fist to her chest in salute.

"Try to have some fun though, and remember that we love you," Galen said, her eyes welling with tears again. "Keep that fact close to your heart and you'll be able to do anything."

"Thanks, Mama." She hugged both of them before closing the hatch so they could detach. With one last check to make sure Ram and Ivan were safely in the space she'd provided for travel, she started the engines. "Okay, let the adventures begin."

CHAPTER FIVE

Two days later Vivien sat outside in her small garden with the maps from her most recent dives and a large cup of coffee. She was usually an early riser, but always a reluctant one, and when she didn't have anything to do she had no problem sleeping past noon.

It was still too early to see the entire yard, but what was visible in the predawn was pristine, thanks to the yard service she'd hired along with the maid service. Home was mostly on her boat, the *Sea Dreamer*, so the big bed inside had been a luxury she hadn't experienced in weeks.

"What a great thing that I love my own company," she said out loud, a habit she'd had since childhood when she thought her surroundings were too quiet.

She'd only partially completed exploring the targeted area in the Atlantic because of the storm she'd told Frankie about, so she started plotting her next trip. Hopefully it'd be right after Triton was fully operational and she wouldn't be missed if she took off a couple of months. "A girl can dream, and with any luck, big, bad Winston won't crush my plans before I'm out the door."

She laughed as she reached for her ringing phone, knowing it could be only one person at this hour. "Hello."

"You should be inside getting your beauty sleep."

"How do you know I'm not? Now that you woke me up, you've fucked it all up for me," she said, enjoying Frankie's laughter. If she had the opportunity to go, she was taking Frankie with her. They'd been apart too long.

"Maybe you've found the secret to turning Steve off then, if you show up looking like shit."

"I'm not that lucky since we both know he's more of a bottom-line kind of guy, and I'm not talking about my ass. Even if I was a hideous crone he'd still want me because of the name and bank account." She pressed the phone to her ear with her shoulder so she could roll up all her stuff and head inside. It was starting to drizzle and the maps hadn't been laminated.

"You forgot toothless," he said, making her smile like no one else in her life could.

"I don't want to jinx myself into losing all my teeth, so I always leave that one out." She made it through the door before the deluge started.

"So, hideous crone you can live with?"

"Yes, but only if I have the ability to chew steak. That's the secret to a happy life." She poured herself another cup of coffee and turned on the news, then muted the sound.

"I'll have to write that down since it's so damn profound."

"Did you call me before five for anything other than making fun of my philosophy?"

"Do you need a ride tonight?"

"I've got a long list of errands and no idea when I'll be done, so I'll meet you there. You're welcome to tag along, but you'd be bored out of your mind."

"You're right about that, so I'll see you there. Love you," Frankie said and hung up.

She tapped the phone against her chin, trying to decide what her first stop of the day should be after a hot shower. If she got all her running around out of the way, maybe she could convince Frankie to take the afternoon off for some fun.

"It's a good thing everyone I know is up as early as I am, which will make this doable."

She dressed casually and drove down to the French bakery at the end of St. Charles Avenue. They were taking fresh croissants out of the oven when she arrived, and she'd need one if she dared another cup of coffee. It was still early so the place was mostly deserted, except for the staff joking with each other in the kitchen. That's what made the woman sitting alone in the corner stand out, not that she wouldn't have even if the place had been packed.

Even sitting, Vivien could tell she was tall and solidly built, and though she was fairly sure they'd never met, something seemed incredibly familiar about her. She realized she was staring when the stranger glanced up from her paper and smiled.

"Sorry," she said and turned to hide her embarrassment. Staring at total strangers wasn't something she did, and now wasn't the time to begin.

"Did you want this for here or to go?" the girl at the register asked.

"For here." She heard the words come out despite the fact that wasn't what she'd planned at all. "Thanks."

She picked the opposite corner and unfolded the newspaper she'd added to her purchases. No matter how hard she tried not to, she peeked up after every paragraph she read. Whoever the Amazon was, she must've had the day off as well since she was in shorts, T-shirt, and sandals. If there'd been a beach around, she was dressed appropriately to bum around on it.

"Have a nice day," the woman said as she stood and walked by her. Vivien had been right about the height.

"You too," she said, cursing herself for sounding out of breath. When the door closed, the air in the room became almost stale, as if the woman had taken the life in it with her. "Good lord, maybe I've been on the water alone too long."

She finished her simple breakfast and headed to Tulane to visit her old professor, Dr. Etta Sinclair. The university's oceanography department wasn't huge, but Etta had done a good job in expanding her love of the water and the treasures it held in its depths. Vivien had missed her when she'd left for LSU and its better engineering program. She'd chosen to start at Tulane to stay close to Frankie as long as she could.

There was a parking spot close to Etta's office, and she was surprised to see her breakfast companion ahead of her on the sidewalk. Maybe the beach bum was an older student, since she appeared slightly north of the average-aged female on campus. She walked without saying anything, and the woman surprised her again when she entered Etta's building.

Etta and the tall woman were already in conversation when Vivien arrived and knocked on the door. "I'm sorry to interrupt, but do you have some time for me when you're done?" she asked Etta. The mystery guest stood and offered her the only other seat in the cramped office aside from Etta's.

"I was delivering something for a friend, so she's all yours," the woman said as she placed her hand on Etta's shoulder before leaving.

"I apologize if I ran her off."

"Don't worry about it. She really was dropping off a package before heading to the aquarium."

"She works there?" The fact-finding question was lame, guaranteeing that she'd never have a career in law enforcement.

"I don't think so," Etta said as she made room on her desk by dropping a few stacks of books on the ground. "She mentioned something about a fish. Enough about that, though. Did you find anything?" The map Etta took out had the section they'd picked together circled in red.

"Nothing this time around."

"Really?" Etta glanced at her over the rim of her wire-framed classes. "I'm pretty sure that's the spot your old map pinpointed."

"The weather turned on me, and I didn't have time to wait for it to clear up. If anything's there, it'll keep until my work schedule frees up again."

Etta leaned back and smiled. "I'm sure it'll be waiting on you since you're the most persistent person I've ever met. Are you in town for a while, or is your father shipping you back out before we can have lunch together?"

"Give me a week and I'll let you know." The file lying on the spot Etta had cleared was incredibly distracting. "I had to come back early, and Daddy does have me booked already."

"So you can wait for this that long?" Etta tapped the file and laughed. "If you can, you must've changed plenty on vacation."

"Who else visits you before eight in the morning? Of course I haven't changed that much." She waited to open the file when Etta relinquished her hold on it, wanting to hear about it from Etta, since she made even the most boring topic sound riveting. "Did you find anything? Was it authentic?"

"It can't be an original because of the pristine condition, considering when it was supposedly written, but it's still old for a copy. Whoever originated it followed the script of some of the other documents you've found, only this one mentions the section of ocean you were planning to investigate."

What had started as a childhood whim had turned into a lifelong obsession to find the origins of the strange writing on her shell. It had led her on interesting dives all over the world and to more maps than any one person should own. Every so often, with Frankie's help, she found actual text to go with the old maps that brought her closer to the answer she was after.

"It's so aggravating. This was the first time I found a spot where I could actually dive without special equipment, and Mother Nature drops a monsoon on my head." She flipped through the papers Etta had put together, looking forward to reviewing the translations she'd included. "Nothing in the form of an alphabet?"

"I never want to curb your enthusiasm, but have you ever considered that you've been chasing a beach bum's artistic license all this time?" Etta pointed to her shell but made no move to touch it.

"My father certainly thinks so, but my gut tells me to keep going. I just know I'm right."

"Then you are, and I have faith you'll eventually find what you're looking for."

"Let's hope it doesn't come in the afterlife," she said before kissing Etta's cheek and heading to her next stop. It wasn't until she was in the car that she realized Etta had effectively changed the subject well enough to never introduce the mystery woman.

"Well played, Etta, and if you were able to hook the Amazon, I'm impressed."

"You like it here?" Kai asked her old classmate Andie Gettis as she prepared the supplies she'd need for the day. "I'd think it'd be difficult to look at all day, every day."

"It was at first, but then the kids come in and want to know how they can make things better. That makes it worthwhile."

"You've been missed," Kai said as she helped carry everything to the side of the large tank.

"One month to go and I'll get to go home for a few weeks. Ready to visit some of your offspring?"

"Funny," she said as she put the air tank on, though technically neither she nor Andie needed one. The aquarium had been the recipient of one of the programs she'd started during some of the stints she'd spent in the area, with her mothers' blessings. Andie had monitored progress in her absence, and from the specimens she'd seen so far, her work was starting to pay off.

"Do they pass the plate test?" From this perspective all she could see was the fish swimming by. "I'd hate to go back to the drawing board now."

"You don't have to worry about that, and if you have time I'll prove it to you at the lunch place down the street."

Kai nodded and jumped in, letting herself sink to the bottom, where her feet sank in the sand. The sharks swimming above her seemed to follow the same pattern and ignored the other fish sharing their space. They seemed satisfied with whatever Andie was putting in the feed buckets, but she was more interested in the game fish. They'd gotten much bigger than when she'd dropped them in a year before, so if a fraction of them had survived in the wild, it was good to see where they were in the life cycle.

She stuck her hand into the bucket, and it didn't take long to draw a crowd while Andie took care of the sharks. When the bucket was empty she glanced out to the large room that faced the tank and noticed there weren't too many people outside, and all but one had on the blue shirts the staff wore. It was her breakfast gawker, and now she was sorry she hadn't stuck around so Etta could've introduced them, since the woman was staring at her as intently as she had that morning.

The woman lifted her hand when she waved, then watched her as she swam back to the top. Kai didn't think she'd still be there once she'd finished changing, and she was right when all she found was the security guard assigned to the area.

"Does that blond woman work here?" she asked as she walked outside with Andie.

"We have more than a few of those." Andie led her into the French Quarter and chose to sit outside. She understood the allure of the table with the red umbrella. Their underwater home was as bright as this on a clear day, but something about the air up top was special.

"You didn't notice the woman watching us?"

"I don't have the same talent with sharks, my friend, so I rarely take my eyes off them to look out at the gallery."

It was strange running into someone that many times in a day, but coincidences did happen sometimes, despite people's theories on the subject. With all she had to do she tried to forget about it and concentrated on the plate the waiter had placed before her.

It was still early for lunch but Andie had insisted. "They definitely pass the plate test," she said when she took a bite of the fried redfish.

Chapter Six

Vivien stared at the two dresses she'd laid on the bed and tried to decide which one was dressy enough for the occasion but in turn didn't give anyone the wrong impression, especially Steve. If she'd been faintly interested in him he would've blown her away by now, since his persistence was unrelenting but also extremely annoying. Steve was handsome, and she could tell he was aware of that fact, but something about him gave her the creeps.

"The blue it is," she said, remembering how much Steve loved her in black.

She dressed and put on only lipstick, knowing the lack of makeup would aggravate her mother. "It's only fair since I'm pissed that I'm here instead of watching the sunset on the deck of my boat."

Her house wasn't too far from her parents in distance, but a world away when it came to everything else. The Palmer estate on River Road at the cusp of the Garden District was truly stunning, and Vivien always thought it was stuck in time. Outside the gates the world had evolved, but inside, the manicured lawns and gardens made the grand home appear even more majestic. It'd been interesting to bring people over when she was younger, but the exercise had proved a litmus test for those only interested in the Palmer money and those who'd become true friends.

Marsha Kessler was the one person Vivien had known since kindergarten who had proved herself loyal. Her best friend's father owned a huge shipping company that put him in her family's league as far as money was concerned, so she'd never been in Vivien's life for opportunistic reasons. Marsha was usually only interested in a good time and was fun to be around when they were ready to take a break from their family business duties.

That wasn't the impression she got when she saw Marsha smoking near the fountain close to the front door. "You look tense," she said as she got out of her car. "Did they run out of booze already?"

"The day your parents run out of booze, I'll know for sure the apocalypse is upon us," Marsha said and laughed. "No, Frankie fixed me a drink, but I'd have had to stay inside and listen to Steve tell me how wonderful he is to enjoy it. After fifteen minutes of that, I thought I'd come pollute the air out here while he does the same inside." Marsha put out her smoke so she could hug her. "If I had a dollar for every time he's asked me to put in a good word for him, I'd double my take-home pay this year."

"Steve's my father's pipe dream so I hope they'll be happy together. I keep telling Daddy that Steve wants to unburden me from my job after marriage so Palmer Oil can have a new executive vice president who dreams of the top spot."

"What are you supposed to be doing while he's running the empire?"

"Having a bunch of little Steves so the company will eventually be Hawksworth Oil. At least that's Frankie's take." The gate opened again, but she didn't recognize the big bike that rolled in. "Steve can't believe I haven't jumped at the offer he keeps wrapping up in different ways."

"Is that the caterer?" Marsha asked as she sat on the edge of the fountain and crossed her legs. "If it is, one or both of your parents is letting their inhibitions out of the box they've kept hidden and locked in the back of the closet since the eighties."

"I doubt it, since Leo would be crushed if they brought someone else into his kitchen," she said about their long-time in-house chef.

"Whoever she is, if she's staying, I'm suddenly glad I came." Marsha stood and smoothed down her skirt. "Shall we?"

"Can I help you?" Vivien asked when they got close enough to watch the woman take her helmet off. It was a surprise to see the mystery woman from her day standing in the drive, and this close, even in the waning light, she noticed how beautiful her light-green eyes were.

"Hello again." The woman smiled as she placed her helmet on the seat of her bike. "I hope I have the correct address. Mr. Winston Palmer invited me for dinner."

"You're in the right place," Vivien said as she glanced at Marsha and almost laughed at her expression. Man-crazy Marsha would eventually commit to just one, but she probably wouldn't mind jumping the gender fence when the specimen was this extraordinary. "We've seen each other plenty today, so I apologize for not introducing myself sooner." She held her hand out. "I'm Vivien Palmer, his daughter."

"A pleasure to formally meet you," the woman said as she took her hand. It was warm, large, and strong, which seemed to fit its owner. "I'm Kai Merlin, your new supervising drilling engineer on Triton."

"That's interesting," she said, her gut becoming as cold as if she'd swallowed a bucket of ice.

"Actually the job's not all that exciting," Kai said, still not releasing her hand. "It's important, but interesting might be a stretch."

"I think Vivien finds it interesting because she's the supervising drilling engineer on Triton," Marsha said when Vivien remained silent. "I'm Marsha Kessler."

"A pleasure to meet you." Kai shook Marsha's hand briefly, then slid both hands deep in her pockets. She stared at Vivien as if trying to decipher the problem. "I'm not sure what's going on, and I'm not familiar with Palmer politics, so I apologize for upsetting you," Kai said, sounding sincere. "I'm only here for a job and, from the look of this place, crab puffs."

"If you don't mind I'll leave you with Marsha. She can show you in." She took a deep breath to control the anger she felt toward her father. The whole heart-to-heart the day she got back had been a farce he'd pulled off beautifully. "Please excuse me."

"Miss Palmer." Kai's voice stopped her. "If you like, I'll leave." The offer made her turn around fast enough for the shell around her neck to break free of the scoop of her dress's neckline, so she wrapped her fist around it for comfort. "I'm new to the area, and I'm sure I could take another job that won't upset you this much."

"If you don't mind some free advice, you should know my father will expect more of a cheerleader than that. To Winston Palmer, nothing's more important than Triton's output."

"Thanks, but I never could pull off the short skirt and bobby socks essential to any good cheerleading outfit."

Kai's tone had changed, so Vivien tried to regain control of herself and the situation. "I'm sorry for being rude. You're a guest and I had no right to talk to you like that, so please stay. I'm sure Marsha will be happy to walk you inside and get you something to drink."

"Take your time."

She nodded, comfortable enough that Kai wasn't going to walk away. Her mother's family dinner turned fiasco wasn't close to getting started, so she intended to hunt her father down and ruin his night more than he had hers. Predictably he was in his office, since he didn't have an off switch, and not surprisingly Steve was glued to his ass, so she plastered a smile she didn't appreciate having to lift the corners of her mouth to make and entered. The way Steve perked up when she came in made her realize he'd misread her expression for something warm and welcoming.

"Steve, would you excuse us? I need to speak to my father in private." Every word made Steve's entire body stiffen more, but he left with a slight slam of the heavy oak door.

"Honey, you really need to soften your stance toward Steve. He's not going to wait forever," Winston said as he shuffled papers on his desk from one pile to another.

Did he practice being this clueless to everything and everyone around him that didn't pertain to business? "I believe those are the most overused words anyone who refuses to see I don't care if Steve waits forever has ever said. No amount of time's going to change my mind, but if you love him that much, I'll break the news to Mom that you're running off with him. He kisses your ass enough times in a day that I'm sure you'll be blissfully happy together." She sat on the small leather couch that faced the French doors and crossed her arms over her chest to draw him from behind his desk.

"That tone isn't necessary." His voice was flat, and if she kept pushing he'd be ready for a fight. "Your mother and I only have—"

"My best interest at heart," she said through gritted teeth as she balled her hands into fists. "Have you actually listened to yourself lately? At least when you're not lying about everything you tell me? When did you become an old Southern plantation owner who needed to sell his daughter off to the best beau that came a-calling?" She let loose a string of curses but didn't let them slip out of her mouth. "Concentrate on what you know, Dad, and it's obvious I'm not high on the list."

"Would you like to slap me too?"

"Tonight isn't the time to tempt me, believe me. Do you want to explain why I found out I'm being replaced by meeting my *replacement* outside? Why tell me all that crap in the office yesterday about listening to what I want?"

"Because I know you, and I know what's best for you. It's time for you to take possession of the office your mother had decorated for you. The future of our company doesn't need to spend her time with all the roughnecks on our payroll." He moved to stand in front of her. "You know your brother won't be able to carry the load."

The door had obviously opened and closed, but neither of them had heard Frankie come in until he snorted at their father's proclamation. Her father loved them both, she'd never questioned that, but he had definite ideas about his children that weren't as progressive as his drilling agenda. Her love life and Frankie's wheelchair were two places she wished he'd evolve and pick his knuckles up off the ground.

"Yeah, Viv, my brain is attached to my legs so we need you to come save the day." Frankie pushed his way in and stared at their father as he opened his mouth. "Save it, Dad. I'm never going to convince you about anything having to do with my capabilities so don't waste any more air on the subject. The house is stuffy enough with all the assholes you invited over tonight."

"This isn't a family-owned company anymore, so you two can have fun at my expense, but if you don't start taking the company and your place in it seriously, someone who's not a Palmer could be in the big chair." Winston picked up a binder on the desk and dropped it next to her. "These are the new leases the board wants to bid on, and with Triton almost on line, that's the next task for both of you. If you get it done, you'll prove to them you deserve the position when I'm ready to retire."

"I was able to get you Triton without being chained to a desk, since Frankie did all the contract negotiations. That's how we work best."

"We'll expect you on Monday," Winston said, as if he'd just joined the conversation and hadn't heard anything they'd said so far. "And I'm bringing Steve in on this one. He's ready to move up."

"You do realize he's not a Palmer, right?"

"He will be if he marries into the family."

"Tell me where you're registered and I'll be happy to send a gift," she said, refusing to give him the last word.

Kai opened and closed her hand, trying to calm the tingling after the temporary shock wore off. The shell around Vivien Palmer's neck had her markings, but that wasn't the surprise since she'd put them there. She was stunned that it was still around Vivien's neck. She'd done it only a few times before, and the gifts had always come back to her when the children had felt they'd outgrown them. Leave it to her mothers to find her a job with the children she'd interacted with years before. Her mothers weren't kidding; she wouldn't have trouble finding them.

The markings had allowed her to tap into their experiences so human interaction wouldn't be so difficult and she could blend into the crowd. That was kind of a strange concept since her ancestors had populated the planet since prehistoric man had walked the Earth, and they'd been responsible for helping mankind's society evolve as well as making them a little less hairy.

"Are you new to the area?" Marsha asked, as if the silence in Vivien's absence had gone on too long.

"Yes, I arrived recently. Have I caused a problem for Miss Palmer?" The anger that coursed through Vivien was so strong she wouldn't have needed the markings to figure it out. She needed to figure out why Vivien's thoughts had been silent to her if she still wore the shell. "That's not what I had planned for my first day."

"Have you met Viv's father?" Marsha looped her arm through hers and led her inside.

The group gathered didn't glance at them, so Kai studied the large, impressively well-stocked saltwater fish tank that took up a wall in the room where everyone was mingling. "I've only talked to him on the phone, but he was very persuasive. After a few conversations he convinced me to move here and that the staff would love me." She nudged Marsha closer to the glass so she could see Winston's collection. "So much for that, huh?"

What would it be like to be caged forever, even if the trap was as beautiful as this one? The tank was masterfully done with its fake coral but live anemones, and she found the leg of a platform coming down at an angle humorous. Some of the colorful fish flitted through the rocks as if still trying to escape, so she guessed they were the newest additions. The ones who perched somewhere and barely moved their fins had evidently figured out their fate.

"Winston's pride and joy," Marsha said as she placed her hand on the tank, which made her red fingernail polish stand out. "He's caught a majority of everything in here."

From her first moment in the water at birth, Kai had been in tune with the shark's spirit more than any other. Even though scientists on the land found them unthinking eating machines, their egg-sized brains could process a lot, and the small bamboo shark swimming in circles at the top of the tank dove down when Kai put her hand next to Marsha's.

She could sense his frustration that was slowly turning to madness, and she tried to ease the despair by temporarily linking their spirits. "He's beautiful," she said as the small striped shark bumped the glass with his tail fin. He reminded her of Ram and Ivan's antics.

"I've never seen him do that or known it was a him," Marsha said. "I guess I should've since Winston named him Mike after the LSU mascot."

"Damn thing's got a screw loose," a man said from behind them. "Winston says he tries to jump out whenever the tank's open for feedings and cleaning. Whoever heard of a shark with a death wish?"

"Sharks, no matter their size, are wild at heart, so maybe he prefers death over confinement," she said, and took some of Mike's sadness when she removed her hand.

"Fish are too stupid to know they're in a tank."

"Stupidity isn't a trait common to only fish, but since you think you know better than me on the subject, we'll agree to disagree. Stupid or not, I'll side with the fish."

"Learn who all the players are before you go calling people stupid," the man said menacingly. "And with an attitude like that one, you won't have much of a future in the oil business." The man laughed, she was sure at her expense.

"By future, do you mean keeping my opinions to myself so people will like me?" The man took a small step forward when Marsha laughed, but it didn't concern her. Whoever he was, he was handsome, with his thick blond hair and his blue eyes that reminded her of her mother's since they were a similar shade. His, though, seemed almost dead and held none of the warmth she always found in her mother's. "Maybe that's why I'm a fish lover."

"I'm a fish lover too, especially when they're battered and deep fried." The guy was the only one who laughed. "Mostly they're just a pain in the ass because environmental groups try to shut us down every time a dolphin gets the sniffles."

"I'll explain later how dolphins really aren't fish, but have you considered there's a way to make everyone happy? You can do business that doesn't come at the expense of the fish and vice versa." She tapped the glass, smiling when Mike swam to that spot. "Think of this as a small example."

"Well said, young lady," an older gentleman said as he put his hand on her shoulder. "That's the kind of talk we want out there when it comes to the company. We love the environment and want everybody to know it."

"Should I have the fish sticks taken off the menu in the cafeteria, Winston?" the younger man asked as he glared at her. "Or should I have T-shirts emblazoned with FISH LOVER on them made up?"

"Kai Merlin, sir," she said, offering Winston her hand. "Thank you for the opportunity."

"Glad to have you." Winston gripped her hand and seemed pleased when she didn't flinch. "What are you drinking?"

"Water's fine." She looked at Vivien and the man in a wheelchair who'd followed Winston into the room. The last time Kai had seen Vivien's little brother he'd been a small but bright boy whose hand had closed over the shell as she'd marked them. She'd given him the greatest wish his mind had asked for at the time—the actual memory of running.

The shell at her neck warmed, and she knew instantly he hadn't removed his either. That was why she'd never received any of their thoughts—their bond had linked the gifts she'd given them to each other, and their connection was so strong it would block anyone else from their minds. That's how it was with her mothers and the other life mates who'd found their true partner. But close siblings could also develop the kind of communication through the necklaces as Vivien and her brother obviously had.

Vivien gazed at her with her hand at the base of her throat, and her brother copied her actions. Had they figured out why their thoughts were so clear to each other? Vivien faltered first by breaking eye contact, and Kai could sense only curiosity now, and something else she couldn't decipher.

"You didn't follow my advice," Vivien said when Kai and Marsha stepped closer to the siblings. "And don't be fooled by his Boy Scout routine. Winston's not a fan of sea life except when it's dropped into that tank."

"It's obvious to me after tonight that I'm not as lovable as my parents think I am. Usually I'm pretty good at meeting people and making new friends." She accepted the glass the waiter brought over on a tray and took a sip. "I also don't want to take something away from you that clearly you're not ready to let go of. Would you mind passing my apologies to your father? I doubt I'll be missed, but in case I am."

She had to get out before the negativity that filled the beautiful house ruined her mood. Everyone there seemed to have an agenda to protect what was theirs and was willing to fight whoever to gain a bigger slice. Navigating this morass for months was as appetizing as eating rotten fish.

Outside, the night had cooled and she felt better after a deep breath. It was hard to believe her mothers hadn't put any of the Palmer-family problems in their report. These people were broken, and they'd added others to their lives that would never allow them to heal. The only two truly loyal to each other were Vivien and her brother, but that wasn't enough to overcome everyone else's plotting and scheming.

"I'm sorry."

"You don't have to be." She turned with her helmet in hand to face Vivien. "There's no law that you have to like me, and I'm not that indispensable to your business, so I quit. If it'll make you feel better you can fire me. Either way you don't have to worry about me."

"Firing you would be a mistake on my part, and quitting won't allow us to get to know each other," Vivien said and seemed to drop whatever crap she was carrying. "Again, I'm sorry for being so rude. My disagreements with my father have nothing to do with you, and please call me Vivien."

"Is this job important to you?"

"The job's actually boring as hell," Vivien said and smiled. "It's boring but important, but I do like doing it on Triton in deep water."

"You're a fish lover too then?"

"I'm more of a water lover and have been ever since I was a little girl, but I love fish too. So many things are still undiscovered down there."

"Then you should keep the job if only to be where you love. I've always believed beautiful tanks like your father's suck the joy out of the fish unfortunate enough to get caught and dropped in, and I have to guess that's what that big corner office will eventually become to you."

"How do you know there's a corner office waiting for me?"

"Your father told me, since he warned me this job was as high as I'd go in the company. I didn't mind that because I believe people, like sharks, are wild at heart too, so we should do what'll make us happy."

"You thought the people in there were wild at heart?"

"Some tame more easily than others. Orca whales aren't fish, but they're taught to do tricks when their greatest talent is killing." She put her helmet down and walked Vivien back to the door. "Take care of yourself and don't let anyone tame your wild side."

"Please stay. My father's given you my job, but it might be fun to go out with you and teach you a few things."

"Are you sure? You can still do that while I work for someone else."

"I'm positive," Vivien said, letting her go first.

They entered together, and the ass who'd given her a hard time watched them as if she might run off with Vivien, a woman he'd obviously claimed for himself. "Who's the guy next to your father?"

"Steve Hawksworth, but please ignore him. He likes to spout off about things he thinks will make my father like him even more than he does."

"Then the company already has a cheerleader, so you don't need another one," she said and laughed, glad when Vivien joined in. That was too much for Steve, it seemed, and he walked rapidly toward them.

"So you're the new drilling supervisor," Steve said as he stepped between them. "I'm surprised Winston invited you tonight."

"I'm sure he's subjecting you to the hoi polloi since we're instituting some changes to the original design and he's anxious to start." Vivien's anger was starting to burn, but this time Kai couldn't blame her if it was directed at Steve.

"Changes? What changes?" Vivien asked, making Kai rethink who she was mad at.

"Enhancements might be a better word. You and your team did a great job on Triton's design, but sometimes even great designs have room for improvement."

"There's no way Winston's taking a chance that Triton gets set back," Steve said louder than necessary, considering he was standing right next to her. If he thought that'd intimidate her, he'd make more progress screaming at Mike in the tank. "He's already upset with how little time we have left."

"He didn't sound upset during our initial talk, but I didn't realize he had to clear changes through you. I thought he ran the company."

"He does, but I know what he expects, and it's my job to give it to him."

"Hopefully he's not expecting a blow job next," she said, and Vivien, Franklin, and Marsha laughed. Steve would be happy in a fish tank. He'd swim around preening for his owner in the confined space because, unlike most, he had no imagination or curiosity as to what lay beyond the glass. "Mr. Palmer's lucky to have you, but sometimes a person doesn't need or want something because it's either an unknown or it's new. Once he knows otherwise, he realizes there's something better. That's why I'm here."

"Snake oil never took off because people learned quickly it was a sham," Steve said and laughed. "Before too long you'll be swimming in crazy circles like Mike, and you'll gladly leave once Winston takes a bite out of your ass for costing him money."

"Dinner's ready," Franklin said, as if to stop Steve before he really got going.

"Let's enjoy it then before it's my ass on the menu," Kai said, her eyes locked with Steve's. "I'm sure whatever comes out of the kitchen has to be better than that."

"I wouldn't take that bet," Marsha said as she took her arm again.

CHAPTER SEVEN

I checked her credentials, and Kai Merlin already knows how to do her job," Winston said loud enough for Vivien to have to take the phone from her ear. "If she needed a sitter she'd still be in the North Sea dodging snow and rain."

"I'm not asking you, Dad. I need to pack my stuff and clear out my quarters for her, so I'm going. Besides, the crew told me she doesn't start for another three weeks, so I might not even see her, and someone has to check the progress made since I was last out there." She sped through traffic, trying to reach Marmande Shipyard on the river before she missed Kai. She'd called that morning to ask what time Kai's helicopter was leaving for the rig and was told they had no record of arrangements for Kai's transportation since she technically didn't start until the beginning of the next month.

Her early call to the guy in charge of setting up things like that had made her curious enough to find out how Kai was getting out to Triton, and she'd asked him to phone her when he found out. It took him an hour, but he finally got an answer from the downtown hotel where Kai was staying. Kai's sailboat was moored at the pier the Marmandes used for the large fishing cruiser Mac Marmande, the owner, kept to indulge his passion for deep-sea fishing. She also wanted to ask Kai how she knew the Marmandes.

"When will you be back?" Her father's patience was as short and nonexistent as a Louisiana winter, but she couldn't live her life strictly for his also-elusive approval. She could hear his frustration, but it didn't bother her like it once had since nothing she said or did broke through the fog of the illusion he wanted her to be, and that in turn widened the divide between them. "The team's ready to go on the new plans and your input is vital."

"Frankie's got everything you need to get started, and it'll take weeks to hurdle the barriers the feds have erected, so don't worry that I'm putting you behind schedule. I know better than to think my happiness and priorities come before the company."

"Everything I've done has been for you and Franklin, so stop with the melodrama."

"You're a funny man when you want to be, Dad," she said and laughed, sad when he didn't join in. "While I'm gone, try to think back to when you were my age and what you wanted out of life."

"Sometimes responsibilities trump our great desires, sweetheart. Hopefully you'll accept that fact like I did, especially after you have a family. Life has to be more than the things that make us happy, especially when so many people are depending on you."

The guard at the gate of Marmande Shipyard waved her through when she showed her ID, since they had a few boats in dry dock for repairs, but she headed in the opposite direction, to the pier where Mac kept his boat. "That's a depressing thought," she said, and heard her father sigh. It was as close as she'd ever come to getting him to agree with her. "I can try my best to be happy and still do what's right. If not, what's the point of all this?"

"A few days, Vivien," he said, slamming the door on any further conversation, "I expect you in the office helping your brother and Steve with this project." The phone went dead, and usually that would've pissed her off for the day, but Kai was walking toward her with a smile. The sight seemed familiar to her somehow, but nothing came to mind as she looked past her to the large, beautiful sailboat.

"Expecting me or someone else?" she said when Kai opened her door and offered her a hand out of the company truck she drove. Kai wore baggy shorts, sandals, and a navy T-shirt that brought out the green of her eyes.

"Your brother said you preferred the water to helicopters, so I gave him a call to offer you a ride. You'd already left, so you're more of a nice surprise than an expected guest." Kai reached in the truck bed and lifted out her duffle, as if her coming along had been settled.

"Did it occur to you that he meant I preferred the water alone? He might've told you I left as a way of letting you down easy." She followed Kai like a tamed puppy, despite her sarcastic commentary.

"When it comes to you, Franklin only speaks the truth that's in his heart. You're not only the most important person in his life, but you're also his favorite." Kai stepped aboard with her bag and stood with her hand out to help her with the step down. She found it almost insulting but took Kai's hand anyway.

"That's a profoundly poetic statement," she said as she let go of Kai's hand and moved around her to the wheel.

"It's true, right?"

"Franklin's my favorite person in the world too, so yes, that's true." Kai laughed as she started the quietest engines Vivien had ever heard and walked along untying the boat from the dock. "What's so funny?"

"I'm relieved you didn't say Steve from last night was your favorite person," Kai said and winked. After the boat was free, Kai pointed to the wheel and made a driving motion with her hands. "You're more familiar with the river so take us out."

"You don't have to be at work for another three weeks, so is this about sucking up to the boss already?" The boat's engines were shockingly powerful for a sailboat, and she liked the way the craft responded to her touch, but she let up on the throttle so she wouldn't empty the small fuel tank these things usually had.

"Speed it up, Boss, or it'll take longer than that to get there." Kai walked the length of the boat unfastening the sail covers but stopped and peered back at her. "And if that was a serious question, I seldom engage in sucking-up behavior. You're either going to like me or you aren't. I don't really need to work for you, but I want to."

"Are those anti-cheerleading statements I hear again?" She laughed along with Kai as the ease of her companionship settled around her like a favorite sweater. She really enjoyed the open water alone, but she didn't want to waste this opportunity.

Kai Merlin had to be incredible if her father, not a man known for his whims, had hired her sight unseen. That he was also considering modifications to his baby, Triton, was also so out of character she'd stared at him throughout dinner the night before to see if she saw any sign of impairment. Her father had to be either high or drunk to chance any delay in Triton's coming online.

Mentally she started a list of questions to ask Kai so she wouldn't seem too intrusive, but the shell at her throat warmed enough to derail her thoughts. It'd done that in the years she'd worn it, and while it seemed strange, it was part of her. The heat was never unpleasant, but when it happened, it seemed like she was touring whatever was going on in Frankie's head. Now, though, all she got from Kai was her great smile, and Franklin seemed a million miles away.

"I'll try to keep my enthusiasm levels high when your father's around," Kai said when she was done and sat behind her.

The two bridges that connected the east and west banks of the river downtown were close, and the crescent that gave the city its nickname was a dangerous spot for crazy currents, so she tightened her hands on the wheel and concentrated on getting them safely through it. "Are you sure you don't want to do this?"

"You can handle it," Kai said, not moving from her seat.

"You don't know that." She wanted to turn around and look at Kai, but concentration was paramount.

"Do you keep the *Sea Dreamer* moored in the middle of the Gulf?"

"Since you know my boat, I guess you know where it's docked, so point taken." The powerful engines took them effortlessly through the bend, and once the river straightened out, she relaxed and glanced behind her. "Question is, how do you know so much about me?"

"Because I checked you and your family out as extensively as you did me, I'm sure," Kai said as she opened her eyes. "I wasn't really desperate for a job, so I wanted to make sure Palmer would be a good fit. If I'm miserable I wouldn't be of much use to you."

"And what made us a good fit for you?" This was an unusual conversation to have with an employee. She hated to admit how spoiled she was because of her last name, but in most cases people went out of their way to be agreeable. Kai made it sound as if they were lucky to have her.

"Your willingness to evolve."

She saw the down side of accepting Kai's invitation to guide them downriver since she liked to face someone when she talked. It was the only way to tell if they were truthful. Now she was like a bug on display for Kai to study without interruption. "Are you mocking us?"

"For someone who says she appreciates the truth, you don't care for it unless it's phrased to your liking, do you?" Kai's feet hit the deck, and she took over so they could reverse their spots.

Kai seemed to have read her mind and changed everything about the situation that bothered her. "That's not what I meant, so don't make the mistake of speaking for me or putting words in my mouth. I don't appreciate it." She cringed since the statement was lame and sounded childish.

"I'm not upset with you, Miss Palmer." Kai's voice was gentle, but like the night before, her tone had changed. "*I* meant that despite what everyone, perhaps including you, thinks about your father, he genuinely sounded interested in trying to streamline your operations by bringing in techniques that big oil doesn't usually embrace. He's an innovator, even if the environmentalists think he's a dinosaur, and if they don't wise up, all that'll be left are the dinosaurs not interested in changing anything."

"Are you sure we're thinking about the same guy? My father's only interested in the bottom line and keeping the dinosaurs on our board happy. Anyone who tries to rock that boat doesn't go far in any company, including ours," she said, forcing herself to shut up. It wasn't a good idea to divulge her thoughts to a total stranger, no matter if she was on their payroll. "That's the reality, and I'd appreciate it if you didn't share what I just said with anyone."

"If you're worried I'm only interested in spying on your operations for some nefarious reason—don't."

There was still plenty of river traffic, but Kai pressed a series of buttons at the center of the helm and the sails went up. "I've never heard a roughneck use the word nefarious."

"I'm rough around the edges, but I have a mother who loves language and insisted I develop an extensive vocabulary. And to answer your question, we are talking about the same guy. Your father's willing to indulge a few of my ideas, and it doesn't really matter to me that he's more interested in the good press than in my crazy eco side."

"That does sound like him, but if you want my advice, stay clear of Steve Hawksworth whenever you can. My father and the board have plenty of reasons to love him, and it's not for *his* crazy eco side." Kai navigated skillfully around the tugs with strings of barges, the freighters, and the other work vessels they met. The wind directions had allowed them to pick up speed, but the ride was still as smooth as if they were gliding over the water instead of on it.

"What do you like besides work and Franklin?"

"Is this the fluff piece of the spy story you're working on?" she asked and laughed, but she sensed that maybe she should sit back and simply enjoy the ride because Kai wasn't all she appeared to be. "What are you really after here?" She didn't make any effort to keep the suspicion from her tone.

Kai glanced back at Vivien, and Vivien's shell warmed and vibrated at her throat again. She held it away from her skin, but Kai knew the sensation wouldn't last long. This trip was about linking Vivien's mind to hers to see why Vivien still hadn't taken the necklace off, but after sensing that it was only because of the bond it strengthened between her and Franklin, she didn't find anything else interesting about her. Her mothers had been right—the only people she could trust until she was done were Isla and Talia.

Vivien by nature was a suspicious person who was trying to delude herself into considering herself an explorer, but she had plenty to learn before she found anything besides the occasional old wreck and pretty fish beneath the water's surface. The wonders Vivien longed for would never be visible because of the blinders she wore through life.

If she had something to do with that because of what she'd done all those years ago, she'd try her best to get Vivien to open up more, but even if she could, she doubted they'd ever become good friends. Vivien seemed to enjoy her solitude too much to ever let anyone but Franklin in. Whatever their future relationship would be, she had enough information to attempt to make a plan to fix what she'd broken in Vivien and Franklin's lives.

She pressed the main switch for the sails, and all of them came down at once. When the engines kicked back on, they slowed enough that she could come up to the crew boat with the Palmer Oil logo on its side.

"What are you doing?" Vivien asked as she stood close to her.

"Making you feel more at ease." She radioed the boat, and it didn't take long for two workers to come out of the cabin to man the ropes that brought them together. "I'll see you soon." She threw Vivien's bags up to Talia and smiled at her old friend. "Could you make sure Miss Palmer gets to Triton please, Captain?"

"No problem. That's where we're headed with supplies."

"You're seriously throwing me off?" Vivien asked, her fists on her hips.

"I think it'd be best if you go a way you trust." She grabbed the lower rail of the crew boat and pulled it close enough that Vivien could step aboard. "Our talk reminded me I don't have to be at work yet, so I'll see you when I'm expected."

Vivien changed vessels with the help of the two crewmembers who'd first come out, then immediately turned around and stared at her as if she was still in disbelief she'd been asked to leave. They drifted apart since Talia had guided her vessel clear, and she was grateful Talia had planned her departure in case this exchange had to happen. Talia had gotten a job as a boat captain and Isla as a diver, and both of the royal guards had been assigned to Triton to be near her without raising any suspicions.

She raised her sails again, passed the crew boat quickly, and didn't think to look back for an hour. By then Vivien and the others were out of sight. "The water will always be a strange and cold place for you, Vivien. What happened to the caring young girl I met years ago?"

The problem didn't have an easy solution since she didn't have any experiences to draw from. "One idiotic act on my part couldn't have caused this much damage," she said softly as she enjoyed the breeze on her face. "But if it did, I owe it to you to fix it."

Kai had no clue as to how to break through the pile of painful memories Vivien clung to like talismans—none at all.

"Have we met?" Vivien asked the woman who sat in the captain's chair with a large mug of coffee in her free hand.

"No, ma'am. I'm new to this route and the company. Talia Hessen," she said, and nodded slightly in her direction.

"Do you know Kai Merlin?"

"No, ma'am, but hopefully you're Vivien Palmer. If you're not, I might have some explaining to do when we reach the rig and I discover I picked up a stranger along the way because someone asked me nicely."

"I'm glad you were there so don't worry about it." Vivien stepped outside and unclipped her satellite phone from her belt. The phone was a gift from Frankie, who liked for her to stay in touch no matter where she was.

"Did you find the big Amazon?" Frankie said as a greeting.

She gave him a brief rundown of what had happened and had to suffer through his laughter. "If I needed anymore humiliation today I'd have called Mom and asked her to appraise my hair and wardrobe."

"I'm sorry, and I'm sorry for sending you out to what was basically a crappy day. After dinner last night I figured you two would become fast friends."

"She asked a lot of questions and I called her on it, so the next thing she did was beeline it to one of our boats and dump my ass." They were close to the mouth of the river, and the water was getting choppier here as the skies became overcast. "Can you pull her file and read me the highlights."

"What kind of questions?" She could hear Frankie typing as they spoke. "Last time someone was that interested in me, it didn't turn out to be corporate espionage. They just wanted to be my friend."

"Go ahead and say it—I'm a jackass."

"The first step to recovery is admitting you've got a problem, sister," Franklin said and laughed. "According to her file she graduated from an Ivy League school, has an excellent work record, and Dad actually recruited her away from an English outfit that had her working in the North Sea. From all this, she sounds cerebral with some roughneck mixed in. No one works the North Sea without having some serious backbone. The conditions are brutal most of the time."

"He went after her? Why?"

"It doesn't say, and you blew your chance to find out when she made you walk the plank."

"Can you have the *Sea Dreamer* brought out? She's got a head start on that speed demon of hers, but I've got a shot of finding her." The mist was turning to a light rain, and she didn't want to arrive soaked so she went back inside. "If you get a chance, try to bring the subject up casually and see what Dad tells you about it. He's not the type to go looking for someone like this without good reason."

"I'll let you know, so be careful."

She went and sat at the table behind the captain and took out her laptop. As it booted up she looked at the row of boxes lining the opposite wall that had Merlin stenciled on the side. She doubted they contained Kai's personal items or snacks, and she no longer cared if she seemed nosy or not.

"Can I see your manifest?" she asked the man closest to her. Every box was listed, but it was like reading gibberish when she tried to make out the descriptions, so she flipped open her pocket knife and cut through the top of the closest one.

Even after she'd opened five, she still had no clue as to what she was looking at, and it was unlikely anyone on board could offer her an explanation, so she sat back down and Googled Kai Merlin's name. Her search found numerous pictures of Kai with the locals of whatever country she was in, smiling in celebration over another successful well, but none of them had to do with crude. Kai's specialty seemed to be finding water.

She saw some of the same equipment in the background of the photo labeled AMAZON JUNGLE. There were monitors in the trees, but the people in loincloths gathered around Kai didn't appear alarmed or upset. Was a ready water supply payment for drilling rights? Maybe the do-gooder traded the convenience of a well for something these people would surely regret when the heavy equipment arrived.

Vivien thought about it for the next three hours as she studied Triton's blueprints, looking for anything that might be a problem as they geared up for production. Triton's capacity would catapult them to the big leagues, which would make the shareholders ecstatically happy, but she primarily wanted to prevent another disaster that would sink the company faster than a torpedo through a rusty hull. Unlike BP, they'd never survive financially if the same thing happened to them.

"Triton, this is the *Sea Witch*," Talia said, and Vivien looked out the window. "We're tying up at the southwest station and request assistance."

"Make sure all your bumpers are out," a man said. "In seas like this you'll get beat to hell if you don't."

Vivien took out her rain gear and stowed her stuff. They were rocking in the high waves, which made unloading a pain in the ass, but she'd rather ride out the storm on Triton's massive structure than here. "Hope you found safe shelter," she thought about Kai, upset with herself for what had happened. "No one deserves to be out in this alone."

But that's exactly how she felt right then.

Chapter Eight

K ai checked her radar again and saw a few blips she figured were anchored fishing vessels, probably because of the weather and rough seas. She'd started making contacts in the area the year before, so she sailed toward them to see if they were some of the people she'd met.

The recent oil spill had decimated their business, but with the help of BP's deep pockets, they were starting to recover and prove the seafood they were catching was safe to eat. With her help, they'd brought in enough healthy specimens that the fish farms she'd helped them start were reported to be thriving. Eventually they could make a living with just that, but like her, they loved the open water. They'd never leave it unless forced to.

"Kai, that you?" A man's voice came over her radio.

"Antoine?" The seventy-one-year-old shrimper had six sons who all worked for him and probably were the other five blips on her radar.

"Come to see if I'm paying you back?" Antoine said and laughed.

"I trusted you from the day you shook my hand, so cut the crap. Are you by any chance putting any in?"

A lot of Antoine's neighbors had taken the settlement money and banked it, but he'd listened to what she was preaching when it came to the future of the fishing industry. With her help, he'd invested in what quickly grew to be a massive operation that farmed redfish, speckled trout, drum, and lemon fish. The only payments she'd asked for her sizeable investment was that he return a fourth of his crop to the wild.

"Come see. We'll wait to put the reds in."

She anchored close to Antoine's boat and swam the fifty or so feet to look at his holding tanks. The vessel, along with the other five, belonged to Kai, and she'd designed each one.

"That's a lot of fish, my friend."

"Too young to keep if they're caught, but big enough to survive. And you were right about the weather. When it's rough like this and the wind is whipping, ain't nobody out here but us, so no fucker who doesn't care what size the catch is bothers."

There had to be over a thousand redfish in the large holding tank, and they were splashing like they realized freedom wasn't far off. The Guidrys were making money, but she wanted them to learn that they could do so while still giving back to the waters that sustained them.

"Your grandchildren will thank you," she said as the bottom of the hold slid back and the fish stopped momentarily before flitting off to the marsh grass a hundred yards away. "More releases like this and they'll still be here when their grandchildren fish these waters."

"Damn right," Antoine said and laughed again, "and my neighbors are kicking themselves in the ass for not listening to you. I got them fancy restaurants from New Orleans lined up after the word got out."

"Good, but don't forget our deal."

"Don't worry. I ain't about to put the gris-gris on myself now." He closed the hold and signaled the others to release their loads. "We added three more tanks and bought out a few more places to be able to spread out. You want to come by and see? The wife's making a big sauce picante."

"Set two more places."

"You got somebody stowed away on that boat, Kai?" Kevin, Antoine's eldest son, asked.

"More like a stalker with her own boat, and I expect she's not too far behind me." The water around her seemed to be full of life, and she had higher hopes for the future. With careful conservation and partners like the Guidrys, she'd spend her life rebuilding this important habitat.

"We can take care of that for you," Kevin said.

"Nah, this could be a good thing because we need to bridge the gap between big oil and the fisherman. If we can get them to buy in, maybe one of your brothers will run a place where all the fish get released."

"Put me in line for that," Kevin said as he slapped her on the back. "I ain't going to be one of those dumbasses who didn't listen to you."

"You got it, and once you're up and running, let's see how many women you attract."

"Women?" Antoine asked as they waited for the other boats to finish.

"Women love a guy trying to save the fishies," she joked as she gazed toward the south. The storm was putting on an impressive lightning show, but her senses didn't ping that Vivien was in danger. Actually the experienced boater was speeding toward them so it wouldn't be long before they would spot her. "Head back and we'll be right behind you."

"You sure you don't want one of the boys to stay with you?" Antoine asked.

"Vivien Palmer's more dreamer than threat, so I'll be fine."

She swam back to her boat with Ram and Ivan on each side of her, then gave them leave to hunt in deeper water so they'd leave Antoine's release alone. It seemed strange that after years of silence, Vivien's shell had suddenly opened her thoughts and feelings to Kai so vividly it was drowning out anything else when she was near. But really all that filled Vivien's head was a rampant curiosity that Kai had doubled when she'd dumped her on the supply boat.

Sudden fits of anger weren't Kai's norm, but she'd never met anyone so guarded, naturally suspicious, and in pain as Vivien Palmer. Unquestionably she'd give Vivien all the attention she wanted as a way to start chipping away at her guarded personality. Not having her parents believe what Vivien considered a childhood trauma had scarred both her and Franklin, and the Palmers had only piled on to that through the years. Kai didn't sense the elder Palmers had done it maliciously, but their efforts to *guide* their children had opened a chasm between them as wide and deep as the deepest ocean canyon.

The *Sea Dreamer* was a nice vessel with what appeared to be some massive horsepower, from the size of Vivien's wake. Vivien's curiosity was driving her, but Kai could also sense the joy she experienced from having the wind in her hair and an expanse of water before her. Even in this weather, it was hard to miss Vivien's happiness in the environment where she felt most at home.

"You don't have any cannons on that thing, do you?" Vivien asked as soon as her anchor went down.

Kai was sure Vivien had no idea how she was able to find her so easily and would probably laugh in her face if she explained the beacon she had tied around her neck. "I'm glad you found me so I can apologize. That wasn't a nice thing to do, and not a good way to start what I hope becomes a friendship." She stared at Vivien's hand since it was clenched in a fist at her throat. "You interested in getting out of this for a little while?"

"We'd have to head inland, or do you want to come aboard?"

"We actually have a dinner invitation, if you're interested."

"New Orleans is a long way off."

"Invitation, not reservation," she said as she maneuvered closer to the *Sea Dreamer*. "You want to go together or follow me?"

"Are you going to dump me in the marsh if I get stupid again?"

"I blame my lack of manners on fatigue, so you have my word it won't happen again." She locked the cabin and set *Salacia*'s security features from the small control she wore on her wrist. Whoever decided to step aboard without permission would have a memorable experience when they jumped overboard and found the guards patrolling the water. Even if they told someone what happened, no one would believe a Great White sighting here, much less seeing two massive sharks.

"You change your mind?" Vivien said with a sigh.

"Let's go on yours," she said as she waved Vivien closer. "This way if I get out of line *you* can demand I swim back."

Vivien allowed her to get them where they were going and sat quietly up on the fly bridge as they went up the bay that would lead to the bayou the Guidrys lived along. The *Sea Dreamer* was big but manageable, and Kai noticed the racks of tanks on the back. Vivien worked for her father and the board, but her life's goal was to find the meaning of the symbols on her shell. Every memory Kai tapped into was testament to that search, and even though Vivien had never come close, nothing killed the drive to find the hidden clues she just knew were hidden below the waves.

Vivien finally broke the silence between them. "No hints as to where we're going?"

"Don't tell my boss, but I'd like to show you the real reason I moved here." She smiled and winked, finally getting Vivien to smile as well.

"All there is around here are small fishing villages, and the only thing the residents like about the oil industry is fishing around our offshore structures."

"You're partially right." She slowed them down and waved at the onlookers who stopped what they were doing and stared. "They do love fishing the platforms out there, but a lot of their family work for you and the others drilling here. You don't bite the hand that pays you, so you won't find too many people planning protests against you."

"You should've been here when the Deepwater Horizon went down. There were plenty of protestors then."

"The outrage over that was justified. Any company who works fast and unsafe should be called out on a world stage, but that's not what this is about." She put the engines in neutral so they'd drift in, and one of Antoine's sons was waiting to tie them off.

Large tanks lined the land all the way to the house, and they were adding more near the trees along the side. Kai had designed the area to save the large oaks and cypress trees that held the land together. A series of elevated walkways allowed the family and workers to reach every tank for observation and feedings. At the back of Antoine's large elevated home, the marsh grasses were thriving, unlike those of his neighbors.

"What's all this?" Vivien asked as she peered into the nearest tank.

"The oil industry didn't kill the fishing industry around here. Overfishing did." Kai knelt next to Vivien and ran a net through the water, filling it with what looked to be guppies. "Like a farmer, anyone who wants to harvest the waters has to seed it first. I'm helping Antoine and his sons show the others a path that'll lead to not only more fish, but a new mindset."

"What are these?" Vivien asked as Kai released her catch.

"Redfish that hatched a few days ago, ma'am," Antoine's son said.

"This is one of the nurseries." Kai pointed to a few more tanks. "Once the fish are bigger, they're separated so none of them get crowded. It's easier to maintain them here since they use the water from the bayou. That way they don't have a huge transition when they're released."

"We planted the grass Kai gave us, and the waste from the fish feeds it," the man said. "It's got all those smart folks from LSU crawling all over us to see how it works, but later about that since dinner's ready."

"You really are a fish lover," Vivien said with a huge smile.

"Especially when they're covered in cream sauce."

The dinner was enlightening, especially when Antoine told Vivien he'd been acquainted with her father for years and that Winston had helped him start his own business. Vivien had never known her father to be overly generous except for anyone who could advance Palmer's business interest. It'd given her a new perspective that'd loosened the anger that for too long had clouded her thoughts of a man she rarely understood anymore.

Kai had brought them back and anchored her vessel a few hundred yards from her own and swam back fully clothed. She hadn't had very much time with Kai, but it was nice to see someone so comfortable in her own skin, since Kai had appeared as at ease with the Guidrys as at her father's table.

The breeze blowing in from the southeast wasn't cold, but it was enough to raise goose bumps as it ticked up another notch. With the rain earlier the boat bobbed more than usual, as if the Gulf hadn't settled yet, but the night was too beautiful for her to go in. She took another sip of the scotch she kept on board and gazed up at the stars, remembering her mom's old stories.

Vivien was sure she'd made most of them up, like the shell legend. If not, they'd have dragged half of Florida back with them after every trip. However, she didn't care if her mom had conjured it from her imagination, because she still cherished it. It was right after the vacation when they'd reported the girl missing and that the sharks she'd feared had attacked her. The two people who should've believed her didn't, which had rocked her self-confidence. She'd never been a fibber as a child, so it'd been like a hard slap to her soul when her parents hadn't taken her at her word, and she'd moped around for weeks after they'd returned home.

Her mother had found her at her bedroom window one night in the dark, staring up at the sky, and told her a story about a girl who thought there wasn't a place for her in the world. The child had no voice, no one who truly believed in her, and since the child felt like those things would never change, her life became one of despair. It wasn't until a loving sprite visited her one night that she knew that, with time, she would find all the answers she sought in the stars.

"Just as there's a place for every star in the heavens, one day you'll find yours," her mom had said. "Once you do, you'll be the point by which someone navigates their way home because that's what you'll be to them—home."

Surprisingly, her mom had apologized for not believing her and Franklin, and it was the last time they'd discussed it. She'd carried the experience with her like the shell she wore, and so far she'd kept her vow never to forget the girl and so to honor her memory.

"I've probably worried about you all these years, and you're most likely happily married with three kids. But if you're up there—I still think about you," she whispered as she took a sip of her drink. It was late and she had an early day on Triton, so she flexed her legs to stand but stopped.

Kai had come out of her cabin and stood briefly on the deck before diving in completely naked, giving Vivien only a brief glimpse. She figured announcing herself now would embarrass Kai as well as herself, but even with the threat of being discovered, she couldn't look away as Kai swam near her vessel.

Kai appeared at home in the water despite the large swells, and Vivien laughed along with her when a few dolphins came up near Kai as if wanting to play. They bumped Kai as she swam, and one even hurdled over her almost like it'd been trained to do so. In all her time at sea, Vivien had never had a pod come so willingly close and interact with someone like this.

"They are creatures drawn by happiness." A voice echoed through Vivien's head, and she put her glass down when she heard it. "Release your sadness about things you have no control over, and you'll be free to find the answers you so desperately seek."

"What in the hell's happening to me," she whispered as she closed her eyes and pressed her hands to the sides of her head. Had the stress finally made her snap? If she had, the only good that would come of it would be getting her parents to stop pushing an agenda she wasn't interested in, but she doubted even a douse of madness would make them give up on the things they wanted for her.

When she opened her eyes again the dolphins were still there but Kai wasn't, and after scanning the area, Vivien figured she'd gone back inside. She was where she most enjoyed her life, but she was alone. Tonight that was a scarier thought than usual because she knew this fractured life she was leading would eventually not be enough. One side would come to demand all her time, and even if she wound up exploring the ocean's depths, without someone to share it with, all of it was meaningless.

"Good Lord, I'm becoming more morose by the minute," she said to the dolphin that stared up at her and made clicking noises. "Maybe I'll get to come back as one of you the next time around, and all I'll have to worry about is fish nets."

She picked up her glass and held it against her chest. Tomorrow it was back to Triton and her last days on the water for some time. The corner office and her father were waiting. "So my unhappiness is almost complete."

Kai swam to their outpost with Ivan and Ram at her sides, wanting to put some distance between her and Vivien. The structure was empty of people, but the equipment she needed for her mission was ready to deploy in their dive room. This technology was much more advanced than anything the military and the oil industry had at their disposal, and it was Kai's intent to keep it that way.

Everyone involved in the oil industry was after better cleanup, but if it was readily available, in her opinion, the drillers would only take more and more reckless chances if they were working with a safety net.

She threw on a T-shirt and shorts before entering the control room and entering the code for the secure chamber in the palace. It was time to report her actions so far.

"Did you arrive all right?" her mother Galen asked with a large smile. Hadley sat next to her and chuckled.

It was all the proof she needed to know that she hadn't stumbled onto her position and the Palmers by chance. "The trip was fast and without incident, and the Palmers and their friends make even the worst of our council meetings seem tame and cordial."

"Do you remember our conversations about how you have to be considerate not only of the realm but of the Earth as a whole?" Galen asked.

"Yes," she said with a sense of shame. Granted, she'd been young when she'd met the Palmer children, but that wasn't an excuse.

"We were glad you chose this place so you could see Vivien and Franklin again. What you did wasn't horrible, so ease your mind about what you're feeling now," Galen said and reached out as if she could touch her through the screen. In a way she did through the shell at her neck.

"Those around them misunderstood what happened, and they didn't take the traumatic event Vivien and Franklin thought they saw seriously. They've gone on from that moment believing large sharks tore you to pieces, and not only were they not believed, but they've carried the helplessness of not being able to help you," Hadley said.

"Because of that, they've built a moat around themselves, and last night you got a taste of what that small act has become. How they face life and people isn't your fault, but you did plant the seed of uncertainty," Galen explained.

"Vivien and Franklin have each other to rely on, and from what I saw at dinner, I'm not solely to blame for their relationship with their parents. Mr. Palmer's progressive in business but treats his children like show dogs. He prances them out for their board of directors and others, but he only values them, in my opinion anyway, for breeding and business."

"Every beautiful kind of flower," Galen said as she took Hadley's hand, "has strains of weeds somewhere in its lines. We'll never know how different the Palmer children would be without that memory, but I trust you to help them."

She nodded as both of them spoke, since she totally agreed. "Do you have any idea how I'm supposed to fix this?"

"You can figure it out, tadpole, but this time around it won't be as easy as leaving etched shells," Hadley said and winked.

"Not helpful at all, Mom, but thanks."

CHAPTER NINE

Steve Hawksworth stared at the plume of smoke rising from what looked like an accident scene on the interstate, but his office was too high up to see clearly. He really didn't care—it was simply something to draw his attention away from the amount of paperwork Winston had piled on both him and Franklin. Winston had promised that the extra workload would level out once Vivien relocated to the office, but Steve doubted that.

In his experience, Winston didn't often compromise. He barked orders and assumed everyone around him would make it their life's mission to carry them out. Steve understood that kind of power, and he also understood the consequences of not marching to Winston's drumbeat. Those two truths had him staring out the window since the only person in Winston's life who didn't give a damn about anything remotely important to him was his daughter, Vivien, and she in turn cared nothing about him either. The idiot had actually rebuffed every advance and overture he'd made toward her, and it had pissed him off longer and more than he cared to admit.

Vivien did everything she could to drive Winston's blood pressure through the stratosphere, and she seemed to almost relish the effect she had on him. But like in all dysfunctional relationships, neither Winston nor Vivien was willing to cut their ties, no matter how miserable they made each other. Whatever it was, it left no room for him or anyone else to make inroads into their lives.

"Do you have the exact coordinates for track fifty-seven?" Franklin asked from his doorway. "I want to double check my figures before filing the initial papers."

"Did your secretary quit?" he asked without turning around.

"No. I just needed to stretch my legs," Franklin said, sarcasm dripping from every word. "You have the numbers or not?"

It wasn't a secret around the office that he and Franklin didn't particularly care for one another, but he wasn't interested in making Franklin his best friend. He just needed him to quit torpedoing his chances with Vivien, which Franklin did constantly, so it was difficult to be civil when the dipshit talked to him like this. Franklin was totally loyal to his sister, and since Vivien didn't like him, Franklin didn't and wouldn't do anything to help him win Vivien over. Marriage was the easiest path to the top of the company, but Vivien acted as if he were radioactive. That left only Winston and his wife Cornelia as his greatest allies as far as that option was concerned.

He moved slowly to his computer and sent an email. "They're waiting in your inbox."

"Saying them out loud was too much trouble for you?" Franklin placed his hands on the wheels of his chair but didn't move.

"Anything else?" He also wasn't interested in any kind of relationship with Franklin because of his weakness. To align himself with Franklin, even as a way to Vivien, wouldn't get him any closer to the prize he was after, and he knew that Winston considered Franklin the plague that'd killed off his family's name.

"Nothing," Franklin said and stared at him before rolling away.

"Steve," his assistant Tanice said as she entered his office and closed the door. "Any word from the water princess?"

"Vivien's teaching the new hire the ropes, supposedly, but Daddy finally put his foot down. The Lady Palmer should grace us with her presence in a few days." He moved back to the window and glanced down at the accident scene now surrounded by flashing blue and red lights from first responders. "What'd you find?"

"Everything on Kai Merlin's resume checks out, down to her time with the Peace Corps. She's got a knack for finding water, purifying it for consumption, and cleaning up dirty waterways that big, bad, industrial scumbags have ravaged."

"Nothing stands out?"

"Only that she's an environmental do-gooder, which is odd, considering her career choice." Tanice moved her fingers down her tablet as she spoke. "If you're talking about unexplained gaps or anomalies, or some big scandal you can use against her, then no."

"No one's that perfect except on paper." He turned and dropped into his chair, where his restlessness made him open and close his hands. "You have to have missed something."

"I called and confirmed all the details on here as well as what was on the background check," Tanice said with a tinge of exasperation. "I'm sure the people on this list aren't involved in a conspiracy about her good deeds just to mess with you. All the information is in here if you think I'm lying."

"I know you're not lying, but we have to find something. You didn't see the reaction Vivien had to that big sarcastic bitch. She creamed her pants, and if this fucking idiot starts giving the water princess any ideas, I'm screwed." He thumbed through the report Tanice had mentioned and paused at all the pictures included. "If I'm right, this explains why Vivien isn't interested. It sure isn't from my lack of trying."

"I'm sure being a lesbian would be the only reason any woman wouldn't be interested in you," Tanice said with a smile he figured bordered on laughter.

"Remember who you're talking to," he said, not at all amused. "Get back to work and find something. You can tell me all about it tonight."

"I'll try my best, Your Highness."

He walked to Winston's office a few minutes before the team meeting his boss had scheduled, wanting to know why Winston had hired Kai Merlin and why he'd risk changes to Triton. Once that facility went on line, Palmer Oil would be directly competing with the big boys, and that's what Steve was waiting for.

"Problem?" Winston asked in his usual gruff manner.

"Maybe," he said as he sat and glanced at all the framed pictures behind Winston's desk. It was an altar to his wife and children at different ages, all near water, and all of them full of awkward smiles and poses. If you didn't know Winston at all and entered this room, you'd swear his family was the center of his universe.

Steve knew better.

"What the hell happened now?" Winston asked, sounding as if he wouldn't mind killing the messenger.

"Before I tell you, would you mind explaining why you lured Kai Merlin out of the North Sea?"

"Because both BP and Chevron were after her for the same reason I was. Merlin's a good engineer who'll do a good job on Triton, but that's true of a large group of folks with the same credentials." Winston took a cigar from the small leather case, usually a fixture in his suit pocket, and lit it without asking if he wanted to join him. Free cigars had ended for everyone when Cornelia limited Winston's daily treats to the three the case held.

"So why not hire someone else more aligned with company beliefs?"

"The good ole days of my daddy running this company are over, so now I need an edge to keep the federal and state regulators as well as the environmentalists off my ass." Winston blew a stream of smoke in his direction, and he came close to coughing but managed not to, since Winston would see it as a fault in his manhood. "Merlin, like you said, is a fish lover, which I know ain't your thing, but the tree huggers love her."

"I could pretend to love fish as much as anybody, if it'll get us ahead in this."

"Sure, but you ain't got the track record she does on the subject, and you don't have all the fishermen on the coast chasing you down for advice."

"So that's why you hired her?"

"I don't have the time or patience to explain myself to you or anybody, so get your petty jealousies under control."

Winston was staring at him in a way that meant it wouldn't do him any good to push him. "Jealousy has nothing to do with it. I'm only looking out for you and the company."

"So Merlin's your *maybe* problem?" Winston blew more smoke at him.

"Forget I said anything—" Franklin and the others arrived for their meeting. When Winston kept staring at him, he realized his mistake. Like he suspected of Vivien, Winston liked Kai, and liked what she'd do for him even more. He wouldn't appreciate or tolerate another outburst.

Enjoy the glory while you can, Winston, Steve thought as he maintained eye contact with his boss. When the next phase of this company comes along, you along with your heirs will only be able to watch as I take over.

❖

"Do you mind if I stick around today?" Vivien asked when Kai's head popped out of the water next to her boat. The dorsal fin in the distance made her panic for a moment, but a second look assured her it was another dolphin.

"I was hoping you would," Kai said, smiling up at her. "How about putting your suit on and joining me?"

Kai's hair was slicked back, and her expression made Vivien think she wasn't only at peace at the moment, but happy. It was almost like a mirror effect since that one glance made her happy as well.

"You're very popular," she said, pointing to the pod that was swimming closer. "I've never seen them do that."

"Maybe you should start swimming with fish in your pants like I do. You'll attract all kinds of new friends."

She laughed when Kai winked at her and left to do as Kai had asked. There wasn't anything remotely interesting to look at under the water here, but it'd been a long while since she'd gone for a swim just for enjoyment and not searching for something. Then again, she didn't have anyone in her life worth spending time like that with—not even from an early age. Franklin was the only one she'd ever wanted to share this with, but his terror of the water had prevented her from experiencing this part of herself with him.

She changed into a one-piece she hadn't worn in over a year and hoped it hid as much as the wetsuit she usually preferred. She definitely wasn't in the same league as Kai, especially since she'd seen her naked the night before, but she didn't have time to worry over something that trivial. "This isn't a date," she said to herself in the mirror attached to the small bathroom door. "Get on with it."

"Bring your mask and snorkel," Kai said when she stepped out.

"I don't find grass and sand all that exciting." She opened the cabinet next to her tanks and removed her equipment anyway.

"Have some faith," Kai said as she floated on her back. She was swimming in shorts and a long-sleeved T-shirt with a large marlin across the chest. "You might have missed a few things since the last time you put your face down here."

Kai had a flirty way of talking to her. Vivien's ears warmed, and she hoped the blush that had sparked that response wasn't too visible. The smile on Kai's face widened, so she figured her wish was pure fantasy. Everything Kai said, though, caused her to react in some way, but unlike Steve, who affected her as strongly, she wasn't dying to get away from Kai.

She glanced at the barrier island in the distance, Raccoon Island, and figured the swim would be worth the effort just to check out how the land was doing after the spill. "If you say so."

Kai nodded and started toward her stern. "I say so, Boss."

She laughed at the title since she doubted Kai had much use for authority and would quit if anyone tried to cram theirs down her throat. Her leap put her in the water feet first, well away from Kai, and she donned her mask as soon as she surfaced since Kai had done the same.

Like she predicted, she saw nothing but grass and long stretches of sand, with the occasional fish as they made their way, but having Kai along made the excursion pleasant. However, about a hundred yards from Raccoon Island she noticed the change in the Gulf floor.

"What's that?" she asked as soon as her head came up.

"Are you sure you want to know?" Kai said, her smile too smug.

"If it's illegal then probably no."

"I'm not that much of a rule breaker." Kai floated on back again and kicked toward shore.

Vivien followed like a well-trained pet but put her head down again to see the large cement structures, laid out randomly. They resembled large pinecones with open tops, and as they swam closer to shore she figured out their purpose. The waves moving toward the beach carried sand that ended up in the structures, and the process was actually building land already planted with a type of sea grass not indigenous to the area.

"What are those?" she asked again as Kai led them to the edge of the island.

"The better question is whose are they?" Kai said as she pointed to the small row of metal boxes on the shore.

"We're paying you way too much if they're yours." She followed slightly behind Kai so as to not be in Kai's line of vision and scrutiny. From the moment she'd first seen Kai, it was like she had free rein to her thoughts and emotions, and she wanted to shut that down for a while.

"They're land expanders, and we have about twelve hundred out there now, with three times that number going in. They belong to you. Or should I say Palmer Oil?"

"I'm certainly not Palmer Oil all by myself." From the shore Vivien could tell where the expanders were installed, since the area was close to becoming a sandbar almost out of the water.

"If you heard your dad go on about you, you'd believe differently. You and Franklin are the future, and he wants the legacy of the company he leaves you to be as much about this stuff as the production side."

She laughed as Kai unlocked the first box. "Maybe I misjudged your cheerleading talents, or maybe you're just a suck-up."

"Will you believe a little of both?" Kai waved her over and pointed to the monitors inside. From what Vivien could see of the setup, the computers were running off the solar panels attached to the outside of the box. "We have enough monitors down here to capture video footage of every wave, as well as how much accumulation we're getting. If my calculations are correct, these will add significant land mass, limited only by how many of them are installed."

"It's got to be significant if you're getting grass to grow and it's staying put."

"The stuff down there is the same strain as what you saw last night. Once it takes hold, it's pretty much permanent, since the roots are things of beauty unless it's growing somewhere you don't want it."

"When did my father become such a conservationist, and why haven't any of us heard about all this? The board would freak if they knew he was spending willy-nilly on stuff like this." Kai moved to the next box and took out some beach chairs and an umbrella. "What, no fridge loaded with drinks?"

"The folks who set all this up weren't big drinkers, but I'll consider the idea," Kai said, her attention on the shoreline. "This project isn't finished, and it certainly hasn't been cheap, but Mr. Palmer made a deal with the state since they own this rather tiny piece of paradise."

"Was the deal to bilk the state out of money?"

"I'm fairly sure you should have a higher regard for your father than I do, and no, that isn't the deal. If we can prove that these work, then Palmer gets the contract to put them in around the other barrier islands, and even if Palmer doesn't, I own the patents on the design so no one can just start installing them for this purpose. I want to restore each of the barrier islands to what they were a hundred and fifty years ago."

"I've known Winston Palmer longer than you, so give him time to shred all your hopes and dreams. Right now I'm more curious about you." She tensed again at the sight of another dorsal fin, but it was still the dolphins right offshore. "If you're more into this stuff, why take a job with us?"

"Can you answer a question first?" She nodded at Kai's question. "What are your dreams?"

"I was around six the last time someone asked me that question, but it wasn't so much an open-ended thing when it came to the answer." When Kai briefly gazed at her as if confused, she laughed. "What I mean is, that question had some wrong answers and pretty much only one right one."

"The CEO of Palmer Oil is probably what your parents were looking for."

"I'm not an indentured servant, but my father was driven to wake up the Palmer genes in us when it came to the company, and he hasn't stopped."

"Back to the cheerleading gig, huh?" She nodded and laughed again. "Now that I know Winston's hopes and dreams, what are yours? Pretend your last name is Smith."

"I'm a treasure hunter at heart, but gold and precious stones aren't all I look for. Ever since I was little, I've wanted to know the secrets that lie beneath all this water, and I love finding scattered bits of it." Vivien sounded melancholy as she peered at the horizon like it could take her away from here and whatever came next in her life. "Something big's hidden down there, and I intend to find it."

In that moment Kai felt the whole of Vivien's life experiences fall on her shoulders, and the weight she'd added in their brief encounters rippled through the span of those years. Her whim so long ago had left Vivien scarred just as much as if she'd come out of the water and gashed her with the shell Vivien wore around her neck. This was why her parents had made the Palmers part of her quest, and rightfully so.

"That's why I do what I do," she said, and Vivien looked at her. "One day when I have children I want to give them a sea as full of life and secrets as it is now. Hopefully they'll love exploring it as much as you do."

"Not if, but when, huh? Who's the lucky guy who'll have these exploring adventurers with you?"

Something from the water pinged Kai's senses, but for the first time in her life she couldn't decipher what it was. It was almost foreign, but she figured it a fluke and turned her attention back to Vivien.

"I haven't had much time for romance, but I'd like to have someone carry on my passions, though only if that's what they choose. In a way, that's what happened at your birth, but it's not something you want." Kai tried not to invade Vivien's thoughts, but the questions that ran through her head were so pronounced they were hard to ignore.

"What happens then? When you don't get to pick willingly, I mean."

"If you're asking what I'd do, I'd follow my heart, but I can't answer for you or anyone else because I also understand obligation. Before you decide to condemn your parents, though, they did name you Vivien—it's French for lady of the lake. Maybe they saw that adventurer and explorer in you early on."

"Sounds like they wanted me to be adventurous but only a little," Vivien said with a smile.

After Vivien answered the question, Kai thought maybe this assignment wouldn't be so hard as she'd imagined after the Palmer dinner party. Getting Vivien to see the world through a less negative lens might help solve her problem. "The Caspian Sea covers over one hundred and fifty thousand square miles, and some legends say it's a mermaid habitat. It's also a lake, as you most probably know."

"Is your outlook always so sunny?"

"The world is a small and rather dull place if you choose to see it only one way."

Chapter Ten

"What is it?" Hadley asked after listening to the low-timbre thumps emanating from somewhere in the Gulf of Mexico's outer shelf. It didn't sound like a natural occurrence, but their detectors couldn't pinpoint it either, especially since they were sporadic.

Natal Robin, the commander in charge of their radar and communications center, stood at attention as Hadley ran the loop again. "We don't know, Highness. We've run it against everything on file and found no matches."

"Have you heard from Kai?"

"The Princess's last communication was with you and our queen."

"Put your best people on it and find whatever this is and where it's coming from," she said as she stood from her desk. "Make sure you check every monitor and see if it's been repeated anywhere else."

"The system's checking now, but so far the Gulf is the only occurrence."

"Only occurrence of what?" Galen asked, making Natal immediately turn and bow. "Please, Natal, when Hadley pulls me out of a council meeting, it's important enough to forgo some formalities. What's happening?"

Hadley played the loop and explained where the sounds were coming from. "Unless the military slipped something past us, we don't know what that is."

"Did you call for Kai?"

"I thought I'd wait for you. Whatever it is, she and her team are closest to it."

"To me," Galen said as she sat on the sofa close to Hadley's desk, "it sounds like one of our vessels but off somehow."

"That was one of the first things we ruled out, my Queen," Natal said.

Hadley moved closer to Natal and placed her hand on her shoulder. "Go back to your post and report directly to me if you find anything else."

"As you command, Highness," Natal said, then bowed again. "My Queen," she said as she left.

"Any ideas?" Galen raised her hand to her as an invitation to join her, which Hadley gladly did.

"I'm sure it's not one of ours, which leaves some troubling possibilities."

"Such as?" Galen rested her head on Hadley's shoulder and placed her hand on her thigh.

"We have people serving in every navy around the world as well as with every major scientific exploration group occurring around the globe. That none of them reported something this sophisticated bothers me."

"They can't report what they don't know."

"I'm probably over-worrying because it's where Kai's swimming right now."

"You get a reward for showing such restraint," Galen said as she lifted her head to deliver a kiss. "If it was anyone else you'd be in the water by now."

"Restraint like that deserves more than a kiss, my Queen," she said as she opened a line to Kai so Galen couldn't answer. They listened to the message Kai had left on board the *Salacia* before going on her swim with Vivien Palmer.

"Sounds like she's making progress," Galen said as her hand went under the hem of the shorts Hadley wore. "Maybe she was paying close attention when you reviewed the lessons on gentle persuasion."

"It's the most important part of any warrior's arsenal," she said as she slightly widened her legs and smiled.

"So if you hadn't been able to persuade me, clubbing me over the head was your next move?"

She hadn't laid eyes on Galen until she was twenty-one and attended the function the royal family hosted in honor of the military academy graduates. Every woman in Atlantis had a purpose and function, and Hadley had chosen the life of a patrol officer. She'd figured that after years at various posts around the globe she'd return, settle down with someone, and teach the next generation of cadets their warrior ways. The lessons were highly important to their security and future, even though they weren't a warring people.

"Do you remember the night we met?"

Galen moved to her lap and nodded. "You were incredibly handsome in your new uniform and all the medals you'd earned at the academy. My date didn't appreciate my open staring."

She laughed at the memory of Galen's date—a tall woman who'd been an instructor's assistant, or so she'd been told. "I didn't notice until my mother pointed it out."

"True, your eyes were glued to the water, so I'm glad Yara elbowed you in the ribs," Galen said as she combed Hadley's hair back. "Your mother still laughs about that."

"She laughs because she knows I inherited my cluelessness from her. Mama told me from the time she conceived me she knew I'd find the same love she's shared with Mom," she said about Yara, her birth mother.

"Do you regret all you had to give up to be my consort?" Galen had asked this same question of Hadley numerous times after their marriage, but she understood why, so she was always patient and truthful in her answers.

Hadley had been born Hadley Marus East, and had Galen been any other woman in Atlantis, when she'd asked for her hand, she would've kept the name East, and perhaps Galen would've adopted it as well, as had her mother Yara when she'd married Brook. Galen was heir to her mother's throne, though, so if Hadley wanted to marry her, the name Merlin wasn't negotiable. The ruling family was descended from Queen Nessa Merlin's line, and it always would be. So Hadley's sacrifices, as Galen thought of them, started with that and continued with the changes to her future plans.

Consorts to the queen didn't leave for months on patrol, they didn't turn down the promotions that came with the title, and they carried out their royal duties with honor and pride. With her marriage, Hadley had fulfilled her dream of active duty, but primarily with a seat on the military council. That honor came to most after a distinguished career in the queen's service.

She'd led numerous missions that were in no way expected of her, but Galen had understood how important that had been to who Hadley was and hadn't interfered. Because Hadley's position on the council had come from what some thought luck, some people had talked about the unfairness of it, but Galen's mother Mari had gone through the same thing. Mari's guidance, especially early on in their marriage, had cemented a friendship between the two that grew with each passing year.

"Love, you know the answer to that." Galen gazed at her with glassy eyes so she didn't hold back. "I had my quest, like Kai's doing now, but my mind and heart were here. Even if patrol and defense had been possible with our match, I would've turned it down because I couldn't have been away from you that long."

"But you didn't mind the gossip?"

"After two broken arms in the arena, most of the idiots stopped questioning my abilities, and those who kept at it aren't important enough to care about." She slipped her hand behind Galen's neck and kissed her hard. "When it's just us, we're Galen and Hadley, and you're mine just like I'm yours. I love you, and I love that you still make my heart pound when I look at you."

"Forgive me for my insecurities, my love," Galen said before she kissed her again. "You have given me such a happy life that it seems like a fairy tale at times, and I want the same for you."

"Anyone with the opportunity to spend time with you who doesn't is an idiot, so not only am I blessed, but I'm one lucky bastard. I want no one else and I never have. Hell, I would've married you even if I'd had to change my name to asshole."

"You're poetic when you want to be, sweetheart." Galen leaned into her and ran her finger down Hadley's cheek and along her jaw. "Are you free for the rest of the afternoon?"

"I promised to check the progress of vector thirteen fifty-two before the foundation streets are laid. Are you up for a swim?"

"We're at that point already? Didn't we vote on that less than two months ago?"

The capital city, or the original Atlantis, was laid out in vectors drawn in a circular pattern, with the palace and main temple at the center. There were fifteen outposts around the world, built in the same pattern and at the same depth; the only difference was their center, since only the capital had a palace. Instead, every outpost had council chambers, and royal representatives appointed by Galen had their office there, their size varying.

Their architects planned every expansion carefully so the land dwellers wouldn't notice their growth, and also so the new sections would blend well with the oldest ones. They also planned these additions well in advance of population growth so the new additions didn't become overly populated.

"The area was leveled when they did vector thirteen fifty-one, since the building committee figured this section would have to be built much sooner than the last two."

"We have experienced a baby boom lately," Galen said as she traced her lips with the tip of her tongue. "If the couples throughout the kingdom find their spouses as hot as I find you, I totally understand it."

"Did you two call me to embarrass me or did you need something?" Kai's face appeared on the screen on the wall behind Hadley's desk.

"We like to show you what you have to look forward to when you decide to settle down," Galen said.

"You'll have to wait a bit on that," Kai said, and from what Hadley could see behind her, Kai was in the cabin of the *Salacia*.

"Did your monitors pick up anything today?" Hadley asked, unable to contain her curiosity.

"I'm checking now, but I felt something while I was out today with Vivien Palmer. It was brief but it was something."

Galen stood and walked closer to the monitor, as if it'd bring her closer to Kai. When they'd become serious enough about their relationship to talk about a future together, Galen had wished for plenty of children, since they both had sisters whom they loved. It wasn't until Galen's pregnancy with Kai did they know Kai would be their only child, and both of them had hovered over her like hens with a chick.

"We miss you, honey," Galen said as she lifted her hand toward Kai's image. "Are you eating?"

"Yes, ma'am, and per you and Mom's plan, I'm making new friends." Kai laughed but seemed to indulge Galen's whim when she lifted her hand as well. "I miss you too, Mama, but I'm having a good time."

"Keep your eyes open and let us know if whatever happened today repeats itself."

"Miss you too," Kai said and winked at her. "Send me whatever you find and we'll check it out."

"Where are Isla and Talia?" she asked as she placed her hands on Galen's shoulders.

"On Triton, since it'd be weird for them to be with me the entire time. Don't worry. They check in every five minutes, it seems."

"It's our job to worry, tadpole, and we will until we're fish food."

"I know and I love you both for it. I promise I'll be better about calling in." Kai blew them both a kiss and smiled as the monitor went black.

"She couldn't have chosen a project here at home?" Galen said after they'd both sighed. "She had plenty to pick from."

"You gave Kai your adventurous heart, love, so don't try to hem her in to only the safe parts of life." She turned Galen around and kissed her.

"*My* adventurous heart? I'm not the one who wanted to swim off in search of glory, stud. Face it. Kai's all yours, even though I got to carry her all those months and suffer through morning sickness that lasted until labor."

She laughed and bent gladly when Galen initiated the next kiss. "Then let's hope she inherited your gifts of persuasion so her time topside is fast."

"Do you think Vivien Palmer will give her problems?"

"Depends on how fast Kai can get undressed," she said, but Galen didn't laugh.

"I told you Oba's vision," Galen said as she clutched her shirt as if to anchor herself in a storm.

"I seldom challenge Oba's gifts, but I don't know how accurate a reading she can get on Kai. She's not seeing things as the high priestess but as Kai's lover, so perhaps this time that's skewed her vision." She took Galen's hand and led her toward their quarters. "Kai would neither betray us nor walk away for anyone, not even me if I asked it of her."

"I hope you're right, and I should've put a stop to their relationship a while ago, but Kai genuinely cares for Oba."

"Don't worry about that either," she said as she closed their bedroom door and stripped her shirt off. "Oba's main priority will always be her service to you and the goddess. In time Kai will see that, and she won't settle for anything but the woman who makes her burn like I burn for you."

"Thank you, my love," Galen said as her dress fell to the ground and her nipples hardened. "You always were good at reminding me of what's important."

CHAPTER ELEVEN

W ill you accept my apology?" Vivien asked as they shared a bottle of wine on *Salacia*'s deck. Kai had offered to cook and was glad when Vivien immediately accepted her invitation.

"First tell me what you're apologizing for, and I'll let you know." She ran her fingers through her hair a few more times to make it finally dry, and the motion made her miss both her mama and Oba. Both of them loved to do that when they spent quiet time together.

"I haven't been very nice since we met, and I'm sorry."

"You were protecting what was yours so don't apologize. Doing that makes me think you're a good friend and you love what you're doing." She poured Vivien more wine and went down to check on the fish she was baking. "I probably would've done the same," she said when she returned and Vivien was staring toward the horizon.

"Well, I'm sorry, and I don't mind saying it so we can move on."

"Can I ask you something?" Kai leaned against the wheel and this time looked at Vivien, finding her attractive.

"Sure, I'll do my best to answer," Vivien said and surprised her by not turning away both her gaze and her emotions.

"Good. I need some background human-interest stuff for my story," she said and winked when Vivien lifted her back a little off the cushion. "You could split me in two with deadly looks like that."

"You have a way of making me question if you're telling the truth, so cut me some slack." Vivien shook her finger at her.

"Tell me about Steve, the guy who's in love with you and doesn't much care for me."

"Steve's not in love with me—he's in love with my last name and what he thinks that'll get him if he's able to bend me to his will. If you're in love with him, he's all yours. You're not stepping on any toes."

She laughed, and Vivien's declaration made her think of Oba again. "Steve the fish-hater isn't my type by a long stretch, and how do you know he isn't in love with you as well as your name?"

"A woman knows these things." Kai thought back to how Oba could make her crave her touch while keeping her at arm's length. "At least, this woman," Vivien pointed to her own chest, "knows that."

"What does he do for the company?"

Vivien stood and stretched before moving closer so she could poke her in the shoulder. "I'm beginning to think you're underplaying your interest in him."

"I'm only curious since I seldom have so much trouble reading someone, and while I'm usually annoying, it takes me longer than a minute to piss someone off like that."

"You're right. It took you about ten to piss me off enough to get thrown off your boat," Vivien said and tapped her glass against hers.

"Nah, you calmed down once you realized what a teddy bear I am."

"Uh-huh," Vivien said, not moving away from her, which made the shell at her throat almost hum. Could Vivien sense it? "To answer your question, Steve's a senior vice president working with me and Frankie on acquisitions and production."

"I'm sure he'll happily lord over me in the coming months then."

"Somehow I doubt he'll get far with that approach. His bark is about all he's got going for him."

"How about some more wine, fish, and less about Steve?"

"That sounds like a heavenly evening, almost as good as whatever you're cooking smells."

Vivien returned to her seat after the compliments, so she went down and plated the meal she'd prepared. They'd have to head back in the morning, and now she regretted they didn't have more time since Vivien perhaps wasn't the empty shell she'd first thought.

"Need any help?" Vivien said, loud enough for her to hear.

"All you need to do is relax and enjoy." She handed Vivien a plate and flipped on the soft lighting she'd installed so they wouldn't be in total darkness once the sun finished setting. Vivien glanced at her when she sat across from her before dropping her gaze to her plate, but looked back up when she cut a small piece of her fish and dropped it overboard.

"Bad bit?" Vivien asked.

"Old custom of mine. I like to give back a little in thanks for what the waters give up whenever I take something from them."

"You're an interesting person, Kai Merlin," Vivien said as she tossed a little piece overboard as well. "I think I'm going to like working with you."

"Maybe we'll show each other different ways of seeing the world both under the water and above it."

"I'll drink to that," Vivien said and tapped her glass against hers again.

The pure sound of the crystal made Kai's optimism rise. Maybe she could heal at least some of Vivien's old hurts. If she could, it'd ease her mind as she moved forward with her life and her future responsibilities.

❖

The sun streaming through the small portal window next to Kai's bunk highlighted the few dust particles in the air, and she watched them, finding their irregular patterns relaxing. She didn't have anything on her schedule until Vivien decided to pull up anchor, so she waited to hear any movement from Vivien's boat. She'd been awake for a few hours, thinking about what her mothers had said, and was being lazy while she waited.

"She still doesn't trust me," she said aloud softly. She wasn't used to this much solitude, but she didn't find it unpleasant. Though Vivien didn't totally trust her, the night before had been nice enough that she'd let her guard down. "Hopefully it wasn't for only that brief second."

Oba drifted into her thoughts, and she closed her eyes in guilt that she hadn't been on her mind as much as she would've imagined when they parted. Her feelings for Oba had cooled without much effort, and her mother Galen's words floated as easily through her mind as the visible dust in the space. No one who you truly love can be too far from your thoughts, her mom had said over and over.

She wasn't ready to admit it fully, but perhaps her bond with Oba wasn't as strong as she'd wanted to believe, and only their proximity had fanned the heat between them. And if it had, would it return when she finished with all this and returned home? Whatever the answer, she'd spend time answering it when she returned to start helping with some of the royal duties.

In the quiet it was easy to hear Vivien step out on her deck, so she got up and went to see if Vivien wanted to spend more time with her. She paused until Vivien got off the phone. Whoever she was talking to wasn't making Vivien very happy.

"I need a few days," Vivien said loudly, but it wasn't quite a yell—yet. She seemed to be working up to it though. "Don't threaten me unless you plan to follow through, so if you want, fire me." A yell out of what sounded to be frustration followed that.

"Bad morning?" she asked, almost laughing when Vivien clutched her chest and spun around to face her. "Sorry. Didn't mean to startle you."

"Eavesdropping isn't very nice," Vivien said, pointing the phone's antenna at her.

"True, but it's hard not to when you have loud conversations out in the middle of nowhere. Are you leaving me for that corner office?"

Vivien stared at her for a long while before shaking her head. "I was hoping to stay around. I really need a few days off, and if you can stand my company we could spend some more time together."

"I'd like that, but you know all my secrets here, so how about a short trip?"

"Where?" Vivien leaned against the rail, suddenly much more relaxed in her stance.

"You said you enjoy diving where there's something to see." She held up a finger before going back down to her desk. "How about we go look at something?" She waved the map Etta had drawn for her.

"Is that one of Professor Sinclair's?"

"It's one of mine, and one of the reasons I took this job. The Gulf still has secrets to tell, don't you think?" She walked along dropping bumpers so Vivien could tie up to the *Salacia*. "Only I don't want to listen to engines the entire way there."

"I'd love to sail with you if you promise not to throw me off if I aggravate you, but you need to give me a crash course. It's been a few years since I've been on a sailboat."

"Great. Pack for four days, and I'll transfer your tanks over if you'll come closer."

It took an hour to lift anchor, and she was glad Vivien didn't mind one of Antoine's boys taking her boat in until they got back. The extra room aboard the *Salacia* was smaller than hers, but all Vivien's gear fit nicely and they'd comingled their rations.

They were headed to a spot off the Louisiana/Mississippi coast, and the wind was strong enough for them to move at a good clip. She'd left Vivien alone with the map and the dossier she'd put together on it. So far Vivien had barely lifted her head, and from her expression she was incredibly happy. At least as happy as Kai had seen her since their first meeting.

"This has to be a hoax," Vivien finally said.

"You want to go back?" She almost laughed at how quickly Vivien shook her head. "Then tell me why you think so, and if you're persuasive enough, we can go barhopping instead."

"It's far enough out, but too close not to have been spotted before now with all the offshore activity in that stretch." She pointed to the line marked on the map. "And usually treasure maps don't come with a big red X where the loot is. I'm surprised Etta gave you this."

"Etta confirmed, or tried to, but like I said, the map's mine. The reason for the big X, one in a long line of them, is I've covered a large portion of the ship's original course." She tied the wheel off so she could sit with Vivien for a bit. "This trip should finish that course. Then I'll have to start widening my search zone, taking into consideration tides and storms since it went down."

"What exactly are you looking for?" Vivien asked as she leaned back as if to enjoy the breeze. The wind wasn't up and the sky was pristinely blue, making Vivien's eyes seem a perfect reflection of it.

"Etta's report was short and fairly non-informative, which isn't like her at all. Usually I have to condense what she sends me."

"Maybe Etta doesn't exactly believe me, and that nonbelief was magnified when she couldn't find any record of the *Valhalla Sun*. The name's as close as I could extract from the ancient Viking language." Vivien gazed at her with a slight smile, as if humoring the fantasy she was hearing. "I can tell you don't believe me either, but I didn't have a whole hell of a lot to do in the North Sea but read, and an old text I found in London led me to the *Valhalla Sun*."

"Vikings being in North America before Columbus isn't a new story, but finding them this far south would be something, if you can prove it." Vivien combed her hair back and put on a ball cap with a fleur de lis on the front to keep it out of her face. "Why here, do you think?"

"The book was a forgery of an even older account of the journey the ship took from Scandinavian shores, only the Vikings weren't the only ones aboard."

"They took little green men from Mars with them?" Vivien laughed but rested her hand on her arm as if to cushion the blow of her joke. "I'm sorry. I shouldn't tease you, considering that's what my father thinks of my wild-goose chases, as he loves to call them."

"You want to hear the rest?"

Vivien squeezed the portion of her arm where her hand still rested and nodded. "I'd love to."

"The Vikings were familiar with the northern sections of what's now the United States, but many of their voyages were made with members of the Knights Templar. Proof of their being here comes from the rune stones they left along the way, which have been found over the years."

"Like the Kensington Runestone discovered in Minnesota? I can't remember when."

She nodded before going to check their heading, wanting to anchor before dark. "Swedish immigrant Olof Olsson Ohman found it in 1898, and scholars have debated its authenticity ever since."

"Do you think it's authentic?"

"How religious are you?"

"No one can accuse me of being a good Catholic, so don't worry about insulting me." Vivien's emotions seemed to swing toward a controlled enthusiasm, and Kai wanted to bring her to a place that'd reignite that carefree girl she'd been. To get Vivien there she didn't mind sharing the search for an answer to a mystery even the libraries in Atlantis didn't have the answer to. "I thought the Kensington Runestone was proved a hoax."

"Depends on who you ask, I guess, but if the Templars were here and left clues to unlocking their secrets, it makes sense the church would try their best to discredit anything found that would in turn discredit them." She made a slight correction to their course and scanned the horizon. They were alone and she seldom felt fear, but she was always vigilant. Her mothers had repeated that lesson on a regular basis.

"So you're a conspiracist when it comes to—?" Vivien's phone rang. "Sorry," she said as she removed it from her bag and answered it. "Hey," Vivien said, then listened for a long while. "Tell him I'll be happy to put in overtime if my not being there throws us behind, but I won't be there until probably next week."

She checked the radar of the Gulf floor while Vivien finished. They were at the edge of where she wanted to start their search, so she lowered the sheets and glided for a bit before dropping anchor. Vivien turned away from her and wrapped up what sounded to be an uncomfortable conversation, though she ended the call by saying, "I love you."

"Do you need to go ashore?" she asked when Vivien dropped the phone back into her bag.

"No, I do want to finish our talk. What exactly do you think you'll find?"

"There are plenty of conspiracies as to what the Templars were hiding, from the truth of Jesus's relationship with Mary Magdalene to the keepers of the Holy Grail, the cup that brings great power to its owner, if the legends are true." She sat close to Vivien and put the map between them. "I don't know what they were hiding. If anything's down there, it's a breadcrumb."

"Which will lead to another one? That's really the only reason you're here?" Vivien asked as she studied the map.

The old ones were works of art compared to their modern counterparts. She enjoyed the artistry that was a testament to the contact sailors through history had with her ancestors. "One of the reasons. Don't try to put me in a box so you can dismiss me if I don't meet your expectations of who I am or what I want. If you do, bringing you here was a mistake."

"Who's jumping to conclusions now?" Vivien asked with a smile. "I haven't been the most open person since we've met, so I guess you'd immediately assume that about me."

"I'm sure you have your reasons, but hopefully you'll see I'm not like most people. The last thing I'm interested in is power within the company. I'm happy where I am because it gives me the freedom to do the things I enjoy."

"You'd be the first."

"I know you don't believe me yet, but how about a deal?" She held her hand out, and Vivien stared at it like she was holding a dead fish. After a pause, though, Vivien took it. "Give me a few days before you make up your mind about me, and there won't be any hard feelings no matter what."

"Sounds like you've got it all figured out."

"Nah." She squeezed Vivien's hand before releasing it. "You're not the challenge here, Boss." She stood, rolled up the map, and tapped it against her leg. "Whatever's down there is, and I'd like to share it with you."

"If it helps—I believe you."

"Then let's get ready for whatever comes next."

CHAPTER TWELVE

Vivien sat at the *Salacia*'s bow and stared up at the stars. It was a cloudless sky, and the low light of the quarter moon made the sky an awe-inspiring blanket of twinkling lights. Kai had told her to relax while she fixed dinner and to call Franklin back and smooth things over. Kai had seemingly figured out what made her tick in a very small amount of time.

Her father was pissed she'd taken off, but she wasn't eager to go back. What Kai had offered and that she'd come into her life at all were so out of the norm for her, she'd questioned her sanity for coming along, but her skin itched with a feeling of being alive.

"Is he sending help thinking I'm going to chop you into little pieces and chum the water, or is he okay?" Kai asked when she reappeared with a bottle of wine and a couple of glasses.

"Frankie's fine, and he said thanks for taking me away from the cluster the office is right now. Seems my father's on a work binge, which means he lives to give orders and the world is supposed to fall at his feet to get everything done." She held both glasses as Kai opened the bottle. "Do you have experience getting away from overbearing parents?" she asked, realizing Kai had given away very little information about her life.

"My parents expect a lot, but we get along fairly well." Kai placed her glass on the deck and lay down close to her. She appeared at ease, and Vivien vowed to work on reaching the same state. "You can put that Palmer rock of responsibility down out here. This is supposed to be fun," Kai said as if she'd read her mind with the accuracy of having a cartoon-text balloon over her head.

"Do you always say the first thing that pops into your head?" The other strange phenomenon she was experiencing around Kai was her sudden attraction to Kai's physical attributes. Up to this point in her life she'd experienced only the opposite extreme in that she could tell when someone like Steve was near her. That innate sense was her one trigger to avoid uncomfortable contact.

"Sorry. I'll keep my mouth shut and enjoy the night."

"You don't have to, since you're exactly what I'm not used to. It'll be good for me to put my normal aside for a little while, since I complain about it enough." She tried the wine and hummed because it was so good. "Need any help with anything?"

"Give me fifteen minutes and you can help me bring up the stuff I've got in the oven."

"So how do you want to do this?" she asked, and smiled when Kai moved closer.

"I'm open to suggestions," Kai said, and she believed her. "But I thought we could start tonight after dinner."

"After dinner?"

Kai laughed, she assumed at her tone. "Still prescribe to the hour after a meal before swimming, huh?" Kai said and laughed. "Let's stay dry and try to do some mapping before we get in the water."

"Do you want me to guess?"

Kai pointed to the very front of the bow, where she saw something under a red-and-white tarp. "It's got enough lights to navigate at night, and the cameras will do a good job of spotting abnormalities on the bottom."

"You're like a scout—always prepared. I'm glad you asked me, so if I haven't said it before, thanks." Partnering with someone like Kai might advance her own search for answers, if she was willing to have a little imagination when it came to investigating these kinds of hard-to-believe stories.

"You're welcome to come with me whenever you like and you're free." Kai stood and went down to retrieve dinner. When she joined her in the small galley, her mouth watered as Kai put what looked like lobster mac and cheese on the counter.

"Keep feeding me like this, and I'll take you up on that offer whenever you make it." She leaned forward when Kai held up a forkful of the dish and closed her eyes as she took a bite of the almost decadent meal. "You really are something else."

"I'll settle for something different," Kai said, smiling.

"Mission accomplished then." She helped take everything up to the deck and sat to watch Kai drop what seemed to be a very light mini-sub into the water.

Once it was below it wasn't hard to see where it was since it was like a glow worm under them. Kai set a laptop between them and set the rover into motion. Unlike the ones on their rigs, Kai's moved on its own in a grid-like pattern that the cameras attached recorded. So far all it showed in the forty feet or so of water was the flat, sometimes grassy bottom typical of the Gulf's bottom.

"You really think anything will be here after all this time?" she asked, wishing like a little kid that something would pop onto the screen. "We're at the cusp of the dead zone, and it's hard to guess what the melt from up north has done to the currents over that many years."

"There's no way to know for sure, but I tried to factor that unknown in and put it all into the track I came up with." Kai's attention was on the monitor, but she seemed aware of everything else near her since she'd flick her eyes around every so often like a good sentry. "My worst nightmare is that someone has already found what I'm looking for and it's part of a fence or filling a pothole in their yard."

"Hopefully you'll have better luck than I've had over the years."

"I'm sure you've found your share of stuff."

She gazed at Kai's profile and wished she could read her as well as Kai seemed to be able to do with her. "How would you know?"

"You strike me as not only someone who plans but follows through," Kai said as she glanced away from the monitor and looked at her.

The scrutiny hit her in the gut, and the warmth in Kai's smile made her drop her fork and put her plate down. It was crazy—she wanted Kai to reach for her, to make some connection no matter what it was. She never craved being touched by anyone, and when did she start using words like crave? "You must get people to go along with you a lot," she said and snapped her mouth closed, not wanting to sound combative.

"Not really. You seem pretty immune to my charm." Kai laughed. "How about you watch this for me and I'll clean up? Could I interest you in dessert or a night swim?"

"Do you usually swim at night even when you're alone out here?"

"I'm not alone now," Kai said in a way that sounded like a challenge. She wondered again how Kai knew her so well after such a short time. She definitely didn't like to back down from anything.

"Should I bother with a suit?" she asked, giving herself away from the first night.

"Miss Palmer, oil baron and Peeping Tom," Kai said with an expression she could only describe as playful. Slowly Kai turned around and put the dishes down and dropped her shorts. Her T-shirt hit the deck as she went over the side. The splash made her laugh.

If she didn't join Kai, and considering she was a Palmer employee it wasn't a good idea, she'd regret acting like she always did. Her normal routine was to act like a rebel but never to venture too far outside the life her parents had given her. That Vivien would've stayed aboard and been happy she was there at all, so she stood and undressed, shedding her inhibitions and fear along with her clothes.

The water was cool but not overly cold, and it completely alerted her to the world around her. Usually she didn't swim at night since the ocean became a different world then, a world she didn't have too much experience with and wasn't ashamed to admit she feared. Like in some places around the world, the larger, more deadly predators came out at night, but one glance at Kai and she forgot that fact.

"Did I pass the test?"

Kai was treading water and appeared almost roguish when the corners of her mouth turned upward. "Hopefully I didn't bully you," Kai said.

"Now what?"

"I'm not sure why you keep thinking I've got an agenda—I don't."

"Should I be insulted that getting me out of my clothes isn't part of your agenda?" she asked as she swam closer to Kai. Eventually she'd figure out what had come over her and when she'd stop surprising herself with her actions and the things popping out of her mouth.

"That's more of a plan than an agenda," Kai said, and she couldn't control her laugh.

This was either part of an agenda or Kai really didn't care about anything she or anyone else thought. "Are you falling behind on anything regarding your grand plan?"

"Depends on how much fun you're having."

"You mean you can't guess?" She moved a little closer and tried not to blush at the fact she was naked. She didn't think she had a problem with modesty, but she wasn't usually naked with a near-perfect Amazon either. "And if you can't, I'm having a blast."

"Then tomorrow I'll kick it up a notch on my evil plan to get you to like me."

❖

"You do that, and I can't guarantee she won't resent you for the rest of time," Cornelia Palmer said to her husband over the breakfast table. She was mindful of the servants milling around, but sometimes Winston needed a dose of reality and not the instant giving in everyone else around him did. "I know you don't want to hear it, but the way you've handled all this so far will take months to cool off."

"It's no different than what my father did to me," Winston said, whacking his hardboiled egg so hard it cracked the cup it was sitting in. "Vivien's too old to be coddled, so I gave her a good shove in the right direction to get her moving."

"And she shoved right back," she said and caught herself before she rolled her eyes. "That didn't surprise you, did it?"

"Do you want her working on rigs until she starts spitting at the table and scares someone like Steve away? He's in love with her, for Christ's sake, and she treats him like a leper."

She stayed quiet, having no desire to be drawn into this conversation again.

"What, no comment on that one? Good. You know I'm right."

"Winston, you're a great many things, but right when it comes to Vivien or Franklin, that is seldom the case. You resented your father for years for bullying you in every aspect of your life, but you've not only become him. You're much worse." She quickly pointed at him, having had enough of his intimidation tactics like staring her down. "I'm not an intern, darling, so lower the glare a few notches."

"With time you'll see I did the right thing."

"With time she'll go to your funeral because it's expected of her, just like when your father passed on, but then all she'll feel is relief and not an iota of grief. I refuse to bring my children to the point that all they think when it comes to me is a welcomed conclusion to a nasty part of their existence when I drop dead." She seldom spoke this way, but she'd gotten up with a new sense of herself that morning. She missed being a mother, and Winston was standing in her way of that. "If that's really what *you* want, now's the time to say so I can stop wasting my time."

"Did I miss the memo where it said take potshots at me, it's really okay?" Another eggcup cracked under Winston's lethal spoon and she sighed—loudly. "I expect you of all people to understand and be on my side about this."

"No, you expect me to fall in line like every other lapdog in your life so you can act however you want." She was about to continue when she heard someone clear their throat behind her.

"Am I interrupting?" Steve Hawksworth asked, and she came close to losing another eggcup when she had the urge to throw hers at Winston's head. "I can come back," Steve said, sounding as if he was offering because it was expected and not because he had plans to do so.

"I'd think you'd have better things to do than to join us for breakfast," she said as she shook her head slightly at her husband.

"Winston insisted, and there's so much going on I thought we could get some stuff done without the phones and constant interruptions at the office."

"Yes, Mom, like that irritating pest on wheels. Such a dead weight, that one," Franklin said as he pushed himself in. "I hope I haven't missed anything."

"Not yet, but don't blink," Steve said and laughed, but he was alone in that joke.

"Do you have time to check out the roses? It's why I called you," she said to Franklin. "The older bushes are in full bloom and I think you'll enjoy them."

"Sure," Franklin said, and she had no trouble hearing his confusion. She'd called him, but not for that. "Lead the way."

"I'd like to talk to you before you leave," she said to Winston, getting only a grunt of acknowledgment.

"Are you okay?" Franklin asked when they were out of the house.

"Your father's being your father, but eventually I'll get over it." Franklin laughed and stopped close to the bench she'd mentioned inside. She sat and took a moment to remember Franklin as the little boy who loved being out here with her digging in the dirt. She used to lift him from his chair and give him a trowel so he could get as dirty as he wanted. Why hadn't she noticed before now how big a hole the absence of not having a close relationship with her children had left in her psyche?

"He can be somewhat overbearing when he wants to, but it's never seemed to affect you." Franklin reached for a branch and bent it closer so he could smell the blooms.

"That's an awfully nice way of saying someone's an asshole, isn't it?" she asked, enjoying Franklin's shock. "I'm sorry for not acknowledging that fact sooner, and it's why I wanted to talk to you."

"This isn't a new twisted version of good cop bad cop, is it?"

The accusation hurt but she'd expected it. "I've been both of those in the last few years, so maybe I should start with an apology. It's the weirdest thing, and I don't expect you to believe me, but it's like I woke up from a fog recently. As excuses go, it's not a very good one, but I also don't want this distance between us to get any worse."

"What do you mean fog?" Franklin asked, still sounding wary.

"That's the best way to describe it." She raised her hands and let them drop to her knees. "For a while I've been so focused on getting you and Vivien to do certain things and act a certain way that I lost sight of why I had children in the first place."

"I thought perpetuating the Palmer name and legacy was the main reason for that."

"All I can do is give you my reasons and it's up to you whether to believe me. I had you because I wanted to bring children into the world and teach them to be happy. That wasn't exactly a priority for mine and your father's parents, but I wanted to be different."

Franklin came closer and reached for her hand. "You were exactly that until a few years ago, and then you turned into Dad."

"You're being kind," she said and couldn't help the tears the admission caused. "The fact you are makes me think I haven't been as horrible a mother as I thought."

"I wish I could forget about it all," Franklin said, his eyes glassy as well, "but some of what you've both said and done has really hurt."

"Can you forgive me?" She grasped his hand with both of hers and squeezed. "The words I'm sorry are so easy to say, but if you give me another chance, I'll prove to you how sorry I am."

"You don't have to try so hard," Franklin said as he kissed her knuckles. "You're my mother and I love you—I never stopped even if I didn't like you very much. What brought all this on?"

"Like I said, I realized recently that you and Vivien were getting out of reach, and it panicked me. I didn't even realize I was acting so poorly until your father started this relentless campaign to mold you two into the perfect Palmers. The more bizarre he got, the more I woke up. It sounds crazy but it's true."

"If you need to hear me say it, then you're forgiven."

She put her arms around him, loving his solidness. "Thank you for a generosity I don't deserve."

"You gave us a good foundation so you deserve that and a lot more, Mom. Maybe you can work on Dad so he can come to the same conclusion."

"That's the other thing I wanted to talk to you about." She kissed his cheek and released him. "Do you think your father's a little off? I don't mean completely insane, though some days I'm not so sure, but he's not himself, and I can't really reach him anymore. At least not often."

"I agree with you, but I'm not sure what good it'll do to admit it. Even if he was a raving lunatic, the board would ignore it because calling attention to his insanity would hurt the stock price, and they'd never tolerate that." Franklin's shoulders slumped as he spoke. "He became more like what you're describing after Steve started working for us, but that's just my own prejudice against that guy talking."

"Your father's fixated on Steve and his family, so I can understand your feelings." She shook her head at her own misgivings for the bright young man her husband was so infatuated with. "I'm sure Vivien's feelings toward him haven't changed, right?"

"Viv would rather date me than Steve, and there's a major ick factor there. Dad's pushing them together is starting to creep her out in more ways than the obvious. The world where parents sell their daughters off in marriage ended a long time ago." Franklin stopped talking and put his finger up when she started to say something. "How about lunch when Viv is back in town? We've both been so busy we haven't had a chance to catch up."

The change of subject made no sense to her, but Steve's sudden appearance was explanation enough. "I'd love to."

"You'll have to let me know when, Mrs. Palmer. I'd love to come along as well," Steve said, clearly not concerned at his invasion of their privacy. "Mr. Palmer wanted you both to know he had to go, so he'll see you tonight."

"You'd make a great assistant, Steve," Franklin said, and she smiled at the dig.

"Funny," Steve said with a neutral expression. "I look forward to that lunch," he said to her before bending and kissing her cheek. "Maybe Vivien, you, and I could make it a date so we can all talk."

"Vivien makes her own dates, so I wouldn't count on that anytime soon since she's so busy." She stood and placed her hands on Franklin's shoulders. "Don't let us keep you." Steve hesitated but plastered on his smile before turning and leaving. "If Vivien never forgives me I can't blame her."

"All you can do is ask, and if she refuses, offer to buy her a new boat."

CHAPTER THIRTEEN

Anything promising?" Vivien asked, her hands wrapped around one of the big mugs from the galley and her shoulder pressed to Kai's. "And this has to be the best cup of coffee I've ever had."

"It's a family recipe," Kai said, pointing to her cup, "and a couple of places have anomalies, but Fido's not done yet."

"Your family grows coffee, and you named the sub Fido?"

"My family buys coffee like everyone else. They just know how to mix better than anyone selling the stuff." She glanced at the top of Vivien's head, liking the smell of citrus from her shampoo. The night before she'd done her best not to tease Vivien as they came out of the water and Vivien's blush colored what appeared to be her entire body. "And the name was better than Rover." She pointed to the two spots she'd picked out of the grid the sub had run during the night.

"That's a sand pile and not a very big one," Vivien said as she ran her finger along the ridge of the spot. "It's worth a look, though."

"I can always go down and put a big red X on it if it'll make you more enthusiastic."

Vivien pressed closer to her and laughed. "You're reminding me why I work alone."

"Sometimes, though, having someone with you makes the finds more interesting."

"Yeah." Vivien leaned back enough that she could look up at her. "How can you understand me so well after a few days?"

"Because we're alike, which means we were born too late."

"Too late?"

She lifted her hand slowly and brushed Vivien's hair back, surprised when Vivien leaned into her touch. "Too late in that we could've sailed searching for treasure and adventure, and no one would've thought it strange decades ago."

"We're pirates at heart, you mean?"

"The world still has plenty of those. We're not stealing anything. We're saving history for all the uninspired people who don't want to look for it. You know the type that likes to glance at it in museums with champagne and little crab puffs and think they're doing their part to further mankind."

Vivien smiled and nodded. "I know plenty of people like that, but the rest of that analogy is how I like thinking about it. As much as I like to complain about my father, my job does give me the freedom to hunt for all that history."

"Next time invite me along," she said as she closed the laptop and gave Vivien her full attention. "Might be fun."

"You may be sorry you said that." Vivien lowered her eyes as she spoke, and Kai decided then to go way beyond what her mothers expected of her and help Vivien find her inner strength.

She deserved so much more than for her to make up for some childhood mistake. Vivien Palmer reminded her of her mother Galen in that she was intelligent, engaging, beautiful, and a joy to be around. The night before when Vivien had joined her in the water, Kai had realized she was truly starting to enjoy Vivien's company. No one had ever made her laugh that much.

"Being on the water with you isn't a hardship, and I'm looking forward to being under the water with you even more." She covered the hand Vivien had placed on her forearm and held it there for a moment. "Are you ready?"

"Let's go find your clue."

"Don't you mean *our* clue?"

"If you find something, it'll be yours. It's only fair since you've been searching longer. I understand that."

"If we do find something you're not going to leave me to go it alone, are you?"

Vivien immediately shook her head.

"Good, discoveries, like so many things in life, are better when they're shared."

"You're right. I love this, and it'll be fun to have someone next to me who loves it just as much."

Kai's shell warmed again, and she greedily tapped into Vivien's excitement. "Then let the adventure begin."

❖

"Anything new?" Hadley asked. She and a number of advisors were in the most secure room within the realm when it came to military secrets. They ran and monitored all their covert operations from here.

Natal typed in a few commands, and the planet appeared on the main screen with a map grid over it. "Once we figured out the random pattern of the pings, we found them in three distinct locations, but we're monitoring globally."

Three sections of water were highlighted, and the Gulf of Mexico was one. "So the English coast, the southern shores of Australia, and the Gulf," she said slowly as she looked from one to the other. "Is there some connection I'm not seeing?"

"No, Highness," Natal said, and the others remained silent.

Mari Merlin, one of Galen's parents, folded her hands together. She'd retired from the military but was still one of Hadley's most trusted advisors. "Can one of you tell us what the heck this is then? Should I remind you that the princess and future of the realm is smack in the middle of one of those hot spots?"

Everyone stood and came to attention when the door opened and Galen entered. Hadley smiled when her wife went over to her mother and kissed her cheek. "Please, everyone, sit and try your best to answer my mother's question."

"Your Highness," Natal said, waiting on her feet despite what Galen had said about the use of her name. "When the signals are on, they resemble our communication pods, but they're off slightly from all our known signals, so we know they're not ours. Whoever's responsible, they're smart enough to keep the messages brief enough that we can't pinpoint where they're originating from."

"If I were speaking to someone topside I could understand, but we have the most sophisticated equipment in the world, at least this world. How's it possible you have no clue as to what this is?" Galen asked, but she was so nice about it, Hadley could see that Natal, as well as everyone, really wanted to respond.

"Let's start with something I hope someone can answer," Mari said. "Where's my granddaughter now?"

"The *Salacia* is currently off the Louisiana/Mississippi coastline," one of the advisors said as the *Salacia*'s icon appeared on the map.

"The rig she's supposed to be on is southwest of there," Hadley said.

"That's easily remedied," Galen said as she placed her hand on the console where it would open a communication link with Kai. The video feed showed an empty room, but Kai's voice came through.

"Is it urgent?" Kai asked softly.

"Just checking to make sure you're all right. It can wait if you are." Galen gazed at Hadley as she spoke, wondering if they were overreacting.

"I'm spending time with Vivien so it might be a few days. Can you wait that long?"

"Hope you're having a great time, my love, and I can wait. Remember to call if you need anything."

"Will do," Kai said, and her voice made Hadley relax. "My love to you and Mom. We'll talk soon."

"Love you too," Galen said and cut their link. "Get confirmation from our sisters in the US, British, and Australian military units that this isn't coming from one of those governments."

"We've already sent word, Highness, and have received word from Australia that it's not. Great Britain and the US are doing extensive searches so it might take a few days," Natal said.

"Have that report sent to the queen as soon as it's available," Hadley said, and Natal put a fist to her chest. "Give us the room for a moment."

"You've never heard anything like this before?" Galen asked, looking from her to her mother.

"No, but we'll figure it out," Mari said and smiled as if to reassure her. "Your mate's more persistent than I am, and that's going some on the stubborn scale. And not to tell you your job, Hadley, but consider sending an elite unit out there until the tadpole's done. Let them keep their distance, but I'd rather they be nearby on the remote chance this develops into something."

"They're gearing up now," she said before taking a deep breath. "I'd rather be safe and redundant on security than not, but I'm sure Kai will not be happy with me."

"Blame it on me if you want, but she'll have to start accepting some of the concessions that come with Triton," Mari said.

"Kai thinks she can take on the world, though, so that'll take time," she said and sighed again.

"She'll learn, just like a young officer I knew once, that duty is sometimes being the one protected. That fact might be easier to accept if she finds a pretty a wife, as you did," Mari said and winked. "The tadpole reminds me more and more of you, Hadley, and we had plenty of talks before you cooled that hot head and took your rightful place."

"According to Queen Sibyl, it took me less time than you, so don't call me a hothead."

"Don't make me separate you two," Galen said as she walked into Hadley's open arms. "And I trust both of you to handle this. I'm due to meet Mama at the archives to help with some research she's doing for Kai."

"Nothing official on the books?" Hadley asked.

"I'm free for the rest of the week."

"Mari and I'll pick you two up and treat you to dinner."

Galen pressed on the back of her neck so she lowered her head and kissed her. "Just as long as you don't try to talk me into anything."

"No promise there," she said and smiled. "Believe me, you'll like most of my ideas."

"It's the ones I won't that worry me."

❖

Kai lifted Vivien's tank and helped her put it on, adjusting the straps to accommodate the helmet she was lending her. "Feel okay?"

"A little lower than usual but it's comfortable." Vivien turned and faced Kai on the dive platform Kai had lowered near the stern on the port side. Kai was wearing another long-sleeved T-shirt with a fish across the back and shorts, which made her wonder how many she owned.

The need for Kai's touch had increased from the night before, but Kai had been a perfect hostess and hadn't done anything to make her uncomfortable. It was damn frustrating. Her problem, though, was being ill-equipped to make the first move, especially with a woman. She'd never really questioned her sexuality, but Kai made her hyperaware of her presence.

No man or woman had ever made her this crazy for no apparent reason. Kai was playful but not overly flirtatious or aggressive in a pursuit kind of way. Nevertheless, somewhere in the last day or so she'd developed a crush, and it would be almost absurdly funny if it wasn't true.

"Let's try the medium collar first," Kai said, breaking her out of her trance.

In Kai's hand was what appeared to be a rubber ring. She'd seen one before but had never gone down with this type of gear. "Do you think we'll really need these?"

"I happen to like the sound of your voice and can't stand not hearing it for the next hour," Kai said as she put it in place. "Trust me. You're going to love the view." The helmet Kai clipped on made her tense for a moment, but the supply of air prevented her from demanding Kai remove it. She watched as Kai geared up quickly and heard her voice clearly. "Let's go, Boss," Kai said as she stepped off the platform.

The water had two-foot swells, but the visibility was good as she followed Kai down. Kai had a swimming style she envied in that she glided through the water with smooth strokes that made it seem like she was barely exerting effort. The coordinates they were searching for were in the GPS unit on Kai's wrist so she followed, studying her dive partner since she really didn't have anything else to look at.

A mound of sand was right under Kai when she stopped, and it was larger than Vivien thought it would be. She couldn't see the shoreline, but this spot wasn't remote, so to find anything here would be the biggest surprise of her life, considering some of the locations she'd explored. She'd dismissed the Gulf a long time ago, since the only treasure she figured it held was crude oil.

"Are you going to say something or daydream all day?" Kai asked as she pointed down. "This is the spot—what do you think?"

"We never finished our talk as to what you hope to find, aside from the *Valhalla Sun*. I know you want to prove its existence, but there has to be more to it than that."

"It's a long story and we've got one more spot to cover, so can I tell you later?"

"Sure, and that might be something or it could be a tide anomaly. I'm not a expert on currents, but I have seen spots like that when the water runs a certain way consistently." She moved closer and touched the top, moving only soft sand. "They change when storms come through here and stir up the bottom."

"True, but let's see if we get lucky." Kai took something she had strapped to her leg and pressed a button, extending the black metal piece to about four feet. She started stabbing into the mound easily, meaning nothing was there. "If it's anything, it's deeper than this, so let's try the next spot."

The next place was larger but they got the same result. She was sorry for Kai, hoping they would've found something if only to stay another day. "What do you think?"

"Well," Kai said as she tried to drive her pole into the bottom of the mound at an angle. "I hate to jinx myself, but this is interesting, or more interesting than anything I've found so far. We don't have the kind of time it'll take to knock these down, but let's try the next best thing."

"If it's dynamite, you're on your own," she said and laughed.

"What about something a little less destructive to the fish?" Kai retracted her tool, re-strapped it to her leg, and pointed to the boat. "Fido's good at more than pictures."

They swam back, and as Kai helped her take her equipment off, she smiled instead of feeling insulted, since she usually did all this herself. "What's the plan?" she asked, grateful that Kai's helmet had kept her hair dry when the wind picked up.

"How about dinner somewhere onshore? I don't want to bore you by keeping you trapped out here."

"I don't mind staying put and cooking for you." Kai was in no way boring. "You can let Fido do whatever Fido does, and if we find something we can map out the next step. Unless I'm boring you."

"Nope, and I was only worried about that," Kai said and pointed southeast. The bank of dark clouds promised rain and chop, but it wasn't enough to drive her in.

"We might not do any swimming tonight, but a little rocking never bothered me."

"Then your ideas are much better than mine. No wonder you're my boss."

CHAPTER FOURTEEN

Steve's phone rang, waking him out of a sound sleep, and he rubbed his face roughly before reaching over to get it. It had been a long couple of days, and he was trying his best to get back in Winston's good graces after his misstep complaining about Kai Merlin and Winston's decision to hire her.

"Who the hell is calling at this hour?" Tanice said as he sat up and turned on the light.

"Not now." He stood and walked out. The double doors that led to the balcony of his condo were sheeted with water from the deluge coming down outside. "Yes," he said when he answered the call.

"You haven't reported in for a few months and we're getting worried."

He tapped his finger against the glass and curbed the urge to put his fist through it. What'd been asked of him and what he'd had to do to get it were beyond what he should've been subjected to, considering his position. "When I have something I'll report, so you're going to have to trust me. Besides, we're getting close so I don't want to take any type of chance that can put us behind."

"Remember to go slowly, since we can't step in to help you right away."

"I remember everything that's expected of me, so don't call me again unless you have something that'll make this easier. I'm tired of the process, but don't worry. I'll deliver."

He ended the call and stood naked in front of the door, not worried that he'd shock any of the neighbors because of the storm. Tanice stepped behind him and kissed his shoulder. "Problems?"

"Nothing you need to worry about." He took a deep breath and opened and closed his hands, trying to stop the restlessness that was making his blood feel like it was swarming with ants.

"We're in this together, don't forget that." Tanice moved to stand before him, and he had to admire the perfection of her body. "Don't lie. We have plenty to worry about since you told me today that Winston's wife turned against you. I thought you had that situation under control?"

"I do, and I'm in charge because I don't panic at the first sign of a problem. We don't need her. I just need for Winston to continue to include me in the big decisions and, more importantly, keep giving me access to the board. If anything along those lines changes, I have a contingency plan."

"Not going to share?"

"No, but I am willing to share something else with you," he said as he picked Tanice up and carried her back to the bedroom. Maybe being disturbed at this hour wasn't so bad after all.

Vivien had admitted she wasn't a great cook, but whatever she was doing in the kitchen smelled good as Kai sat in the common area of her vessel waiting for Vivien to finish. The weather had turned nasty a few hours after she'd stored their gear, and after a glance at the weather report she doubted it would clear anytime soon. It was a strong front coming from the Atlantic, drenching Florida and the southern coastline all the way to Texas.

Kai had decided to wait to release the rover until the weather cleared some, even though Fido was capable in any situation. She didn't want to make Vivien suspicious by showing off the capability of what was on board. The weather service said blue skies and calm water would return by morning, so she'd use the ground-penetrating radar then.

"What's the word?" Vivien asked as she leaned against the counter wiping her hands.

Outside, the rain was coming down heavily and at an angle. The wind was gusting so much the waves had picked up considerably, but she'd put out the stabilizers once they'd gone in, so the rocking wasn't as bad as it could've been. "Should clear up by four in the morning, so tomorrow we can see what's under those mounds."

"Ready to tell me a story?"

"If you tell me what you're making with your non-cooking skills, sure." The smile Vivien gave her made Kai's fingers twitch.

Beautiful women weren't a foreign concept to her, though her mother Hadley had warned her about too many liaisons. In Hadley's opinion, Oba was bad enough, but sleeping with every woman who showed interest demonstrated a certain disrespect for the citizens she'd one day rule. She wasn't a piece of driftwood, though, so she'd given in to some of the women who'd been persistent.

"Shrimp étouffée with jasmine rice, but I can't take credit. Frankie orders from my favorite places around town and has them freeze stuff for me. I can't cook, but I'm an excellent re-heater."

"That counts in my book, so let me help you plate it and I'll tell you my tale."

The *Valhalla Sun* was one in a string of ships she'd searched for since her early teen years so her mother Galen and her grandmother Sibyl could add their histories to the archives. Granted, the main library in Atlantis's capital held a thousand times more books than the Library of Congress, but the people of Atlantis didn't know all man's secrets. They had more accurate accounts of the world's historical timetable, but groups like the Templars held their inner beliefs and secrets in their heads, so many of the true facts had been lost through time.

By finding them one by one, Kai figured she could show both of her mothers the part of themselves they'd given her. Hadley the adventurer loved the search, and Galen the historian loved the find. The adventure of the search and then archiving it would be Kai's life's work, along with her future responsibilities on the throne. That would be years from now, since her mother Galen wasn't close to retiring.

She opened a bottle of wine and, as they sat, poured a glass for Vivien first, enjoying the hum of approval when Vivien took a sip. "For a roughneck you've got superb taste in wine," Vivien said.

"Thank you." She got her plate. "It's nice to share a bottle with someone who can tell the difference between this and Boone's Farm.

Not to knock the Boone makers, but their stuff's a little too sweet for me."

"To good food, drink, and most importantly, good company," Vivien said and held up her glass. "Now talk." She laughed.

"Let me start by saying I'm one of those people who believes the Templars left a treasure that hasn't been found. I don't like to guess what it might be, but in their quest to hide it, they advanced navigation and travel by more than we give them credit for." She stopped to eat, and Vivien appeared almost disappointed.

"Don't stop now." Vivien sounded whiny.

"Remind me not to start these things when I'm hungry." She took another bite and smiled as she chewed. "I've followed the crumbs they've left, and if I find something valuable it'll be great, but I'm more interested in the historical aspect. Imagine what they had if they took the chance of crossing the sea to hide it."

"Do you think this means anything?" Vivien showed her the shell around her neck without taking it off. "That's what I've been looking for—the alphabet that will unlock this."

"Why do you think you'll find the answers under the water?" she asked, interested in Vivien's answer. Most people might've been interested, but their searches would've started and ended topside.

"Something that I don't like talking about happened the day before we got them, since Frankie got one too, so it's led me to the water." Vivien leaned back and shrugged. "Even if I never find it, this has been my lucky charm for finding plenty of other things."

"To finding things then." She held her glass up again, trying to cheer Vivien up. "Maybe if we put our heads together for a while we can come up with something."

"Do you mean under the water?" Vivien asked with an attractive pinking on her cheeks.

"And above—you just never know."

❖

"Still nothing?" Sibyl Merlin asked her daughter Galen as they looked over the real-time information the *Salacia*'s onboard systems were sending.

"This is something, I guess, but if you're talking about the mystery signal, then no." Galen clenched her hands in an effort to not run out of the room and swim to where Kai was, even though, judging from Kai's messages, she was in no real danger. "It seems odd that we'd find this now while she's out there essentially alone."

"Kai's a lot like you, even if you only see Hadley when you look at her. Your mother, sister, and I worried about you while you ran around Rome for more than a year." Sibyl took Galen's hand and walked her to the tea service one of the archive employees had brought in. "The Vatican Library was a good learning experience, I thought, not only for the sheer amount of ancient texts, but for the freedom it gave you."

"Kai isn't safely hidden in the stacks surrounded by only molding paper and geeks, Mama." She hated whining and clicked her teeth together to stop talking. "The water and her secrets hold her interest."

"You make it sound like I don't know Kai at all. From Hadley she inherited the need to explore, to stand up for the defenseless, and those looks you instantly couldn't get enough of." Sibyl poured but handed her a cookie first. "From you, though, came that incessant curiosity that's only satisfied by finding the why of everything. This search for a boat that might or might not have sailed will probably take a lifetime to answer for anyone else but Kai. You gave her the most important genetic trait anyone could inherit, and that's the pursuit of everything."

"I'm not sure about that, and thanks for trying to take my mind off all this." She bit into the peanut butter chocolate-chip cookie and smiled. They'd been her favorites ever since Hadley had made them for her when she was pregnant.

Sibyl laughed and shook her head. "Deny it all you want, but Kai will find whatever she's looking for because her mind works like yours. Your sister Clarice is more laid-back in her approach to life, but you both never get tired of learning and teaching. I've always thought it was the best way to not get bored. Besides," Sibyl handed her another cookie, "between Hadley, her mother Brook, and Mari's overprotectiveness, nothing will happen to our tadpole. I had to hold your mother down to keep her from suiting up and heading out with the team Hadley deployed."

"I'd laugh, but I had to do the same thing." She'd had trouble sleeping since Hadley twitched all night long, and she knew it was from her desire to go keep watch over Kai. She and Hadley would agree about that until their last breath.

"Then until all these military types find something, let's get back to Kai's search for this phantom boat."

"Let's hope that's all she finds."

CHAPTER FIFTEEN

The water was like green glass the next morning, and Kai turned her face to the first light to breathe in the smell of salt water. She extended her senses out and smiled as she connected to Ram and Ivan, enjoying their leisurely swimming pattern. They were full and content in each other's company and only about an hour away. All of that reflected her mood at the moment because of her night with Vivien.

The rain and wind had kept them inside so she'd suggested a funny movie, thinking it would cool Vivien's attraction, but the opposite had happened. Vivien had an infectious laugh that gave you no choice but to join in and enjoy the moment with her, and she had. They'd talked after that until late, and it made her wonder something she hadn't been able to answer even after they'd gone to bed.

Vivien had an inordinate list of things in common with her that spanned both likes and dislikes. Could the gift she'd left have actually bled more than simply the lines that would open up the link between them and she'd seeded a bit of herself in Vivien? Vivien seemed to be a mix of everything she desired in a mate, but with the differences her mother Galen said were important to keep a relationship fresh. She'd come close to opening their link in such a way Vivien would understand exactly what was happening.

"How many of those T-shirts do you own?" Vivien asked as she handed over a mug of coffee. She smiled when she saw Vivien was wearing the one she'd had on last night.

"You found my stash, huh?"

"It was hanging in the bathroom so I hope you don't mind." Vivien sat and put her hand on the cushion next to her. "Join me?"

"I don't mind at all," she said, wondering what Vivien was sad about. "Didn't sleep well?"

"You're an incredibly perceptive person, and when I see my father again I'll have to thank him for hiring you." Vivien pulled her shirt over her legs when she bent her knees and lifted her feet up. "I'll do that after I complain to him about ruining my fun. Unfortunately I have to go back."

"Right this second?" She didn't want to let Vivien go until she had to report for work.

"Today sometime, but not right this second. If you want, you can drop me on shore and I'll fly back."

"If I've got the day I'll take you home."

"Good, since you still owe me some lessons, but I think I've learned one well." Vivien leaned against her and hummed for some reason.

"Should I guess?"

"Skinny-dipping," Vivien said as she moved to put her coffee down. "Think you can indulge me one more time before I have to go?" Vivien stood up and stripped the T-shirt off and dropped it on her lap. It was like a declaration of some kind that quickly turned to not quite fear but uncertainty.

Vivien had a swimmer's body despite her height, in that she was fit but not skinny, but none of that mattered when she faced her in a nakedness that went well beyond the lack of clothing. The display was more about a sense of acceptance and belonging. Vivien Palmer had belonged to no one in her life, and she was perhaps making steps to change that fact.

"Don't take this wrong, okay," Kai said and held her hand when Vivien reached for her shirt again. "You're an incredibly beautiful woman." She took her shirt off as well and blocked Vivien's attention from her shell as she dropped her shorts.

"Why would anyone take that wrong?" Vivien's eyes were the only thing restless about her.

"When you work for someone and they might think I'm saying it to gain favor."

Vivien laughed and moved an inch closer. "You're the only person who's ever worked for us that's even seen me naked more than once."

"So Steve's in the once club?" She almost didn't want to know the answer, because if it were true it'd piss her off.

"No one's in that club, and I don't think you said it to get me to like you since you also threw me overboard. Do you in some part of your head think this is a little nuts?"

"No," she said and dove over the side.

The sun was a large orange ball half hidden by a bank of clouds, so Kai swam up behind Vivien and held her so they were both facing it. "Crazy isn't how I'd describe this moment."

"Then explain it to me," Vivien said as she pressed closer and relaxed, as if trusting her to keep them afloat.

"Maybe we're two old souls that recognize an old friend in the other, or we're new souls who recognize the joy of new friendships."

"Naked friends?" Vivien said and laughed.

"Either new or old—those are the best kind." Vivien had sparked her desire but she kept her hands still, though she wanted her as much or more than Oba. The surprise of that made her a little glad Vivien had to go. Seduction wasn't how she wanted to help Vivien or Franklin. "That's true, because you can't hide anything."

"Will you let me know if you find anything? I'm sorry I'll miss it," Vivien said as Kai guided them to the dock where Vivien's vessel had been tied up.

"If the rune stones or any speck of wreckage are there, they can wait a few more weeks until we can make it back. You don't think I'll forget about you because you have to leave?"

Kai grabbed her bags and helped her up to the dock. Vivien found her chivalry humorous once again but didn't mind now that she was sure it was who Kai seemed to be. "You're not going back? The need-to-know would drive me crazy."

"I'll try to control myself, and even if I wanted to, I can't. The office sent an email and asked that I head out early."

"That's why you're putting your search off," she said, the bliss of the last few days deflating as if Kai had pricked it with a pen.

"Have some faith in me." Kai jumped on board and put her bag inside, coming back out with her hands jammed in her pockets. "Did you forget that I'm no one's cheerleader? If you did, go ahead and add I'm no kiss-ass either."

"Thank God we're on land," she said, trying to return to more solid footing, which seemed to be harder on land than on Kai's boat. "Might've been a long swim."

"Go to work, Miss Palmer, and when the time comes I'll take you exploring and swimming, but I promise it'll be fun." Kai seemed to release her tension enough to smile before holding her hand out to her. "Be careful going back. That river is something else when it comes to currents."

"I have time to go out and give you a tour, unless you'd rather skip it. Triton is yours to take care of now, but do you mind if I call you? Not about the rig, I mean." Jeez, how many times had she heard that line in her life and wanted to be completely honest with a resounding no? Maybe people like Steve wanted that yes as desperately as she did, as she smiled because Kai did.

"When you get back to the office tomorrow, have Franklin give you my number, along with everything you asked him for." Kai spoke as if she had a cheat sheet of everything in her brain. It always sounded so clichéd in books when a character was described as having transparent thoughts, but it was spooky how well Kai not only read her, but how well she knew her.

"You sound a little narcissistic."

"That's like being a little pregnant. Narcissism is all-encompassing." Kai laughed when she stuck her tongue out because of Kai's sarcastic comment. "We'll talk about it the next time we get together, and there *will* be a next time."

"Planning to kidnap me?" The shell at her neck vibrated and so, she swore, did her blood.

"I can fly the Jolly Roger if you'd like me to. Think about it, and hopefully it won't be too long before we see each other again." Kai waved and didn't surprise her by glancing back. She didn't interpret it as noninterest but the space to make up her mind. The way Kai held her in the water showed how interested she was.

"I can promise it won't be long since you're making me crazy. That's a first."

❖

"Well, what've you been up to?" Isla asked as she joined Kai and Talia at Triton's railing to watch Vivien speed north too late in the day for Kai's comfort. Vivien had insisted on giving her the tour, and she'd readily agreed for the same reason Vivien probably wanted to do it. She wasn't ready to see Vivien disappear into the horizon just yet.

"Besides helping Miss Palmer pack and hanging on her every word, that is," Talia said and laughed.

"Actually I might've found another clue to the *Valhalla*, and we're being paid by these people to listen to every word. Don't accuse me of being a kiss-ass on my first day. That's not my style," Kai said in a tone that sounded defensive even to her. "Sorry, I can usually take a joke," she said after she winced.

"Problems?" Talia asked.

"The experts at home picked up some weird blips that seem to be emanating from here, but we can't find what they are. They didn't come out and say it, but I think my moms are about to freak, and I don't want to be called home before we finish." Vivien's boat was out of sight, so that clued her in to the silence around her. "What are you two not telling me? Come on. I know when you're hiding something."

"We've had a rover down there checking out operations and spotted some strange equipment attached to this monster," Isla said.

"Was it monitoring the rover while you were monitoring whatever it was?"

"We backed off precisely for that reason and haven't sent our equipment down unless the guys here with the company that owns the unmanned submersible have their sub in the water as well," Talia said as she handed over a small monitor with the footage of what they'd found. "The rover we brought looks like the one they use, so it wouldn't raise an alarm in case someone spotted ours. We wanted to wait on you before we did anything."

Her mother Galen had explained this part of ruling from the time she was able to grasp what the lesson was. Most people, not all, handed off the difficult decisions at times because of many different reasons, so she'd have to develop broad shoulders to carry the weight. When it was her time on the throne, she wouldn't have anyone else to hand over the responsibility to—the decisions would be hers.

She'd never considered either Talia or Isla lazy or cowards, considering she'd known them all her life, but they'd waited before they did anything because they were afraid. None of them wanted to be discovered by what some in their realm thought to be ignorant creatures, and it was always safer to leave that possibility to someone else.

"I can see by your expression you think we're assholes for dumping this on you, but that's not why we waited," Talia said.

She smiled, thinking she needed a better poker face and a better hold on her emotions if she didn't want to be read like a popular library book. She also had to stop making assumptions before it became a habit. "Sorry, and in my defense, I never thought asshole."

"I didn't want to call the queen while you were out of our sight and drop that on her."

Talia had a good point, but this might also be a case of panic without all the facts. "Are you sure this isn't part of the rig's overall makeup? From what I read about this project, they're monitoring every aspect to assure the regulators that another disaster isn't on the horizon."

"The ones we saw were tucked alongside the rig's security," Isla said and zoomed in the picture to show her what she meant.

"Interesting," she said softly as she studied the piece of equipment.

"It looks like one of ours but not as advanced." Talia said what she'd been thinking.

"Keep watch up here. I need to call my mother Hadley."

"Do you want to share?" Talia asked.

"I will, but I have a few questions first." She slammed her hands down on the rail and headed to the room Vivien had given her.

It'd been her parting gift before she left for the corner office she'd talked about while she'd taken her through this rig like a proud mom showing off her child.

She locked the door and sat for a moment with her hands between her legs and took some deep breaths. It'd be irresponsible to start off being accusatory, but she was having a hard time believing her moms hadn't found a way to keep eyes and ears on her. If that was true, it proved they thought she wasn't ready for what her future held. That hurt more than it angered her, but she was a little upset.

"Hey," Hadley said when Kai finally put the call through. "You okay?"

"I'm fine, but we found something." She pulled the footage Talia and Isla had taken and cued it up. "Where do you think that might've come from?" she asked, a little anger seeping into her tone.

"From your demeanor, why ask the question if you already have the answer." Hadley crossed her arms over her chest and seemed to study the pictures she'd sent. "If you need me to say it, I don't know."

"It's one of ours," she said, and forced herself to stop talking. Both her mothers had warned about the words spoken that couldn't be erased or taken back.

"No, it *looks* like ours," Hadley said as she typed a few things into her system, then took the foreign equipment and cut it away from the loop and enhanced it. "But it's not. When did you find this?"

"I didn't, my team did, but they waited because they didn't want to upset you and Mama since I was with Vivien." She studied the slowly rotating sensor and could see the differences from what they used in different situations for monitoring and communications. "I realize it's not one from our stock, but there's nothing remotely like this out there that belongs to us? Maybe one of the elders thought I needed looking after and didn't bother to let you or Mama in on their plan."

"Kai, I trust you to take care of yourself. From the time you could stand, we had people we trusted train you to be the best warrior you could become. You're the heir to your mother's throne, so no one, especially me, is going to coddle you. Not allowing you to stand on your own would prevent you from becoming an effective queen." Hadley peered right at her and smiled. "And if someone else did this, you have my permission to kick their ass."

"I'm sorry, Mom. When they showed me that thing I lost my head for a second and blamed you before I asked. I should've waited to call you."

"I can take it, pup," Hadley said, using the other nickname she'd given her when she'd turned four and followed her into the training fields like an eager seal ready to learn some new tricks. "We can always be honest with each other, and nothing will break our bond."

"Maybe I need to go to bed early tonight and get some sleep so I'll stop snapping at people."

"Let's concentrate on what's important right now," Hadley said and tapped on the sensor in the corner of the screen. "This might be what gave off the blip we picked up earlier, but we need to proceed cautiously. Whoever put it there has technology that's almost as advanced as ours. The anomaly we discovered was probably activated when the rover got too close."

"Where do you think it came from?" She watched as their system broke down the pieces and tried to identify what they were. "Think the military came up with something and we don't know about it?"

"Anything's possible, but my gut tells me this is something completely different."

Kai leaned back and thought for a minute, not wanting to act rashly again. "How about we give the unmanned sub guys all the credit?"

"Have the Triton crew bring these things up, you mean?"

"If this is some new technology that could possibly track even us, we need to take a look but put suspicion on someone else when it comes to actually finding and retrieving it."

"That's a good plan, and we'll keep researching on our end." Hadley pressed the tips of her fingers together and looked directly at her. "Don't take this the wrong way since I totally believe in your abilities, but be careful, pup. This isn't normal, and you're there with very little backup. Get mad at me if you want, but I've already sent a team that'll set up in the facility you put out there. They'll keep their distance, but until we figure this out, we want someone close just in case."

"I will, and I'm really sorry for misjudging this so badly. Tell Mama I'll get back in touch as soon as we get our hands on this thing."

"Will do, and I'll contact the team leader to warn you if they're swimming anywhere near you. I love you, so take care."

"Love you too," she said as she tapped over her heart with her fingers. "Give Mama a kiss for me."

Kai briefed Isla and Talia before putting on her hard hat and heading for the mess hall. She was in a good position to ask for what she needed since she was new, and most of these men probably thought she was clueless. Of course, crews like this thought everyone was clueless until you proved yourself. Once they started working in the morning, she planned to get one of the devices topside to take a look at it.

"Let's see if I can channel my helpless-female side."

CHAPTER SIXTEEN

It's a good thing the windows don't open," Frankie said the next afternoon as he reached for Vivien's hand. She'd been so lost in thought she hadn't heard him come in. "You look like you're ready to jump."

"And miss out on the stockholder dinner tonight?" she said mockingly. "I had an appointment to have all my finger and toenails ripped out but rescheduled to feel even more pain tonight. Even if I could fling myself out of here, Daddy would make me go encased in plaster. Never mind that I was in the middle of the Gulf until last night—he wasn't buying that I was tired."

"Cheer up, a long weekend's coming, and I promised I'd go with you to wherever you want to dive next. Unless you want to do something else."

"How about something we can do together?" She kissed the top of his head and put her hand on the side of his neck. "Maybe we should go shell hunting."

"Or we could sit on the sand and drink," he said and laughed. "We're old enough to get away with that now."

She smiled and nodded. "Did you get all my numbers for me?"

"Steve's not too happy every time I wheel in there, but yes, and I'm putting everything together. He thinks you're avoiding him."

"Vivien." Steve interrupted them almost as if the mention of his name had conjured him up. "I made a reservation for lunch, so if you're ready."

"Did we have an appointment?" She let Frankie go and checked her book. "I already have plans with Franklin and Marsha."

"I'll call and add two." Steve walked toward her and touched her hand before he picked up her phone and asked her assistant to do just that. "I don't like taking no for an answer."

"That's obvious, but we'll have to meet you there," she said, and Frankie's eyes widened. Her answer made Steve smile in a way that made his feelings of victory obvious.

"Um," Frankie said when they were alone again, and she raised her finger to stop him from saying anything else.

"Come on, we don't want to be late." The sound of footsteps followed her statement, and she curled her fingers into fists. Her days would be long if she had to worry about Steve spying on her, along with the pressure she was under from her father.

She followed Frankie down to his car before calling Marsha and making her brother laugh when she spoke in pig Latin. They were quiet as she pointed out the places where she wanted him to turn until they were close to the Rum House restaurant on Magazine Street in uptown New Orleans.

"Are we running some kind of covert operation?" Frankie asked once they were out of the car.

"It's creepy that he always knows where I am and what we've been talking about. I'm probably just paranoid, but I'm beginning to think he's found a way to spy on me that's not Daddy trying to push us together." She nodded to the hostess who held the door open for them. Marsha was already waiting and had obviously ordered drinks.

"He's not my favorite person, but that's a little out there," Franklin said as he maneuvered himself next to Marsha since it was the spot without a chair.

Her fantasy had always been that the two people she loved most in the world would find each other, but Frankie was way too shy for Marsha's taste. If he learned to be a little more adventurous, Marsha would tilt his world off kilter, but in a good way since his self-perceived disability had never been an issue for her.

"What's a little out there?" Marsha asked as Vivien dropped into the chair across from her.

"I think Steven's bugged my office," she said as she dipped a tortilla chip into the guacamole covered in mango chunks. "Frankie thinks I'm crazy, but since I've been in my overly decorated office, he knows my every move, and he's got insight into all my conversations."

"What do you mean?" Franklin asked as he gave Marsha a thumbs-up after trying his rum punch.

"He pointed out the mistakes," she made air quotes, "you made in the paperwork you forwarded me yesterday. All the stuff on his list was from our talk about it, and before you think he's a good guesser, that was something you worked on at home. It's not on our system."

Franklin sat back and stared at her, appearing as disgusted as he obviously felt. "How do we find out if that's what he's doing?"

"Let me help y'all out with this," Marsha said, waving her hand. "I'll make a few calls and let you know before I do anything."

"Thanks for believing me." She reached for Frankie and Marsha's hands. "Where the hell would I be without you both?"

"I'll explain why you don't have to worry about us not being there for you later," Marsha said and squeezed her fingers, "but right now glance to your left real quick."

"What the fuck?" Since Steve was the kind of guy who drove a car to be noticed, it was hard to miss the brightest candy-apple-red Corvette she'd ever seen parked right outside. At any other time she would've admired the beautiful lines of the American classic, but it was one more prop in Steve's carefully crafted image. "Part of me wanted to be convinced I was being paranoid."

"If I didn't know better, I'd say you were trying to avoid me," Steve said as he sat next to her. "I thought we had a date?"

"And we're beginning to think you don't get it when people are trying their best to get away from you," Franklin said, and Vivien could hear his teeth grinding. He only did that when he was truly angry. "Why don't you either get out of here and let us enjoy each other's company, or order a taco and choke on it."

"Careful, Franklin," Steve said and laughed. "I almost feel threatened."

"So is my sister by your stalking. How'd you get here? I doubt this place would've been my first guess to look for Vivien if I was searching for her, and I know for damn sure you're not that lucky." The volume of Franklin's voice was starting to rise, and the bartender came out from behind the carved oak bar.

"Hey, man, you got nothing better to do than bother these people?" The guy was bigger than Steve, but Steve didn't appear intimidated. "If that wasn't real clear, get the fuck out."

"See you both back at the office. It's plain to me that a conversation is necessary so you understand what's expected of you." Steve left, not giving them a chance to respond, and Vivien realized it also gave him an out in answering Frankie's question on how he'd found them.

"What an asshole," Marsha said as she placed her hand on the bartender's forearm. "Thanks, Harris."

"Did I miss a meeting and that asshole became my boss?" Vivien asked. Her skin itched from the anger coursing through her. "Because he sure sounds like we're at the office to please him."

"I think it's time to enjoy the trust fund Granddad Palmer left us," Frankie said.

"Are you serious?"

"While you were offshore I had to deal with Steve, and I'm sick of it. He acts like that whenever Dad's not around, then a perfect kiss-ass whenever he is."

"But you love your job, Frankie," Vivien said, sorry she'd complained so much. The only interest Frankie had aside from spending time with her was his job.

"If I get bored I'll find something with one of the majors. Being an attorney who specializes in maritime contracts has to be good for something, right?"

"Then this time I'll follow your lead."

"What's the alarm?" Kai asked as she entered the operations room. She'd tasked Isla with hacking Triton's system and overloading the sensor closest to the foreign one.

"One of the security gismos is going ape shit," the supervisor said. "Want me to turn it off and get someone in the water?"

"Why don't you let the Oceanagraph folks earn their keep," she said nonchalantly. "They can check the rest of them in that area once they get their equipment wet. In my experience, once one goes out they all do, but this time it could just be a fish with a bad sense of direction."

"Thanks, Boss. The divers will love you for keeping them topside in this mess."

The weather had been nasty when the sun came up and had gotten progressively worse as heavy rain lashed the windows, casting dark-gray shadows over everything. "Good nap weather, for sure," she said as the sub team headed for their command module on deck. "I haven't met those guys so I'll head down there. Call if anything else fucks up."

The module was cold and cramped, but the chill was necessary to keep the equipment cool. Kai stood between the two comfortable leather chairs the pilots used and watched the monitors. She might not have known the crew, but she was familiar with Oceanagraph since the guys who'd found the *Titanic* and her final resting place had utilized their equipment. The owner seemed to be a lot like Vivien in that he worked so he could afford the explorer in him.

"There's our problem," the guy on her left said as he pointed to the sensor lit up in red. "It's still in one piece, so if they can reboot it tell them to try."

Kai touched the shell at her throat and focused on the man on her right. While her mothers were better at implanting thoughts into others they didn't know, if the subject was open enough, and since she wasn't asking for anything complicated, she could usually pull it off.

The guy guided the rover to the right. "Let's do a three-sixty to make sure before we tell them to do anything." He moved the joy stick a little more and there it was. "What the hell?" the man said with no prompting from her. "Did they fuck up and put one too close to this one? If that's the case, the interference could make this thing wiggy all the time."

"That don't look like the security sensors Palmer installed," the other guy said. "Do you know what it is?" he asked her.

"Are you sure you've never seen it before?"

Both men shook their heads.

"I'd tell you to bring it up, but I can't know for sure that it's not dangerous because your buddy's right. That doesn't resemble ours at all." She radioed for her number two to come down and sit with these guys. "You two do a sweep of every inch of this thing and see if you find anything else that doesn't belong down there. If you do, don't touch it and come get me."

She waited for her replacement outside, enjoying the Gulf breeze and rain on her skin. With any luck this incident would bring

Vivien back. "Don't let anyone in the water near what we found, and if anyone tries it, shackle them when they come back up."

"You got it," Barney Hickman, her assistant operator, said as he shielded his eyes from the weather.

She went back to the command center and waited before calling it in, glad she did since they found six more of the foreign modules. They still needed to check the deeper sections, and if the spacing was consistent she figured they'd find another hundred or so.

"Do you want to evac the rig?" Barney asked when she went back down to check the map they'd made of where the extra sensors were.

"Not right now, but if upper management wants us to remove whatever these things are, I'm going to recommend it."

Barney took his hard hat off and scratched the top of his head where his hair was thinning. The rain had slacked off but the humidity was brutal, so Barney started fanning himself with his clipboard.

"That'll go over like a ton of shit hitting that pretty building downtown. Old man Palmer doesn't like shutting down for nothing, and evacuating this mother will cost a bunch of money."

"It'll cost even more if we're sitting on something that's rigged to blow," she said as they walked to where the crew was placing new pipe down the well. "I don't know that for sure so don't let that go any further than us two, but we all know once we're fully operational, Palmer will jump in status as far as the majors like BP and Shell are concerned. This isn't a mom-and-pop anymore, and they're all after Triton's design. If they can't get it, they'll try everything to discredit it."

"You really think someone would do that to get ahead?" Barney took his safety glasses off next and wiped his eyes on his sleeve. "How are you not sweating in this soup?"

"Business is ruthless, you know that, and I think cool thoughts." She laughed when he lifted his middle finger in her direction and decided it was time to move on with her plan. "Keep an eye on everything, and I'll go see what our bosses want us to do."

She dialed the number Vivien had given her and put her feet on the desk while she waited for the ringing to stop. It surprised her that she'd actually missed Vivien as much as she had after she'd gone. "I'm losing my mind."

"You've only been out there a day, so insanity shouldn't be a problem yet," Vivien said dryly.

"Actually it's you who might go a little insane once I tell you what we found today." Kai heard a male voice asking Vivien what was going on, and she wondered if it was Steve.

"Was it a spill that destroyed Triton?"

"No."

"Then believe me, nothing you can tell me will be worse than what's happened today. Actually you should call the office and report whatever it is, since Frankie and I might be leaving for a really long vacation." The man with Vivien laughed at that, so Kai guessed it had to be Franklin.

"How long?" Kai dropped her feet to the ground and opened the small book on her desk that contained all the contacts for the Palmer offices. Vivien seemed to have quickly forgotten whatever they'd done together once she got back to her life, and Kai clicked her teeth together as a way to stay quiet. If that was the case, she'd have time enough later to analyze what an idiot she'd been.

"Until we run out of the trust our grandfather left us," Vivien said and exhaled loudly. "We should be broke by the year thirty-five hundred or so."

"Good luck then and sorry to bother you." She hung up and thought about her next step as far as who to call. It had to be someone who wouldn't strip her of the authority to get anywhere near the sensors. They were the answer to a puzzle she didn't know existed until she'd seen them. Vivien would've taken the lead but would've included her in the process—that she was sure about.

The next logical person was Winston Palmer, but the gamble there was he might turn things over to his lackey Steve. "Hopefully he's got more sense that that," she said as she picked up the phone again, only to have it ring.

"What'd you find?" Vivien asked.

"Are you sure you want to know? If I tell you it might mess up your vacation plans."

Vivien laughed softly. "You are a bit of a pain in the ass, aren't you? And it saves me from calling you later. I wasn't going to disappear on you, so don't sound so defensive, guppy."

"I'll agree with you this one time because of what I'm getting ready to dump on you, and if you never call me guppy again." She explained what was happening, and all Vivien did through the process was grunt to let her know she was still on the line. "That's the extent of it."

"You've been there a day, for the love of God," Vivien said and laughed. "I guess we can't quit today, Frankie."

"You want me to get everyone off this thing?"

"Let's wait until we talk to my father, but I'll call you back as soon as we're done."

"You got it, and hopefully by then I'll have an answer for you as to how many more we have to deal with." She accessed a map of the other production platforms close to them and wrote down the coordinates of the closest two. If she found any other sensors or whatever they were, then perhaps they were attached not to spy on Triton but to triangulate between platforms to perhaps map something. "I thought I'd go visit some of our neighbors and see if we were the only lucky ones."

"Give me a couple of hours and you can carry out your plan, which sounds good. I don't want my father rupturing an artery or taking you out if you jump ahead too much."

"Thanks for the warning, and I look forward to hearing from you," Kai said as the last of her anger disappeared. "But if it comes to Winston blowing up over this, I'll take the blame."

"Why would you do that?"

"Two reasons," she said and put her feet back on the desk so she could push back far enough to stare at the ceiling. "It isn't your fault, and Winston would probably be happier screaming at me."

"Like I've said before, you don't know my father very well."

"That's okay, but I think his daughter is a far more interesting person."

CHAPTER SEVENTEEN

Galen glanced at the clock next to their bed before sticking her tongue out at the ringing phone. She'd spent a great afternoon in bed enjoying Hadley's romantic mood, so it had to be important if whoever it was decided to bother her here.

"Are you going to glare at it or do you want me to answer?" Hadley said from behind her as she tickled along her abdomen.

"I'll get it since, if it's about Kai, I'll feel guilty for putting it off." She answered, and Natal started off apologetic but did assure her it was important. "Give us twenty minutes and bring it to my office."

"Was it about Kai?" Hadley asked as she guided Galen back down and covered her with her body.

She relished the sensation of Hadley's hand slowly moving up her inner thigh, but they had to go. "Remember where your hand is right now so you can start there later, but we've got to shower and meet Natal in a half hour. To answer your question, though, it's sort of about Kai, or at least what they found."

"I guess they were ours after all, and Kai will think we're spying on her no matter how much I deny it."

"Isn't it you who always preaches not to guess until we have all the facts? And you won't have all the facts until you take a shower." She pushed on Hadley's chest and laughed when she wouldn't budge. "You smell like you just had sex."

"Think if I had another hour or so," Hadley said and kissed the tip of her nose. "I'd need two showers."

Since neither of them knew who Natal was bringing with her, they decided to dress a little more formally than they wanted, but Hadley held her hand as they walked toward her office. Their life seldom held this much mystery, but she knew Hadley wasn't lying, and no one who reported to Hadley would've dared to overstep themselves to spy on Kai.

"What's your best guess?" Hadley asked as they neared the door.

"Sometimes I wonder if we need to speak since you're so good at reading my mind." She stopped and gazed up at Hadley, profoundly glad this strong, intelligent woman had agreed to share her life with her. Hadley not only loved and adored her, but she was also fun and the best champion she could've hoped for.

"If someone screwed up, she's not going to believe me, is she?"

"Honey, Kai will believe you because she trusts you more than anyone else in the world, and more importantly, she knows you trust her."

"I'm glad you're so optimistic," Hadley said and kissed her. "Let's go see whose ass I'm going to kick for this mess."

Natal was alone, and from the ramrod-straight posture, whatever she had to say wasn't something she particularly wanted to hear. When Hadley squeezed her fingers she figured that's how her consort felt as well.

"At ease," Hadley said and waved Natal to the table Galen used for small meetings with her immediate staff. "You look like you're about to crack in half."

"I have an opinion about the sensors Kai's team found, and I thought it best to tell you first, your majesties," Natal said, her hands flat on the table. "In a sense, they are ours, but not ours."

"Well, I don't know about you," Galen said as she looked at Hadley, "but that clears it up for me."

Hadley laughed at her attempt at humor before refocusing on Natal. "Let's try less cryptic descriptions and tell me what all this is about."

"When Queen Nessa first colonized Earth," Natal put an archived image on the screen of the inventoried supplies the expedition had taken with them, "her team took these sensors with them. Either someone made replicas of the originals, since none outside the museum exists, or they found a cache with functional equipment and utilized it. Even if the second scenario is possible, I'm not sure how the sensors were charged and made operational. Nothing then or now resembles Earth's electrical or motorized engines."

"So no one to your knowledge would know how to power and operate these," Galen paused, searching for the right word, "antiques."

"Yes, Your Highness, to my knowledge. At least no one on *Earth* has the knowledge."

Both she and Hadley understood what Natal was saying, and the thought chilled her. "Dear goddess," she whispered.

"Indeed," Hadley said as she closed her eyes.

❖

"Who is this fucking idiot?" Steve said loudly after Vivien reported what Kai had found. "Do any of you have any fucking idea how much it'd cost to evacuate Triton? Not to mention what the inspectors will do to us going forward."

"If all you have to offer is how to use the word fuck in different sentences, then go outside and wait," Vivien said, having reached her limit of Steve's personality for the day. "This isn't Kai Merlin's fault. She didn't put these things, whatever they are, on Triton. And she didn't technically find them."

"That's not what you just said," Steve said, not backing down, and when her father didn't interrupt he seemed encouraged to be even more obnoxious.

"You drew your own conclusions, but I never blamed this on Kai or anyone. These things are there, they were found today, and we've got to decide what to do with them."

"Steve," Frankie said, making the now-panting man stop staring at her. "Wait outside. Vivien and I have to speak to our father."

"I'm one of the leads on this project, so don't think you can lock me out."

"You are part of *this* project, but you aren't a part of my family, so get out."

The artwork in her father's office shook when Steve slammed the door, and for a long moment they all seemed to enjoy the silence.

Winston looked at Frankie, then her, before raising his hand to cue one of them for an explanation.

"At lunch today, Vivien and I made a decision," Frankie said, and she could sense his need to do this so she remained silent. "We've had enough of that guy, and you, frankly."

"Me?" Winston pressed his index finger to the center of his chest and laughed.

"Don't act like a clueless idiot, Dad. It's insulting. Ever since you brought Steve aboard, you've become," Frankie tapped his fingers on the table as if thinking of a good word, "a prick."

Vivien laughed since that was the word she had in mind, but her father didn't appear amused. Yet he took a deep breath and waved Frankie on instead of slapping him down.

"So we quit," Frankie said without fanfare.

"If you want me to talk to Steve, I will. He's been giving you a tough time, but I figured you could handle it," Winston said as if he'd slapped a Band-Aid on a small cut, patted the top of Frankie's head, and now expected him to stop whining.

Vivien told him about lunch and Steve's escalating stalker behavior, convinced it wouldn't do any good but at least it'd all be out. "Don't bother having a talk with Steve, because you agree with him on most things," she said. "This isn't a him-or-us proposition."

"It sure as hell sounds like it," Winston said, his words fast and short, a sign he was getting really angry.

"It's too late for that, Dad. Frankie and I love our jobs, but we aren't going to be whipping posts for you to try to make us into something we'll never be interested in being. Add to that the constant abuse from Steve you see as courting behavior," she said, making air quotes, "or the old boy's club. We're leaving, and Steve is only a small part of that equation."

"Have you forgotten this is Palmer Oil, and you're both Palmers?"

"No, we haven't, but you and that asshole have forgotten common courtesy, and I'm tired of tensing up every time I pull into the parking lot," Frankie said, matching his father's tone. "Life's hard enough without having to face a battle over absolutely everything every day."

"We'll help you with whatever this is, and then you can continue whatever it is you and Steve have planned for this company's future.

But Frankie's right. Fighting you and Steve at every turn is getting old."

"So I have no say in this?" Winston asked, a little more calmly.

"All you can do is wish us luck and invite us to dinner every so often, but I'm not in the mood for broken promises," she said.

"Neither am I," Frankie echoed, and there was nothing left to say, at least from their side. It saddened her that their relationship had come down to taking sides.

"Then this is a him-or-you scenario," Winston said and smiled.

"Here you go." Frankie took their letters of resignation from his leather folio and slid them across the table. "That's our scenario. Steve won't hand you one as well, no matter what happens or how he's treated."

"Why do you think that?"

"Because he wants your position too much to quit now," she said, then walked out with Frankie right behind her.

❖

"Kai," Hadley said as she watched her daughter's face. "I've never pulled rank on you, so don't think I mean this as an insult, but I strictly forbid you to go near these things unless it's in your capacity as a Palmer employee." Kai said nothing and her face was void of expression. "Tell me you understand that."

"I swore I wouldn't and I won't," Kai said, but she didn't sound upset. "You really think we have visitors from home here, or maybe a spy?"

"We don't know either thing for certain," Galen said, clenching her fists tightly. From their years together, Hadley knew how angry she was. "Natal did research, and our systems show this might be what the original sensors would've morphed into had we continued with the same design. This type of sensor proved unreliable on Earth since the water has a different chemical makeup than in Atlantis."

"Chances are the ones you found aren't operational, but we can't gamble giving away your position if they are."

"Mom, you don't have to repeat yourself again. I called Vivien Palmer so I'm sure she'll be here before tomorrow. Once *she* brings them up, we can get a closer look and hopefully figure out who they belong to."

"The team is in place just as a precaution," Hadley said.

"Hopefully it's not that many, since the outpost isn't that big." Kai's desk phone rang and she answered. "Should I try to find a red carpet before then?" Kai said after listening to whoever was on the line. "How about the other rigs in the area? Will do, and see you tomorrow."

"Vivien Palmer?" Galen asked when Kai gently replaced the receiver.

"She and her father are arriving in the morning," Kai said and laughed. "He thinks this is an attempt by an environmental group to shut down Triton."

"If only it were that simple," Galen said, finally relaxing. "What we need to know aside from whom, is why there."

"This could be the first cache we find," Hadley reminded them both. If the rulers on Atlantis sent someone, they most probably had conquests on their minds, since they'd never mentioned it in their last communication with Galen. "No matter what, we don't expose ourselves, and we crush whoever tries to take what's ours, especially you and your mother's birthright."

"Yes, ma'am," Kai said, pressing her fist to her chest. "On my sword and honor, I *will* defend your throne, Mama."

"You're definitely the best of both of us," Galen said, kissing her fingers and pointing them at her. "It might come down to a fight, but remember what your mom always says."

"Plan smart, fight well, kill once," Kai said.

Those words had been Hadley's motto throughout her life. Whatever the situation, she planned to excess, which made anything not only easier but discouraged anyone from wanting to face her ever again. It'd be no different even if the threat came from someone who thought they owned them as a people. These assholes had been absent from their lives for too long to think they had any say here.

"Remember to report anything out of the ordinary, and we'll be in touch if we find anything else." Hadley stood behind Galen so Kai could see them both. "We love you, pup, so don't take any chances and break our hearts."

"Listen to her," Galen said as her head dropped back to her chest. "Your mother's a wise woman."

"Both of them are," Kai said and smiled as they signed off.

"She'll listen to you, right?" Galen asked in a tone that begged reassurance.

"Kai knows better than anyone in the realm the importance of following orders. It's anyone's prerogative to ignore a ranking officer, but then they can expect the same behavior from others when they're the ones giving orders. Discipline's something you must give before you earn the respect to receive it."

"You're as talented outside the bedroom with that mouth as you are in," Galen said and laughed with her, since her face obviously showed the blush she could feel the heat of.

CHAPTER EIGHTEEN

K ai skipped the mess hall and settled for a sandwich on the helipad to enjoy the breeze and clear skies. When the stars were as bright as they were that night, she remembered the stories she'd read about their home planet. However, that was really no longer a true statement—home planet. Earth was as much a part of their history, if not more, than Atlantis ever would be.

From the books she'd read, some of them numerous times, Atlantis had been once much like Earth in the early days of man. It had been filled with pristine forests, mountains that yielded precious ore, and hundreds of thousands of miles of water. Their history was full of words like paradise and heaven, but as in all things the people loved their environment only as much as they were taught to love it.

Not long after Princess Nessa left to explore places where new colonies could be formed, her father's selfishness led the people to revolt against his heavy-handed rule. With Nessa gone he'd lost the one thing the citizens truly loved about him, so they replaced him with Nessa's aunt, who was next in line for the throne. Only it didn't take the revolters long to figure out the true ruler wouldn't be the king's sister, but her husband, who'd learned well from the deposed and now murdered king.

The name Poseidon became a memory that people remembered more fondly than their new line of rulers, the Oberons. In a short time the first King Oberon showed that the throne, complete power, and the loyalty of the people under his heel were not enough. He started down a path that took only a few decades to destroy the beauty of Atlantis by destroying their environment both in and out of the water.

To start fresh after her father's death, Queen Nessa took a consort and for the first time ever took her name. From that day on their heirs had been Merlins, but their blood and wisdom to rule had been inherited, they believed, from the young woman with the courage to change the fate of those who truly believed in her.

According to the communications Kai's mother still received periodically, Atlantis was in a continuous mode of recovery, but that would only go so far with an Oberon on their throne. Each man after the first king had claimed Earth and the Atlanteans on it as part of his empire, and every queen since Nessa had declared her independence once she and the original settlers decided never to go back. That choice was easy after the visions of the original high priestess gave Nessa a glimpse into their future.

"I wonder if you ever saw me?" Kai whispered into the wind. "And if you did were you proud of the sight?"

"You really might be cracking up if you're avoiding people so you can talk to yourself," Vivien said from the stairs. "Or are you out here feeding the fish again?"

"How'd you sneak on here with me not seeing you?" She glanced back to see if Vivien was alone.

"You're facing the wrong way to have seen me moor the boat, but don't worry. My father's grand entrance tomorrow will more than make up for my low-key approach." Vivien joined her on the edge, placing her meal between them. "I brought you one of Corey's brownies to make up for sneaking up on you," Vivien said, mentioning this crew's head cook. Every company prided itself on its kitchen talent, and Corey hadn't disappointed so far.

"I already had one."

"You're an instant-gratification kind of girl, huh?" Vivien pointed to her half sandwich.

"I think that's something we have in common," she said, breaking the brownie in half and handing a piece to Vivien. "Can I ask why you're leaving the company after our little adventure is over?"

Vivien filled her in without hesitation, and that surprised her, considering how little they knew each other. "What is it about you that makes my mouth run like I don't have any control over it?"

"Even though you think I'm a reporter working undercover, you can trust me, Vivien. Believe me, if you'd read some of my papers in school you wouldn't be under that delusion." She ate her portion of her second dessert and tried to read Vivien's thoughts. None of them were clear, but she did sense a building confusion mostly aimed at her. "Are you sure about everything you and Frankie decided?"

"Honestly, part of me thinks we're letting Steve win. Without Frankie and me there, God knows what he'll talk my father into, but I've had enough. Life's too short and all that." Vivien laughed before resting her elbows on the railing. "Why, do you think I should've stuck it out?"

"It would've been one way to know for sure what Steve's motivations are," she said and shook her head when Vivien started to interrupt. "That's not me trying to change your mind, but I do want you to think."

"About?" Vivien said, but didn't seem upset.

"Even if you aren't there, the company will always be Palmer Oil. Leaving it to someone like Steve is inviting whatever will be done in your name to happen." She pointed to the east, where the Deepwater Horizon was still resting at the bottom of the Gulf. "Do you want something like what happened a few miles from here to happen again and have that forever linked to your family?"

"Are you trying to guilt me into changing my mind?" Vivien asked as she turned to face her. Even in the low light, Kai could see the blueness of her eyes and the beauty that'd captured her even as a child back on that day they'd met on the beach.

"Do you want me to?" She smiled and Oba came to her mind. For once she understood what Oba had tried to tell her about love and the woman in her future. If that did turn out to be Oba, she'd never own her whole heart because of how devoted Oba was to the gods. While Kai's title would come with a lifetime of duty, she wanted the same kind of relationship her mothers had. Her mother Galen was queen, but her life with Hadley was full, and they both were sure of what they shared.

"I asked you first," Vivien said as the corner of her mouth turned slightly upward.

"I'm not trying to guilt you, but I do want you to change your mind."

"Why?" The wind picked up and blew Vivien's hair into her face.

Kai impulsively reached up to comb it back, which made Vivien blush. "Because one day I might have to sail into the sunset, and I'd feel better if you and Franklin were the ones steering Palmer into the future."

"Why?" Vivien sounded like an old vinyl record that was stuck.

"For plenty of reasons, but the one that comes to mind is you have a foot always in the sea, no matter your duties to your job. Someone like that will protect both the company and the places you'll drill."

"Thank you for your confidence in me, and I'll think about it." Vivien went back to looking at the water and swinging her legs over the side of the platform. "I can't speak for Frankie, but *I'll* consider what you said."

They were silent for a while, and Kai broke the stillness by asking about the sensors under them. "What's your game plan tomorrow?"

"Don't you mean *our* game plan?" Vivien gazed at her with one eyebrow raised higher than the other. "My father's flying in once the crew boats get here, along with a crew from OSHA. If it does turn out to be some stunt by environmentalists, he's going to blow someone's world to shit." Vivien picked up their plates and handed them over when Kai stood and held her hands out for them. "I agree with you that we need to get everyone off before we go near them."

"I doubt they're dangerous, but it's better to be sure about these things." She followed Vivien down to the main deck and nodded when one of the crew relieved her of everything she was holding. "We need to figure out where I'm going to bed down tonight since you gave me your room."

"You stay put and I'll bunk in the *Sea Dreamer*. It's comfortable, and I've done it plenty of times."

Kai followed Vivien to the lift that would take her to water level and got in with her. "Thanks for the extra brownie and the company," she said as they stood at the dock built off one of the legs that held up the structure. It was one of two, and Vivien's vessel was already sharing space with a large crew boat waiting for evacuation tomorrow.

"Thank you for the pep talk and for not kissing my ass like most people when they want something from me, not that you do," Vivien said and shrugged. "But even if you want something, you're much more subtle about it than everyone else is."

"Believe me, Vivien, when I kiss your ass," she said close to Vivien's ear, "it'll be a memorable experience for both of us."

Winston Palmer arrived at nine the next morning and walked directly to the control room the unmanned sub guys operated from. It was tight with him, Vivien, and Kai all watching the monitors, but no one complained as the submersible ran the line of every foreign sensor they'd found.

Kai concentrated on Winston and his mind since she didn't see a change in any of the sensors after the tenth one appeared on-screen. For a man who ran a profitable company, his thoughts were surprisingly revolving around Vivien and Steve. The daydream of their wedding seemed to play in a loop, drowning out almost everything else happening around him. It was one of the strangest things she'd ever encountered when tapping into someone's thoughts.

She focused on the monitor everyone was staring at and took a deep breath before crossing her arms so she could touch the shell at her throat and not have it be obvious. Oba and her mother Galen always said it was a matter of concentration, so slowly she broke through the fog and made the sensors and why they were there the most important thing in his head.

All Winston did for about five long minutes was blink repeatedly, as if he were in some discomfort, and eventually he rubbed his temples before asking to sit down. "What's your plan, Viv?" He sounded oddly different from all the other times Kai had heard him.

"Like I said, we don't know why they're there, who placed them, and if they're dangerous, so we need to get everyone off before we go near any of them," Vivien said as she stood close to her and glanced up at her as she spoke.

"Kai, any suggestions once we do that?" he asked as his rapid blinking started to relax.

She placed one more thought into his head before she answered and almost laughed when he nodded. "I have some experience with explosives, not that I think that's what those are, but I want an up-close look before we touch them."

"No," Vivien said in a way that conveyed the finality of her answer. "We'll talk later about how you know anything about explosives, but you aren't going to put yourself in danger to save Triton, no matter how in love the board is with this thing."

"I didn't say I'd touch or remove one," she said and put her arms down. "One look to see if we need to call experts in, and that's it. No sense in letting someone blow us out of the water without a fight."

"Go ahead," Winston said with his finger pointed at her, "but touch it, and I'll let Vivien kick your ass if it's still in one piece when you get out of the water."

"Don't worry, Dad," Vivien said, her eyes focused on Kai's. "I'm going with her, and I might take a spear gun with me to keep her in line."

They figured out which three were closest to the surface to see where they had to put in, and Winston promised to stay in the control room to warn them of any changes. "Be careful, Viv," Winston said as he took Vivien's hand. "I love you," he whispered, and Vivien's expression changed to one of shock. "You were right."

"About what?" Vivien asked, not trying to move away from her father.

"Lots of things, but let's start with the evacuation. Once you two are done, we'll get into the rest of my extensive list."

"You feeling okay?" Vivien asked, and Winston laughed.

"Must be all this fresh air, but I'm good." Winston hugged her briefly, as if he'd almost forgotten how, and left the confined space.

"That was different," Vivien said as she stared at the door Winston had disappeared out of.

"Nah, he's your dad. Different would be if all of us hugged you before we got on with our day," she said and winked. Perhaps her mothers' assignment that was meant to right old wrongs had placed her at the center of a bizarre situation. Oba would know for sure, but it was like someone had purposely put Winston in a fog. Why and how had they done it?

It was possible, but even in their realm such a tactic was used sparingly as a way to try to turn someone away from a life of crime or worse. That was a bit harder to do when it came to the women of Atlantis, since their talisman and their genetic makeup gave them the talent of joining their thoughts, but it was possible.

"Come on, comedian," Vivien said, waving her through the door.

"You never know. It might improve morale if you started giving hugs," she said and smiled when Vivien laughed and shook her head. She nodded slightly in Isla's direction, since Talia was down getting her crew boat ready. Isla had gotten their dive equipment together so she was confident it was ready to go. "Meet you down at the water," she said as she left to change clothes.

"See you, since my suit's on my boat," Vivien said as she followed Isla, helping with the gear she was hauling down.

Kai glanced back once and found Vivien doing the same. Had Vivien's talisman picked up what she'd done to her father? If Vivien had felt it, she didn't seem upset by the possibility, which made her wonder just how much Vivien and Franklin had figured out about the gifts she'd bestowed years before.

"One step at a time, Kai," she said to herself, but that was hard to do. When it came to Vivien, her curiosity was becoming dangerously piqued.

Kai secured Vivien's helmet in place before sitting so Isla could do the same for her. Usually the rig divers geared up with regular diving equipment, but she was using the same ones they'd dove with before so they could communicate with each other and with Winston. In the time it took to evacuate everyone, the sub crew rigged together another control room they could operate from on one of the crew boats.

"Thanks." Kai faced Isla and gave her a thumbs-up. "Get clear."

A few minutes later they were the only two people left on Triton, and Vivien raised her thumb as well once Winston radioed they were ready. Even in the bright sunlight, Kai could see the lights of the sub not far from where they were.

"Ladies first," she said to Vivien and heard Winston laugh.

They scattered the fish congregating around the leg of the rig that plunged into water, and Kai kicked hard to get in front of Vivien. Not that she wanted to get there first but to put herself between Vivien and whatever this was. The sub was to their right with its powerful lights on, illuminating the small box. Kai looked directly at it, bringing it into better focus because of the lights on her helmet.

"Nothing's written on it," she said as Vivien placed her hand on her shoulder to hold her position behind her. "No blinking lights or anything."

"You think whatever it is could be operational?" Vivien asked.

Kai had skipped the wetsuit and gone in wearing a pair of shorts and a dark T-shirt. She took out a small mirror on a telescoping arm from one of her pockets and positioned it so she could see the back. She couldn't see any markings on the surfaces, and she didn't think it was a sensor, at least a sensor like they used.

"It's a closed system since I don't see anything that gives a hint as to what it is." She moved the small mirror all along the back of it to see how it was attached. "Whatever these are, we have to hope whoever placed them left fingerprints to track them down."

"How's it attached?" Winston asked as the sub came closer to them.

"I can't really tell without ripping it off."

"Should I remind you my daughter's right behind you," Winston said rather loudly.

"I'm not suicidal, sir, but I do have an idea." She turned to look at Vivien and pointed to the surface.

Once they were above the water, Kai saw Talia's vessel close to them. "Vivien, get aboard and I'll be right behind you."

"What are you doing?" Vivien asked, treading water, then putting her hand up when Isla lowered a ladder for her.

"I need a small chain or strap like we use for cargo. Then I'm coming up to join you." She glanced up at Isla and held onto the ladder to keep herself in place. "Think you can put one together long enough to keep us out of the way if something goes wrong?"

"You bet," Isla said before heading inside fast.

Vivien grabbed the strap of her tank after she'd stripped out of her equipment so they could look at each other. "Don't do anything stupid."

"I'll be right back—promise."

Isla came back with a roll of straps they'd tied together and handed her an end. All she needed was one of these things to prove her mothers' theories. So far she wasn't sure this was anything like they'd ever had. Those first pieces of equipment Queen Nessa had brought back were built differently and had a warning system as a way to keep their secrets and their contents in place. She'd brought the mirror to save herself from the slight but attention-getting shock theirs put out.

She headed back down with the sub nearby and carefully tied the strap around the closest box. Sure that it was on tightly, she headed back, following the line to the surface. One of the crew took her tank and helmet to make it easier to climb aboard. As she stepped on deck, her talisman slipped out of her T-shirt collar, and she couldn't retrieve it before Vivien reached out and touched it with one hand. Vivien's other hand was on her own, and she momentarily formed a link between them.

"You ready?" she asked, taking hold of Vivien's hand. "We need to get this done." She tried to divert Vivien's attention and had thought she'd succeeded when Vivien nodded, but it was clear that wouldn't last.

Talia steered forward slowly until the strap became taut, then pushed the engines a little more until it became slack again. "Well?" Winston asked from beside her.

"It either popped off, or," she said as she pulled the length back in, slowly when she saw the metal box at the end, "it worked."

Talia's boat held only the sub crew, the Palmers, Talia, Isla, and Kai, so Vivien and Winston nodded when she held it up but over the water. "It's not ticking, is it?" Vivien asked.

"No, but if you want I can take it on board my boat to try to crack it open," she offered, which in turn made everyone with them take a step closer.

"We've followed all the inspector's recommendations, and according to his rulebook, once someone attaches something to a rig, it's no longer theirs," Winston said but made no move to take it away from her. "Anyone who wants to leave can, but I want to know what's in there."

"Me too," Vivien said.

Kai took it inside and placed it on one of the tables bolted to the floor. She put on a pair of latex gloves and unrolled a sleeve of small tools she'd given Isla to bring along. The metal appeared normal, but it was starting to erode, as if whoever placed it didn't realize how fast the salt water would eat through it. That had been the problem with their first sensors that were constructed from an Atlantean metal called genga. On their home planet, genga was widely used in underwater construction, from what Kai had read, but the water covering most of the planet contained no salt at all.

She let Vivien pick it up first and watched as she turned it to study all its sides. It looked like a solid metal box with no weld marks or screw holes. "We're going to have to have it x-rayed to see what's inside," Vivien said.

Kai opened her bag and fished out a powerful magnifying glass. "May I?" she asked with her hand out. Like their helmets, the magnifier had lights around the perimeter, and she started with one of the longer sides. These appeared to be solid as well, and she had to really hunt for the releases.

"What's that?" Vivien said when she spotted the faint line along the bottom edge.

She took a small screwdriver and ran it along the line, searching for a release button. She found four on each of the long sides and one on the smaller ones, and when she finished poking each one in, the box opened like an egg. Vivien's hands shot up when the green glob appeared to be headed for the tabletop, but Isla was waiting with a container, so Kai concentrated on pouring the stuff inside. It was odorless, but Kai asked the guys to open all the windows as a precaution. Once most of the glob was gone, Kai placed the two sides in a tub Talia had brought and studied the series of glass tubes of various sizes that lined the inside.

"Well," Winston said as he put his glasses on and sat on the other side of her. "What the hell is it?"

"I really don't know, sir," she said, and Vivien didn't add to that. "I've never seen anything quite like it, but it must mean something to someone, since there are enough of them down there to fill our hull."

"What do we do about that?" he asked as he rubbed his face as if out of frustration.

"I need to bring up a few more to see if they're all the same," she said as she packed the first one away carefully and sealed the container. "If they are, we can use the submersibles to retrieve the rest."

"Then what?" Winston asked.

"This seems to be a lot of trouble for someone to go to, so I think we need to find a lab and ship them off," Vivien said as she held up the container of the green substance. "After we start with extraction, we need to visit the other rigs in the area and see if this is just about us, or if we find more."

Kai made two more dives, and the other two sensors were exact replicas, along with the rust along the outside. She and Talia exchanged glances as they opened the third one, since these sensors weren't designed to study water health, temperatures, and organisms. They were communications modules. The only thing was, none of their systems had picked up any exchange except the weird random blips.

"I agree, only let's take them out a few at a time, or leave them until we know what that is," she said, pointing to the green slime.

"How long do you want to shut down?" Winston asked.

"Give me two days, and hopefully I'll get us cleared. Head on back, if you want, and I'll do what needs to be done to get us operational again."

"I appreciate the offer, but I'm staying put," Winston said as he signaled Talia to take them back to Triton. "You might need my help, so I promise not to get in your way."

"Let's get started then."

CHAPTER NINETEEN

I never noticed the shell around your neck," Vivien said as they traveled to the Shell Oil facility closest to them. Winston's call to their operations manager in New Orleans had cleared the way for their visit. "It's like mine."

"It's similar," she said, since Vivien was holding hers out of her shirt. "I've had it a long time. It was a gift from my parents, but I've always thought they're like snowflakes. No two are exactly alike."

"You're an interesting person," Vivien said loud enough to be heard over the whirl of the engine. "I've said that before, but now I'm fairly sure there's something about you I haven't figured out."

"So you don't think I'm an open book?" She smiled, and her smile widened when Vivien blushed and turned her head as if she realized her face was completely red. "But if you're worried, you've already figured out my secret."

Vivien held her hair back and her eyebrows came together, but at least she'd forgotten her nervousness. "I'm a fish lover but a terrible cheerleader."

"That's true, but—" Vivien's voice was loud all of a sudden, since Kai had cut the engines to slow them down. "You seem overly qualified for this job, so I'm not sure why you took it."

"You should be happy about that, since you're getting a bargain if it's true. Suspicious isn't the way to go here."

"Stop speaking for me, please. I didn't say suspicious. You did."

She brought them around and waited for the Shell crew to tie them off before fully facing Vivien. "Just remember that I'm not out to get or harm you in any way. I might have loved other jobs more, but sometimes—"

"You have to work for the evil spawn to pay the bills?"

"You have to find ways to make both necessities work together because the world needs both. We need fish and oil, but one can't come before the other. For me it's that simple."

"You guys ready?" the roughneck on deck called out. "Or you want me to wait until you make out?"

"Lose the attitude with the lady or I'll kick your ass," she said, but slapped the guy's back anyway after shaking his hand.

"Took you long enough." The guy kept his hand on her shoulder. "Thought you got lost."

"Vivien, this is Trout Guidry." She pointed to Trout. "He's one of Antoine's boys."

"That's a great operation you and your family have going," Vivien said, as if making small talk was necessary for the ride up to the deck.

It didn't take them long to deploy their submersible and start checking the parts of their operation that were underwater, and even less time to find the same placement of metal boxes. Kai joined one of their divers and dislodged another three so they could be photographed to share with the other rigs in both deep and shallow water.

"What the hell?" Vivien asked as they made their way back.

"I wish I could say for sure, but I really don't know." In her head she plotted the locations of the other outer-shelf rigs, and what it meant if all of them had the same communicators.

"You don't have any clue?" Vivien's hand was wrapped around her shell.

"No," and for the moment that was true.

By the time they'd reached Triton it was being evacuated again, only this time more than ten coast-guard cutters surrounded the facility. This evac didn't seem voluntary. Winston's voice on the radio broke the silence, and Vivien answered him as Kai scoured the horizon as if looking for someone or something.

"What now?" Vivien asked her father as she pointed to one of their crew boats leaving a berth.

"The OSHA guy took one look at the green shit that came out of that thing and shut the entire Gulf down."

"They can do that?" She threw the crewman a line and waited for Kai to finish. "We're on our way up," she said before her father could answer, figuring it wasn't a conversation they should have over the air.

The new people on the rig were more than OSHA and coast guard, and they were carrying DVDs and files from their offices and from the submersible command module. The fact her father stood by and let them meant that wasn't voluntary either. If these guys were part of some federal alphabet soup, it surprised her how quickly they'd arrived. The unknown boxes had been out of the water less than a day.

"Are we in danger?" she asked her father when they reached him. "We inhaled whatever that was when we opened it."

"They said the hazmat guys are suited up for precautionary reasons, but their preliminary field tests were negative for any airborne pathogens." Winston put his arm around Vivien's shoulder and kissed her temple. "The problem, though, is they have no idea what this is. At least the one guy I knew on the team told me that."

"So why shut down the whole Gulf?" Kai asked.

"If all these things are some kind of explosive devices, it could be terrorism, so the Washington honchos want to play it safe." Winston's voice wasn't loud, but Vivien could tell by his clipped tone that he was angry. "I can't blame them, but boy, is this going to put us behind."

"Do we have to leave?" she asked, her eyes never leaving Kai's. "They can't evict us from our own rig, can they?"

"We haven't gotten that far yet, but they're going to have to carry my ass off here." Winston let go of her when a man in a coast-guard uniform approached them.

"Sir, we appreciate your cooperation so far, and I hope that continues. From what we can tell from your records, we've got a tick over a hundred of these things down there." The guy stood at parade rest with his hands behind his back and completely ignored her and Kai. "Until it's cleared by the agencies involved, we're going to have to ask you and everyone else to leave this facility."

"For how long?" she asked.

"For however long it takes to assure this isn't a safety concern," the man said with a bit of sarcasm.

"You're talking about thousands of people losing their jobs," Kai said, and Vivien enjoyed how the condescending asshole had to cock his head back to look Kai in the eye. "I believe Mr. Palmer and his employees deserve a timeline so they can plan accordingly. The operation he runs isn't exactly small."

"I'm sure someone will get back to you on that."

"Not good enough," Kai said, crossing her arms over her chest. "If you don't have the authority to give him an answer, then we'd like to speak to someone who does."

"Is that a threat?"

"No, it's a promise that a representative from Palmer will accept every interview opportunity offered where we'll describe in detail the draconian actions you've taken here today."

"She's right about that," Winston said. "And if this turns out to be some environmental nut job, I'll be happy to tell the world at large how much the hit to the economy rests on your shoulders."

"In a PR battle, I believe the side of caution will have the upper hand," the man said with a smug smile.

"Are you finished in the submersible module?" Kai asked, confusing Vivien. "I left some gear in there, and I'd like to take it before you kick us off."

"You all have an hour to vacate the premises." The guy walked away with the swagger of someone who'd gotten his way.

"Draconian actions?" Vivien asked shaking her head. "That's as good as nefarious, but it didn't do any good."

"She's right. You sure give in easy," Winston said.

"There's one more thing I'd like to check out before you brand me a weenie."

"What?" Vivien asked but followed Kai anyway, her father not far behind. "We've seen the boxes and can't prove it since they took our files. Do you think they'll start singing and dancing when you see them again?"

"Allow me to satisfy the conspiracy theorist in me." Kai sat and powered everything up, leading the sub from its berth toward the coast-guard cutters docked below.

"How'd you know," Winston said as he stared at the screen. "Goddamn good call."

Each of the three cutters had five of the same boxes attached to its hull well below the waterline. It was a hunch on Kai's part, born from the hours she'd spent studying strategy with her mother Hadley. If you wanted to plan an invasion or even consider one, information was central to your success. By attaching sensors to ships allowed everywhere, including military facilities, it was easy to take note of the enemy's potential to fight and work countermeasures to assure victory.

As she maneuvered to the next vessel, the door swung open and the officer who'd spoken to them, along with three others, had their guns drawn. "Take your hands off the console and place them behind your head," he ordered, and she complied after pressing one last button. "What the hell are you doing?"

The sub was still moving closer to the next cutter, and they had a few seconds before they collided. "Do you mind if I cut the engines? I don't want to get charged if I wreck your vessel."

"Go ahead, but don't try anything funny. We saw the lights in the water, so answer my question. What are you doing?" He kept his weapon pointed at what seemed the center of her chest.

"I'd like to know why you're evacuating us while having the same devices attached to your vessels. Either they're dangerous or not, but you can't have it both ways." She stopped the sub at the cutter's center hull and focused the camera.

"What the shit is that?" the man said loudly. "Get down there and do your job," he said to the guy next to him. "If you just put those on my ship, I'm going to drop you in a black hole where you'll pray to die."

"Watch the recording from the beginning to now. I didn't put those there. You brought them with you. Convince me *you* didn't put all the rest on this rig." She placed the sub on autopilot to keep it in place so she could fully turn around and watch him.

"Are you sick in the head? Why would we put those things on your rig?"

"You just accused me of the same thing," she said, and Winston laughed. "We've got a problem, but you have an even bigger problem."

"Yeah," the guy said as he holstered his side arm. "What's my bigger problem?"

"Our security out here revolves around safety. We want to send our guys home in the same condition they arrived in. Companies like Palmer, though, aren't patrolling the waters under every facility constantly, so if something like this happens, we can't be sure of who or when." She spread her hands out, and he nodded quickly, as if understanding her point so far. "You're the United States Coast Guard, though, and I don't think you're docking those snazzy boats down there just anywhere. Our lapse in security is easier to explain than yours, so you've got the bigger problem."

She waved to the seat next to her and scanned the next two boats, finding the same thing on both. "You opened one of the damn things—you've got no idea what it is?" the guy said, calmer and now talking strictly to her.

"If your lab people give me a rundown of the ingredients of the green goop, I could make an educated guess maybe, but right now I have no idea."

"Let me make a call." He stood and took a deep breath. "If I can, I'll try to clear a skeleton crew from your outfit to stay aboard while we do the extractions."

"I should give myself a raise for hiring you," Winston said as he slapped her on the back. "That was brilliant."

"Lucky guess, sir, but I had to chance it. If we're not close by while they do whatever it is they're going to do on Triton, we'll never get any answers."

"The only thing left to decide is the skeleton crew, aside from me and Kai," Winston said.

"The three of us should do fine, and the bonus is Frankie can show you his stuff while you're stuck out here with me," Vivien said, staring at Winston as if daring him to contradict her.

"Think you can manage without me for a few days? I want to report to the board and sit with your brother as to what comes next." Winston placed his hand on Vivien's shoulder and sounded sincere.

"You promise to give him a chance?" Vivien asked just as sincerely.

"You've got my word."

They watched him leave for the office on the upper deck, and Vivien finally took her hand. "Thank you."

"What are you thanking me for?" she asked, aware of how good Vivien's warm hand felt in hers.

"I don't think he really noticed me until today, and my gut says you're responsible for that."

"I appreciate the endorsement, but you did that all on your own. We're sometimes blind to the things and, more importantly, the people closest to us."

"What do you think changes that?"

She sandwiched Vivien's hand between her own. "Sometimes a blow to the head, or one to the heart. If I had to guess, your father has seen Triton only from a helicopter or from pictures. Today was the first time he's walked its decks and stared up at this beast from water level."

"That's true, but what does that have to do with anything?" Vivien asked her in a way that reminded her of the child she'd met years before.

"How can you not be in awe of a woman who's given him so much more than he asked for? Today, here," she released one hand and pointed around them, "Winston Palmer finally saw you in an element of your life you're passionate about, and perhaps it changed his perspective."

"I agree that he should give himself a raise for hiring you, and thanks for saying all that."

"Maybe that should be the happy ending to the book I'm planning now that I've scrapped the article idea." She laughed when Vivien slapped her arm.

"Happy endings work only in romances."

"True, but we'd have to find a stand-in for Steve," she said, and Vivien simply squeezed her hand and peered up at her with an open expression, as if daring her to come up with a name.

The day had been interesting for more reasons than their mystery boxes.

CHAPTER TWENTY

G alen sat and watched Hadley put on her uniform, trying to arrange her thoughts so they made sense. One of the team members Hadley had sent to the area had removed a box from one of the coast-guard cutters. Judging by the report Kai sent, it resembled one of their early communication pods, but with some differences. Either they had a traitor or visitors, and neither scenario was something to celebrate.

"I won't be long, so cheer up," Hadley said as she put the intercom around her neck that allowed her to speak underwater. "It's not safe to examine whatever this is here. The remote lab was built for precisely this reason. We knew one day it'd be indispensable."

"I'm going to miss you no matter how long you're gone, but I was thinking about what Kai said. None of the advisors disagreed with her assessment, and neither do you." She didn't want to be the first queen in years to have a trial for treason against the throne.

Because of the competitive nature all her subjects had, including herself, in their history there had been challenges to the throne. Some queens had faced their opponents and others had champions stand in their place, but both options were deemed fair and honorable. None of the recorded challenges had been won, so that in all the generations they'd been on Earth a descendant of Queen Nessa had ruled and been loved by a majority of their people. Galen didn't delude herself that everyone loved or agreed with her in all things.

Hadley finished and sat next to her so she could put her arm around her. "I can't stop you from worrying, but try to save it for when we know what this is. If it's an attempt by a dying planet for control, we'll deal with it, and if it's an attempt to dethrone you, I'll gladly face them in the arena."

"I know you would, and I love you for it and for so many more reasons," she said and couldn't hold back the emotion that brought tears.

"What's this about?" Hadley picked her up and set her on her lap.

"Do you know why I'm so grateful to the gods no queen has ever lost a challenge?"

Hadley shook her head and wiped her face with her fingertips.

"Because if they loved as deeply as I love you, the loss of the throne was minor compared to losing your heart. The power to rule means nothing without you. Those women who lost left behind more than their lives and blood on the arena ground—they left broken hearts and partners behind."

"Don't put weapons in my hands yet, my love. I need to know what we're facing, but I also believe it's important to keep this as quiet as we can until we do." Hadley kissed her and held her for a long moment. "For now I'm only allowing Mari, my mother Brook, and Yara into the lab."

"You're going there alone? What if it's a trap?" Her head and chest physically hurt and tightened from the overwhelming sense of dread.

"You know what a prima donna I am," Hadley said and turned her head quickly, as if to flick her hair back had it been longer. "We're going in the big macha cruiser full of bad-ass warriors wanting to prove themselves. Don't fuss, baby. We're taking an entourage."

"Make sure to tell them all that I'm the jealous type," she said as she ran her fingers along Hadley's dark eyebrows. "I know you'll insist on silence on all communications until you get back, so please be careful."

"And you too," Hadley said, hugging her again. "I really don't want to be away from you right now, so please cancel anything that doesn't have to do with security."

"You'd probably wrap me in bubbles if you could."

"That's true for more than keeping you safe. I'm the jealous type too."

❖

By nightfall Kai and Vivien were two of only five people left on Triton, and with the machinery off it seemed like a ghost ship adrift in a sea of black ink. One of the cooks had volunteered to stay, so their skeleton crew was gathered in the kitchen enjoying a meal. Kai and Vivien had joined them, but Kai had left early for the solitude of the now incredibly dark helipad.

She didn't think she'd be alone long, and from the sound of the footsteps on the metal stairs she'd guessed right. "I realize you're losing a butt-load of money, but it's beautiful out here," she said, not getting up. She'd brought up a blanket and two pillows so they could enjoy the stars, since the sky was completely clear.

"Expecting me?" Vivien asked as she put the dessert and coffee she'd brought down and lay down in the opposite direction so their heads would be close.

"More like I was hoping for you," she said, turning her head slightly to make eye contact. "You're better company than Barney."

"Barney's a nice guy and a great number two to have, so don't make fun of him."

"Should I go get him so you can be alone?" she said and smiled when Vivien glared at her. "Look up, Miss Palmer. Believe me, it's a much more attractive sight."

Vivien didn't move her head but did reach over for her shell. It took concentration to not allow a link to form, exposing her thoughts to Vivien's. She didn't need someone like Oba or her mothers to lecture her about how easy that would be when the attraction was this strong. If she allowed it she'd have no secrets from Vivien, and no one in the realm would forgive her easily for that.

"Why didn't you tell me you had one of these with the same markings?" Vivien held the shell, and Kai had no problem reading Vivien's thoughts, which at the moment centered around questions about her feelings. For once in her life, Vivien Palmer seemed to be confused as to what came next.

"Tell me why it's so important to you." She shook her head and rolled so she could face Vivien. "Scratch that. What secrets do you think the markings hold? And why do you think they're buried in water?"

"Do you promise not to think I'm crazy if I'm honest?" Vivien released the shell but left her hand on Kai's chest.

"I promise, and I didn't tell you because mine is so much a part of me that I sometimes forget it's there. My parents gave it to me a long time ago, and I seldom take it off." She took Vivien's hand and laced their fingers together. "It's like me introducing myself to you and mentioning I've got nipples—true, but I'm sure you're not totally interested."

"That would've certainly been memorable," Vivien said and laughed. "For a long time I thought the shell was a peace offering from my mom." Vivien's voice was low, as if she was shy all of a sudden.

"Want to get more comfortable for your story?" she said as she sat and turned her body around. When Vivien didn't refuse, she lay down and opened her arms to her, smiling when Vivien rested her head on her shoulder. "You okay? I don't want you to think I'm taking advantage."

"No, I don't think that. Do you think this is strange?" Vivien asked as her hand came to rest on Kai's abdomen. "I don't ever do this, especially with someone who works for us."

"Want to sit up near the edge? I really don't want to weird you out."

Vivien moved closer and placed her hand on her hip. "That's why I asked. I'm so comfortable with you, and I can't figure out why. Don't take this the wrong way, but I'm not a touchy-feely kind of person. With you, though—"

Vivien's hand tightened around her waist. "How can I take that wrong? Knowing you're comfortable around me is a step closer to becoming good friends. At least that's how I'm going to see it."

"You don't mind?"

"Usually when a beautiful woman wants to share the sky with me and be close, it's not a bother."

"So you wouldn't share much with Steve?" Vivien asked, and she smiled at the hesitation in the words.

"If you're asking if I like you better than Steve, the answer is yes in more ways than the obvious ones."

Vivien lifted her head up and looked down at her. "Obvious ones?"

"Steve's an ass with an ego that could sink this thing, but even if he were as nice as Franklin, I'd rather be out here with you."

The answer was enough to get Vivien to put her head down and hum for a moment.

"You're one of the only people I've met who doesn't seem to want anything from me."

"Tell me your story, for now that's all I want."

Vivien's recollections of the day they met were fairly accurate, and she had no idea of the lengths the Palmers had gone through to make her and Franklin forget it. From the sound of it, the shells had been their comfort and one of the many things that had brought them together. "The girl was never found, and for some reason I think it was because she swam away."

"Seems reasonable to me," she said as she tracked a satellite overhead.

"No, I mean, she swam away under the water without equipment of any kind like she could breathe in the water."

Kai didn't speak for a few minutes, trying to think of something to say that wouldn't make Vivien's nightmares of not being believed return. "You mean like a mermaid or something?"

"You promised not to make fun of me."

"No. I promised not to think you're crazy," she said and pulled Vivien to her when she started to move away. "And I'm not making fun. I'm asking a question."

"She didn't have a fish tail or scales—she looked like a normal person who could obviously hold her breath for a really long time." Vivien sighed and Kai rubbed her back in comforting circles. "The next morning Franklin and I had these, and we've worn them ever since."

"Do you believe your life would be much different if you'd never seen that girl?" She heard Vivien sigh again and closed her eyes at the sound. "Do you think you'd be happier?"

"Granted, I don't usually play what-if games after forced therapy, but I'd like to think I'd still be who I am with or without that experience." Vivien seem to relax as she spoke since she slumped against her. "It wasn't a great feeling to not be believed, but I'm glad that happened to us—to me. Franklin was my witness I wasn't crazy, but the feeling I had when I looked at her in the water isn't something I'd trade."

"What feeling?" Kai asked, curious and glad they were having this conversation.

"That's weird and personal, but I'll tell you if you really want to know."

"I would."

"It was like finding something important and precious I didn't realize I'd lost. Since I was so young I didn't understand the full ramifications of that sense of belonging to someone, but maybe that was good. If I'd totally understood it and then realized it'd never happen again, at least not yet, I'd still be in therapy." Vivien laughed, and for the first time since they'd met, her laughter actually sounded light and joyful. "Maybe you should send me a bill."

"Good friends never charge for listening, and that was an interesting story."

"It's okay if you don't believe me. Trust me. No one else did."

She moved so she could see Vivien's face but didn't let her go. "If you said it happened, and Franklin says the same thing, why wouldn't I believe you? I hope you find the answers you're looking for. What exactly are you looking for?"

"I wish I knew for sure, but my gut tells me it's in the depths. Every map I've found with similar markings always leads somewhere, but they never answer every question." Vivien held a shell in each hand and seemed to study both of them closely. "Do you think this is part of an ancient alphabet? That's the thing I'm most curious about."

"It could be," she said and smiled. "The joke will be on us if they turn out to say Made in China."

"Now you're making fun of me."

"Just a little, but it's because I like you so much. If this job ends tomorrow I'll still be glad I met you." She brushed back the strands of hair that'd blown over Vivien's eyes and simply stared for a long moment. Vivien was truly beautiful.

"When I saw you I thought of that day. You made me feel something new, and I'm glad I didn't totally screw it up."

"I'm lucky you weren't completely taken with Steve or anyone else." The words slipped out, and for a second she thought she'd said too much.

"Maybe that's been my mistake all this time." She didn't move when Vivien ran her hands up her arms to her shoulders. "Do you agree?"

The shells were doing their jobs in that they amplified feelings when a true connection was made. Kai knew all its secrets, but this was new, wonderful, and so different than her link with Oba. "I do," she said, and despite knowing the risk and that it was wrong, she kissed Vivien with all the passion pent up inside her. She wanted this woman badly, but she cleared the fog in her head when Vivien moaned.

In a way she couldn't turn back, since it would be like walking on a beach and trying to arrange the sand like you found it, but she couldn't regret her actions. The burning in her total being was what both her mothers had told her to wait for, and to discover it was for a woman who couldn't share her future shattered something inside her. Unlike Vivien during their first meeting, she was old enough to realize it might not ever be duplicated, no matter how long she searched throughout the realm. No one else in the whole of Atlantis would be Vivien.

"Are you okay?" she asked Vivien, since her eyes were still closed.

"I will be if you kiss me like that again."

That, she was afraid, would be a bigger mistake than doing it in the first place.

"Scanning the area now, Highness," the copilot of the large shuttle Hadley was in said as they reached the laboratory they'd built three thousand feet deeper than they had the city. The facility was most often used to study and care for the giant squid that man found so elusive.

"Anything?" Hadley studied the monitor, looking for a small anomaly, which is what the behemoth they were in resembled, if any of the world's navies noticed it.

"Only some of our squid friends and a US Navy bus about twenty miles from us."

"Good. Contact us if you spot anything, and send out a group to search for any type of monitoring equipment, even if it's ours. Mark them, but don't move anything."

"I'll put swimmers in the water as soon as you disembark."

Mari slapped her on the back as she led her group to the portal that would allow them to leave without flooding the ship. After retiring from active duty, both Mari and her mother Brook had taken an interest in conservation, so they'd visited this location often. The water was cold at first, but their suits soon regulated the temperature so they could swim the short distance comfortably.

The soldier who'd brought the box back was standing at attention when they stepped into the large lab space, until Mari gave her the at-ease command in a kind tone. The young woman had also neatly laid out all the tools they'd need next to the foreign box.

"Thank you for your speed in getting back," she said as she put gloves on and picked up the X-ray probe. "Did anyone on the team open one or take it anywhere near the command post the princess will be working from?"

"No, ma'am. Our team leader sealed this one in a locker after spraying all sides with cloaking spray." The spray jammed any spying attempts, if any such tactics were placed on the outside of the device. "I went ahead and submerged it, so nothing will transmit from the gel inside. Anything found, including all the others recovered, will be included only in reports to you and the queen."

"Excellent," she said as she watched the screen, their system collecting data that would be stored only here. "According to the composition analyzer it's made of genga, and we know the only place to find that now is in our national museum."

"How did it get here?" Brook asked as she put her glasses on to read along. "None of our systems detected an incoming ship, and judging from the number of these things, it didn't get here yesterday."

"A ship can enter without detection in a few ways," Mari said. "We need to figure out what intel they're gathering. They've used an odd placement pattern to try to find us, don't you all think?"

"Let's see," Hadley said as she cracked it open and placed a probe in the gel that emerged.

Their system started downloading information, and Hadley gripped the table when the exact location for every colony they'd established and Galen's daily schedule appeared on-screen. An invading force would have no trouble centering their attacks from space, if they planned to annihilate them. The fate of their world and every living thing on it could be in danger.

"How is this possible?" Mari said, her face tense from what appeared to be shock.

"Wait, let me think," she said as she tried to remember Galen's itinerary for the coming week. The most recent list, before Galen had actually cancelled all her activities, had two differences or updates from this one. That made it easier to pare the list of people who could've compiled this information. "It doesn't matter now that we communicate with the palace, so, Mari, please call and have the palace cleared of all unessential personnel. Have Laud double the guard outside the royal chambers. If something happens to my wife, I'll kill anyone who allows it."

"Calm down, Haddy," Brook said as she placed her hands on her daughter's shoulders. "It's no time for idle threats."

"That was more of a promise," she said with force. "Natal, go ahead and see how this thing is communicating with all the other boxes found so far. I'd like to know how they could be connected without any of our systems detecting anything."

"I've already run the analysis and that's the strangest part of all," Natal said as she typed. "The location of our assets and the queen's schedule seems to be almost hardwired into it, but it doesn't communicate with any of the other boxes, even when in close proximity like these were. They only gather location intel where the individual box has been. This one has schematics of the coast-guard base the ship was assigned to in Louisiana."

"They can't be hardwired," she said, ready to get back to Galen even if they weren't finished. "That schedule was correct three days ago."

"That's all that's on here, though. All the memory is just a week old," Natal said. "We only recently detected the strange blips, but the locations and the queen's schedule were the only things shared with this box. It was an incoming transmission, with no recorded outgoing messages."

"Is it possible for it to send something and not record it?" Brook asked.

"This technology is antiquated, so I'm certain that's not the case, ma'am. There seems to be enough of these for someone to get the information they need no matter where in the world they are. The only mass communication was the locations and schedules, which makes sense if you're trying to be covert." The system finished extracting everything it could, so Natal removed all the probes.

"Destroy it," Hadley said. "Whoever placed them has to know they're compromised, so it won't make any difference now."

"Let's get back," Mari said.

"Head to the shuttle and order the swimmers aboard. I've got one more call to make."

Chapter Twenty-one

O h my God," Vivien said when she opened her eyes. It was ludicrous that a kiss would put her life into perspective, but something deep inside her seemed to have come alive.

"That was inappropriate—I'm sorry," Kai said but didn't move away.

"Don't say that. It's not like you forced yourself on me." She'd never begged for anything in her life, but she'd be willing to now. This had been like someone opening a door and saying "this is the promised land," then slamming the door in your face. "I wanted you to do that."

"Don't think I didn't want to—I did, but maybe this isn't the best time."

"I'm sorry, but the company and whatever all these things are don't take precedence over this," she said, placing her hand against Kai's cheek. "Maybe we don't have a definition for it yet, but I'd like to find one."

"Answer something for me first. Have you ever looked at a woman twice, much less kissed one?"

"Is that the route you're taking to blow me off? Seriously?" She pushed Kai away and got up. "When you decide to stop acting like a jerk, come find me."

"Wait," Kai said, jumping to her feet so quickly and gracefully it made her stop. "I'm not acting like a jerk. Just the opposite. I don't want you to do something you might think differently about when the sun comes up tomorrow."

"That's mighty chivalrous of you, but let me ask you something. Why butter up a girl with stars in a secluded spot, skinny-dipping, and dinners if you weren't interested?" She put her fists on her hips to have something to do with her hands, but that wasn't helping her get rid of her anger. "You've led me to an inevitable conclusion, then backed off. Deny it if you want to, but that's what this is, and because that's what this is, you're a jerk."

Vivien took the steps two at a time, needing to get away before she did something as juvenile as cry. She shut the door to the room next to Kai's and sat on her bunk breathing hard. When the phone rang, it startled her enough to break through the irrational despair of Kai's rejection. "Hello."

"What's wrong?" Frankie said.

"What are you talking about?" She loved him, but now wasn't the time to get into this, even if it was Frankie. "I'm fine but tired. It's been a long, strange day. One of many, actually."

"That's all? It doesn't feel like that's all."

The knock on her door made her want to blow him off, but when they were young she'd vowed never to do that. When they were growing up, a lot of who Frankie was or thought of himself was tied to that cursed wheelchair, but she'd refused to let him buy into that. Not that she believed she missed out on a lot—it'd been important to her to be the one person in Frankie's life who not only loved him, but also pushed him way beyond the limits of his legs and chair.

"That's all. I promise." She opened the door and put her finger up to Kai. "Did Dad make it back okay?"

"Did you slip something into his drink? He's back and acting like a caring human being for a change."

She stayed on her feet and kept her eyes on Kai as she sat on a bunk. It didn't really matter to her libido that she was angry—the sight of Kai on her bed was turning her on. She shook her head when Kai smiled as if she'd read her thoughts. "He might've come to the conclusion on this trip that he needs us more than the board and Steve. Granted, someone might've pushed him in that direction, and we might owe a little something for it, but I don't mind."

"You mean you didn't win him over with your bulldozer personality?"

"Actually, Kai Merlin did with her charm and logic. I'll be happy to tell you about it later."

"Have a good night and I'll call you tomorrow. Love you."

"I love you too," she said, her eyes on Kai as she put the phone down. "If you're here to apologize or to protect me from myself, good night. I'm old enough to understand the consequences of my actions."

"I'm not that much of a slow learner." Kai leaned back and stretched her legs out.

To Vivien she looked like the definition of power, if the word had to have a human face. "You might be too late if you changed your mind."

"I thought we could go for a ride and talk. That's it. Whatever you think, I'm not a tease, jerk, or asshole who's yanking your emotional chain for laughs." Kai stood up and got close enough to her that she could sense the energy Kai possessed. Strangely, it accumulated as much in her shell as in her groin. "Maybe Triton isn't the best place for the conversation we need to have."

"Your boat or mine?"

"Yours is moored downstairs and will save us a dinghy ride," Kai said as she stepped behind her and placed her hand on her abdomen. "I'm sorry for upsetting you."

"Let's go see how good you are at making it up to me."

The orb under Oba's hand glowed with the white light she always attributed to the purity of the goddess. The vision she'd been given, though, made her cry just like the first time she'd seen it. It was as if seeing a prophecy that had been written about and part of their scriptures for generations before her time with the orb come to life like a stage play.

When the high priestess who'd been gifted with the vision first wrote of it for her successors to learn from, the orb had provided a specific time frame. Kai's actions could start the domino effect that could lead to the fulfillment of the priestesses' writings.

"Can you share what you see?" Galen asked as she sat at the edge of the throne in the main-temple altar area. The space had been cleared for this meeting, and even Hadley had left them to speak freely.

"Why ask when you can demand that I share?" she said, lifting her hands to her face after giving thanks to the goddess. "I'm sorry, Galen. These images are unbalancing me. I didn't mean to be rude."

"I'm a little unbalanced myself, if you're telling me I might have given birth to the ruler who might bring about our destruction. Kai might not pick up after herself at times, but world annihilation is hard to believe." Galen stood and faced the statues of the gods that stood watch over the orb when it sat on its grand perch made of pearls and other precious stones.

"It's not a total world annihilation."

"To be exposed to the human world and causing worldwide panic might just be the end of our world," Galen said, and sat again. "The sharks among us believe it our right to rule humans and stop their assault on the environment we must share. At times it's hard to be heard over their objections."

"They're loud, true, but in no way the majority," she said as she poured them both tea.

"I realize that, but they do exist and will continue to exist since they raise children with their beliefs. They don't understand how ambitious those who dwell on land are to get their way, and some are just power-hungry to rule over everything. It's in the nature of every species to destroy what they don't understand." Galen accepted the cup, her smile, though, not as relaxed. "We are something they will definitely not understand."

"But like in all prophecies, this one can be changed, Highness."

"By calling Kai home to a quest of my choosing? Something the orb, you, Hadley, and I deem safe? I could, but my child would never have faith or trust in any of us, and I wouldn't blame her for that." Galen stared at her in a way that she never had, and she wanted to look away in shame. "Could what you see be tainted by what you feel for Kai and what she wants from you?"

"My Queen," she said but couldn't say anything else because she could think of no words to excuse her behavior.

"Oba, I do remember what it was like to be young and attracted to someone, especially someone who looks like Kai," Galen said, and winked. "But you have to have known what you shared with my daughter wouldn't last, and not because of whether I approve."

"What I did was wrong, so I wouldn't blame you if you choose to punish me for my lack of judgment. I'll accept it willingly." She dropped to her knees and pressed her forehead to the floor.

"Oba, please rise. That's not what I meant." Galen placed her hands on her shoulders and encouraged her back to her seat. "When I first saw Hadley and then got to know her in my heart, I was certain of the truth of my future with her. There would never be anyone else who owned so much of, not only myself, but my dreams and future. You might think that's too much to give, but Hadley gave back of herself more than what she's received. Too much of you belongs to the goddess, and too much of Kai belongs to the throne for either of you to sacrifice what you must to prove you are soul mates. So it doesn't matter if Hadley and I approve—what you and Kai share isn't built on a foundation to last a lifetime."

"Perhaps though, Highness, she is about to find exactly that, and it will result in the same shaky ground."

"This girl Vivien, you mean?"

She nodded and stayed on her knees. "The prophecy can be interpreted in a number of ways since it reads—'She will turn from the path set by the first and that will bring about the end of our world as we know it.'" As she spoke, the orb shone again but with a dimmer light. "Kai emerged from the water for a reason that day years ago, and when she did, she didn't fight the first chapter of her fate."

"Vivien Palmer is Kai's fate?"

"If she is and Kai turns from the path decided for her at birth, then it could bring about the end of our world as we know it. She could choose Vivien over the throne."

Galen fell back in the throne and closed her eyes. "Is that what you saw?"

"Yes." She saw no reason to lie. "I told her as well before she left. Love may draw her away from us and our people, but eventually that choice will bring nothing but pain."

"Some will think it insane to consider making that choice, but I believe I understand your concern."

"If she loves as deeply as you do, the choice will be easy, even if it does end badly."

Galen's eyes grew glassy with tears. "Of course, because no one wants to believe it'll end like that if they love enough. What of the rest of what Kai found? Did the orb show you anything else?"

"It only shows me the prophecy, so perhaps they're connected."

"Let's hope not," Galen said as she closed her eyes again. "It might bring new meaning to the end of the world as we know it."

Kai set a course west of Triton and tried to clear her head as the *Sea Dreamer* cut through the choppy water. The night was cloudy, hiding the moon, so Vivien's profile was visible in the glow of the instrument panel. She sailed until they were relatively alone, at least by the display of the radar. It was too deep to drop anchor here, so she left the engines above idle, so with the slow speed they'd stay almost in place when she turned them into the current.

"Why don't you want me?" Vivien asked softly, but she still heard her over the hum of the engines.

"You're way off if that's your first question." She stood and motioned Vivien down to the deck and slid down the ladder to join her. Vivien stood and watched her but didn't move as she knocked all the cushions off the bench seat to the deck and sat with her back against the stern.

Vivien followed her and stumbled on the last step, as if from nerves. "More stargazing?"

"Not in this cloud cover." She held her hand up, but that's all the encouragement she'd give Vivien. "If you want me to answer all your questions, I will."

"What do you want from me?"

"My list includes nothing someone like Steve's does. All I want from you is your time and you." Vivien took her hand, so she tugged gently so Vivien would straddle her legs. "I have to admit it wasn't what I had in mind when we first met, but I'm glad our first impressions don't get in the way of all this."

"Could you please explain before I screw up again?"

She hadn't thought of Vivien as a vulnerable person, but the question did have hints of uncertainty that made any other words unnecessary. When she placed her hand on the side of Vivien's neck, Vivien closed her eyes and stopped breathing. This time she took her time as she pressed her lips to Vivien's. Every woman she'd ever been with fell from her thoughts when Vivien opened her mouth slightly, as if inviting her in.

She tried not to make the kiss too demanding, but it was hard when her mind filled with all the things Vivien wanted and was thinking. "You weren't wrong, and I really didn't want you to get the wrong impression. I'm sure enough people in the past have wanted what you could give more than they wanted you."

"Could we stop talking for a little while?"

"We can do whatever you like."

The invitation made Vivien laugh and stand, so she had to cock her head back to see what Vivien had in mind. When the button of Vivien's shorts was undone, she had a clue, and any shyness Vivien had displayed before disappeared along with her clothes. The splash a few moments later made her think she wasn't as irresistible as her history had proved, but this was a refreshing change. Like Vivien, it was a relief to be wanted and pursued for herself and not for the power that would come from landing the title a union with her would bring.

She stripped and jumped in without making much of a ripple in the water and swam until she was behind Vivien. "Be careful in this chop," she said as she put her arm around Vivien, bringing her close.

"That's why you're here—to keep me safe and afloat," Vivien said as she turned and put her arms around her neck. "You have to since I'm beginning to understand the wonders of skinny-dipping more and more."

They kissed again, Vivien's nipples hard against her chest. The constant breeze chilled her wet skin, but she didn't think that was the reason for Vivien's reaction. Some of her hesitancy melted away at the thought that Vivien wanted her, so she put more need into the kiss and pushed her leg between Vivien's, which caused both of them to moan.

"Let's get out of the water," Vivien whispered in her ear, and she nodded.

Back on the deck Vivien spread a towel over the cushions and lay down as if issuing another invitation. The radio came to life just as she covered Vivien's body with her own.

"Ms. Palmer." Kai recognize Barney Hickman's voice.

She enjoyed Vivien's walk to the control panel even in the low light. Vivien wasn't tall, but her curves and the shape of her ass were impossible to look away from. "What can I do for you, Barney?" Vivien asked with a shake of her head when she glanced back at her.

"The coast-guard guy wants to talk to whoever's in charge right away."

"Of course he does," Vivien said, pinching her eyebrow as if in frustration. "Give us twenty minutes and we'll see him in the mess hall."

"Will do."

Kai stood and collected Vivien's clothes and handed them over. Maybe this distraction had saved her from something she couldn't undo, but she refused to think of it as a mistake. What she felt for Vivien wasn't wrong, but it wasn't fair to either of them since it had no future. Since she couldn't control herself around Vivien, maybe getting back to the job site was for the best.

"Once this is over, I want a few more days out here with you to hunt for more than stones," Vivien said as she kissed the spot over her heart.

"That sounds like the best offer I've had in forever."

"Just don't forget it," Vivien said. "I've finally found something I consider real treasure."

CHAPTER TWENTY-TWO

Triton was lit up like a star on Broadway when they approached, so Kai cut their speed and reached for the radio. "What the hell's going on, Barney?"

"The coast guard said they found something and they want all our people off," Barney whispered as if he wasn't alone. "Are you guys close? This shit's getting intense."

"We're close, so don't let anyone push you around."

"If someone punches me I want a raise."

"What else could they have found?" Vivien said with her arm around her waist. "The boxes were bad enough."

"Did you bring your phone?" She had the engines set to the lowest speed that propelled them forward. Vivien held up the device so she relinquished the wheel. "Make a loop around from the east, then park it."

"Why not go right in?" Vivien did as she asked despite the question.

"I want to see if they've got divers in the water. Look for lights away from the rig, because if something else was attached to Triton we would've spotted it." She stepped away and typed a text message, erasing it when she was sure it'd been sent. "Thanks," she said, handing it back. "Call your dad and see if anything else has been reported to him."

"Has anything like this ever happened to you in any other situation?"

"There's always some strangeness on every job, but this is a first." Vivien didn't leave her side as she spoke to Winston, and when she stared in the direction Kai pointed, she saw a line of light in the water. "Keep circling but don't get too far away."

"Why?" Vivien asked not moving.

"I don't think these guys are planning to share with us what they found, so I'm going to go peek. I won't get too close, so don't worry—in and out so we have a clue as to what's happening."

"They might shoot you, too, so I don't want you to go," Vivien said before blowing out a long breath. "But I guess I can't stop you."

"You can if you asked nicely, but I also don't want you to lose Triton."

"Be careful at least."

It would've been easier to go over the side unencumbered, but she had no choice but to strap on a tank and put on a mask. The darkness didn't bother her as she swam as fast as she could toward the lights, and after a few minutes she didn't see divers but Triton's unmanned subs. They were hovering over a spot, and she cursed when she focused on what it was.

A command module that resembled an upside-down mushroom was floating in about eighty feet of water, from what she could tell in the inky water and with no moonlight. Again the object appeared to be theirs but a more antiquated version of what was in their arsenal. The info the boxes were collecting was evidently being recorded into this and sharing it. It was like an office's server, and the boxes were workstations. If she could get close enough she could find the answer to so many questions—the most important being who was responsible for all this.

She couldn't pull the brains out of the thing without appearing in the sub's video feed, so for now she'd have to think of something else, but she had time. The unmanned subs were in the water for only one reason: the coast guard didn't know what the hell this was. When you were afraid of something in the water, the government wasn't any different than the rest of the world—it proceeded cautiously.

She swam back to Vivien more confused than ever, since she and her team couldn't have missed something like this given all the time they'd been in the area. The boxes were at times hard to find unless you were tuned into them, but a command module sent out a stronger signal.

"Hey," she said, tossing her mask aboard the *Sea Dreamer*.

"Find anything?" Vivien peered down at her with what Kai assumed was worry.

"A big something but they've got it surrounded." Vivien grabbed her tank so she could come up. "Let's dock so we can make some calls."

"Is it another clump of boxes?" Vivien put a towel over her shoulders and gave her a quick kiss.

"This is something bigger and looks like the capsules from the *Apollo* flights. Now that I've seen it, they'll speed up their timeline to get it out of here without telling us anything."

"Did they see you?"

"They don't have anyone in the water, but once we make the first call or ask the first question, the jig is up, as they say." She wondered if this would be some of the last moments she'd spend with Vivien. A quest was important to everyone in the realm since it officially finished your education and prepared you for your future, but security would reign over all that once she reported this situation. "The subs are down there, so they probably don't know what it is either."

"You think they'll boot us back onshore for good now?" Vivien stood next to her as she guided them back to Triton.

"This is a bizarre set of circumstances, so probably yes. Might save your dad a trip back out here."

"Promise me you won't disappear on me," Vivien said softly, and the need in her plea made Kai want to hold her.

"I wouldn't do that to you," she said, and she meant it.

"Highness, we patrolled the area yesterday and that wasn't there," team leader Edil Oliver said to Galen and Hadley by video link.

"Did it drop from the sky?" Hadley asked, making Galen poke her for the sarcasm.

"No, ma'am."

"I'm more interested *now* in what we're going to do about it," Galen said before the blame game got going.

"The coast guard has the unmanned subs monitoring it, so we've kept our distance, but we plan to get close enough to stick a probe in it and backtrack the information. Once we know who, it'll be easier to ask why. Both of you have my apologies for this failure. If you'd like to replace me, I'd certainly understand."

Galen wanted to do just that, but Hadley took her hand, which calmed her. "Throw yourself on your triton later, Edil. Right now we just need you to do your job," Hadley said without a trace of humor.

The screen went blank without them dismissing Edil, so they both leaned forward, knowing why. Galen's emotions swelled when she saw Kai's face on the screen, but she took a deep breath to tamp down the urge to sob in relief. From the surroundings, Kai wasn't on the *Salacia*, but she didn't appear tense or afraid.

"Highnesses," Kai said with her fist over her chest as she bowed slightly. Their child was only this formal when she knew they weren't alone and she was acting in an official capacity. "I'm sure you've heard about what was found, so I was reporting in for instructions."

"How—" Hadley said.

"Vivien and I were on the water and saw the lights from the unmanned subs. I took a quick look but stayed out of camera range."

For all the times she was glad Kai was like Hadley in most things, Galen didn't care for her need to jump into anything without much thought. "Has the *Salacia* picked up on anything?" she asked as she studied Kai's face for signs of anything amiss. She wanted to call Kai home before any real danger presented itself, but she had to balance her maternal instincts with her daughter's future and how the realm would view her.

"Can I speak to you two privately for a moment?" Kai asked, as if reading her mind.

The room cleared instantly, and Hadley sighed as she tightened her grip on her hand. If anyone in the realm had worshipped Kai from her first breath, it was Hadley. "Kai, don't take this as a criticism, considering I would've done the same thing, but think before you act from now on," Hadley said softly. "I'm your mother's consort, so if something happens to me she'll still be queen and the realm will survive, as will she, but you are our future. Our people need you to survive this or anything else that's found."

"I promise to let Edil's team handle the underwater missions, but I don't want to be locked in my room at home either."

"Is it about your purpose there, or is this about Vivien Palmer?" she asked, Oba's warnings on her mind.

"Both," Kai said, crossing her arms over her chest. "I won't abandon her or the goals I've set. If I leave now, Vivien will be more lost than before, and I won't do that to her. Not again."

"Kai, we'd never presume to arrange a union for you, but..." Galen said.

"I know the rules better than anyone in the realm, Mom, but you can't order me not to care about her and what happens to her."

Galen knew in that moment that Kai wouldn't come back the same. Vivien Palmer had somehow woven a spell that she'd cast years before, and Kai was happy to be mesmerized. She'd had her suspicions back then, since Kai had risked leaving the water for her out of all the mortals she had swum by in her life. Something about Vivien had called to her, and Kai had listened like a sailor following a siren's song.

"All right," she said as a coldness settled in her chest that made her place her hand over her heart. "Remember well what Oba told you. We will love you no matter what path you choose, but our choices are so much more catastrophic than most when they are different than what's expected."

"I know my place, and more importantly, I know my fate. Trust me enough to not betray you and everyone else on a whim," Kai said with a smile that made her appear more sad than pleased. "I love you both, and I'll be back when I'm done."

"Take care, tadpole, and we love you too," Hadley said, and the screen went blank.

"She'll remember everything, right?" Galen needed reassurance.

"Kai will no more betray you than I will," Hadley said as she helped her to her feet so she could hug her. "She'll need us when she returns, though, to help her heal the crack in her heart that will happen when she leaves the woman she loves."

"Do you think it will heal?"

Hadley pulled back so she could see her face. "Do you want me to lie?"

She shook her head, in no mood to be coddled.

"If she loves as fiercely as I love you, then no. Time will dull anything, but it will not make you forget." Hadley pressed her hand to her cheek. "That's my answer, but yours might be different when it comes to love."

"If I lost you, an eternity wouldn't dull the pain. That would shatter my will to go on, so I pray to the goddess she doesn't fall that deep into Vivien's abyss."

CHAPTER TWENTY-THREE

W e're evacuating everyone and clearing the area," the coast-guard representative said. The guy was new and had plenty of colorful ribbons and bits of medal on his chest and collar, so Kai figured he wasn't used to being questioned. "And before you complain, I'm clearing everything within a ten-mile radius."

"Did you figure out the boxes were dangerous?" Kai asked.

"This isn't a Palmer problem anymore, so pack up and go. If you decide to get cute I'll hog-tie you and carry you off myself."

"I don't think you'd like the results of trying that, so quit with the threats. I'm asking since some of my team was exposed to whatever the hell those are."

"Someone will contact you about that, but for now, Mr. Palmer's sending a helicopter for everyone left and someone to collect those fancy boats down there. Be ready in thirty."

"I'll be happy to make those arrangements," Isla said, making Kai smile since she wasn't about to let anyone aboard the *Salacia*. "We'll be in New Orleans by tomorrow."

"Thanks. I'll call you to get all the information," she said, and Isla nodded, not needing things spelled out.

When they were left alone on the deck Vivien reached for her hand. "Do you have a place to stay?"

"That's why I brought the boat."

"Come home with me, and when I get Daddy settled I'll be happy to join you."

"Sure," she said, not ready to let Vivien go yet.

The helicopter flight was smooth, so Kai closed her eyes and tried to organize her thoughts. They needed to find one clue as to where all this hardware was coming from and what purpose someone had for placing it. Once she was alone she wanted to talk to her mothers again so they could hash out all the points.

Vivien's truck was at the heliport, so she climbed into the passenger side after dumping their bags in the back. "Are you hungry?" Vivien asked.

"A little, but let's stop and get something to go. Those clouds have held off, but not for much longer, so let's get inside before the deluge starts."

The pizza place was close to Vivien's house, so in less than an hour she walked around the den while Vivien talked to her father and brother on the phone. It was a big space with a lot of antique framed maps on the walls, as well as relics Vivien had obviously found on some of her dives. The room seemed inviting and comfortable with the pictures of Vivien and Franklin at various ages scattered throughout the built-in shelves.

She stared at the one that had to have been taken the summer they'd met, since she recognized the bathing suits they were wearing. Their smiles were so genuine she couldn't look away, at least not until she felt Vivien's arms around her waist. She laughed when she saw the pile of clothes by the kitchen counter Vivien had been leaning against.

"If I crank up the air conditioner, can I interest you in a fire?"

"I'm getting warm already, but a fire would be nice." She kissed Vivien before she let her go light the gas fire. The way Vivien didn't look away as she got out of her clothes made her feel wanted, so she didn't waste time worrying about the consequences of her actions. Right now she wanted Vivien as much as she'd ever wanted any woman, and from the way Vivien's eyes followed her every step, the desire was mutual.

"Do you want a slice of pizza?" Vivien asked with a smile.

"I find cold pizza is better, but if you're hungry," she said, picking Vivien up so she could wrap her legs around her.

She dropped to her knees with Vivien and laid her down on the blanket Vivien had taken off the sofa. Through Vivien's shell she sensed her nervousness, but also her need to be with her, so she took the lead. "Tell me to stop if anything makes you uncomfortable, okay?"

"Unless you tie me up and steal my jewelry, I don't see me stopping you from doing whatever you want."

Kai lay next to Vivien and positioned herself so she could kiss Vivien and place her hand on her abdomen. "I won't tie you up unless you want me to, but right now I only want to touch you."

Vivien's body was creamy white with pronounced tan lines that made her arms and legs appear like they'd been kissed by the sun. She liked that Vivien enjoyed the water as much as everyone she knew. It seemed almost unfair that Vivien hadn't found the secrets she'd searched for.

She must've been moving too slowly since Vivien pushed her onto her back and straddled her hips. "You've been winding me up for days, so touch me before I have to resort to begging," Vivien said, her breasts swaying right in front of her face.

Kai didn't want this to be rushed or about lust, so she sat up slowly, moving her hands from Vivien's hips to the undersides of her breasts. Vivien pushed her hips forward when she cupped them, and it was all the invitation she needed. She kissed Vivien, her tongue gliding into Vivien's mouth, causing her to moan and her nipples to harden against her palms. The response made her wet, but right now all she wanted was to please Vivien and build her to an orgasm that'd leave an imprint of her on her heart.

"Kai, please," Vivien said as her hips pumped forward as if chasing some sort of contact. "I need you—" Vivien's plea ended in a long, almost torturous moan when she placed a hand between her legs. Vivien was so wet she took her time to run her fingers up and down, enjoying how easily her fingers slid over Vivien's clitoris that was as hard as the steel her people's tritons were made of.

The grip Vivien had on her shoulders tightened as she turned her hand palm up and gently put two fingers in. She wanted to prolong the act, but Vivien seemed so ready she didn't want to deny her. Vivien moved with her, but her eyes were shut tight and her mouth was puckered as if she was about to say a prolonged oh. When the walls of her sex clamped down on Kai's fingers, Vivien finally made some sort of sound. She moaned loud enough to make Kai smile, especially when it started low and ended in a high keen that stopped only when Vivien slumped against her.

"Jesus," Vivien said, extremely out of breath. "Don't move yet," she said when Kai began to take her fingers out. "What the hell did you do to me?" Kai peered into Vivien's blue eyes and smiled again. Vivien looked incredibly relaxed but still—she thought for a moment, trying to find the right word. "What?" Vivien asked almost shyly.

"You look…" She kissed Vivien's slightly swollen lips and felt a twitch in Vivien's vaginal walls. "The best word I can think of is lush."

"Like a plant?"

"Like a beautiful, sexy woman," she said as the doorbell rang.

"Don't make any noise." Vivien glanced back toward her phone. "Whoever it is can wait until tomorrow." The phone started next, like Vivien seemed to expect, and Vivien groaned when she heard the distinctive ring Kai recognized as Franklin's.

"How about you point me toward the shower and then get the door?"

Vivien gazed at her with an expression that made her appear as if she'd asked her to walk across hot coals. "What about me?"

"The hot-water supply depends on how quickly you get rid of guests," she said as she took her fingers out, enjoying the way Vivien squeezed them as if getting the last bit of pleasure she could before they parted.

"You're seriously leaving me to face them alone? One look at me and they're going to know what we were doing." Vivien hadn't moved away from her, and really all she was in the mood for was touching Vivien until she begged her to stop.

"Don't go anywhere," she said, kissing Vivien's cheek before getting up. She answered the phone when it rang again, hoping it was Franklin. "Hello, Franklin," she said when she recognized his voice. "Vivien's in the restroom, so I hope you don't mind me answering her phone."

"Could you open the door then? It's starting to rain."

"Sorry, we're at Tulane meeting with Professor Olivier. Vivien was a little restless so we walked. We can head back if it's important."

She smiled when Vivien nodded as if approving of her performance. "Or we can come by your parents' house later and talk over everything that's been happening."

"Sounds good," he said and laughed for some reason. "Tell my sister to call me if eight tonight isn't acceptable."

She put the phone down and stared at the way Vivien was lying back with her legs spread open, inviting her. The sight made her clitoris pound with want, so she covered Vivien's body with her own and pressed her clit to Vivien's. The move made Vivien wrap her legs around her hips as if to increase the pressure, and the intense pleasure made her completely open to Vivien.

Kai placed her hands on the floor close to Vivien's head, and as she lost control the shell at her throat warmed and seemed to almost reach out for Vivien's. She knew the consequences if they did connect, but right now all that mattered was Vivien and the need to make her want her as much as Kai needed her. As they slid against each other, the shell opened that part of herself not even Oba had reached, and Vivien's responded with no resistance. The orgasm unlocked the very essence of who Kai was, and glimpsing every one of Vivien's most private thoughts made her lose complete control.

"Oh, my God," Vivien said as she raked her nails across Kai's back, and the way she tightened her legs made Kai speed her hips.

It was as if they'd clicked together like two pieces made for each other, and as Kai's body reached the peak the shell did its job. The process now couldn't be stopped unless she left Vivien wanting on the floor and walked out the door.

"Kai, don't…unh." Vivien finished her demand with a groan that in turn started her tears. It was almost too much for Kai as well, as she jerked against Vivien wanting to wring the last bit of pleasure out of both of them.

When they were done, Kai's arms shook from the effort it took to hold herself up, so she began to roll off, but Vivien held her in place with her legs. "I'm about to collapse."

"I don't care," Vivien said, her tears still falling into her hair. "What the hell did you do to me?" The question did make her move, but Vivien followed and ended up on top. "It wasn't a bad thing—quite the opposite, actually."

"You're an inspiration in this department," she said, wiping Vivien's cheeks with her fingers.

"All my lushness, huh?" Vivien laughed as she put her head on her shoulder. "It's like you possessed me completely, and it was everything I ever wanted."

"Thank you for sharing this part of yourself with me." She lifted her head and kissed Vivien's lips. "In hindsight I should've told Franklin we'd all meet tomorrow."

"I'll make it up to you tonight."

"It can't come fast enough."

Vivien's hips slammed into her when she squeezed her butt, and it made her smile. "Jesus." Vivien lifted her hips again and Kai put her hand between her legs. "Maybe you should've said *I* can't come enough."

They took their time in the shower, and a few hours later they were seated at one end of the Palmers' dinner table. Winston had reported over drinks that he didn't know anything new and was as frustrated as everyone else with assets in the Gulf. After that fact was established and talked about, Cornelia took over the conversation and steered it away from business.

"So how in the world did you end up here?" Cornelia asked Kai after she'd answered questions about her past. "You're an environmentalist in a world of wolves."

"I'm more a realist than an environmentalist, ma'am. We've got problems, so I decided to do something about them instead of picketing. The world needs oil and gas until something else comes along, but it also needs fish and clean water."

"Why can't the rest of the wackos out there understand that," Winston said as he refilled everyone's wineglass.

"Maybe because they don't like being called wackos," Vivien said, making everyone laugh. "And, Dad, why didn't you tell us about all these projects you and Kai are working on?"

Kai sat back and enjoyed the banter. The gentle teasing seemed to be new to this family, and perhaps it was the first step in getting them to see each other in a new way. So far tonight had gone very differently than when they'd all first met.

"Are you accusing me of being one of those wackos we've been talking about?" Winston said but smiled at Vivien. "Kai was persuasive on the phone and in her emails, so I'm glad I got to her first."

"Wait, you approved all those projects before meeting her?" Vivien glanced between her and her father as if waiting for someone to tell her this was a joke. "Raccoon Island alone must've cost a fortune."

"I used a little of Kai's rationale combined with my own for one outcome, and that's why I made the decision to spend the money, so to me it was a good investment." Winston spoke softly, in an almost gentle tone, and from what she could determine from the shells Franklin and Vivien wore, this tone was something new and welcome.

"What's your reason?" Franklin asked as he raked his nail up and down the linen tablecloth, making a slight scraping noise.

"One day whenever it's right for you and your sister, my grandchildren will play on that island, and no matter what other opinions they form of their grandparents—hopefully they'll be proud we did that." Winston's voice became gruff as he spoke, but she figured it was from the building emotion he wasn't used to expressing. "A company isn't the only legacy I want to leave you two."

"Why didn't you tell me?" Vivien asked, staring only at her.

"Because it was your father's story to tell, so I didn't want to ruin his surprise." Kai glanced at Franklin for a moment to include him in what she was saying.

"Thanks, Daddy," Vivien said before she stood and kissed Winston on the cheek and then her mother.

"You're welcome," Winston said, wiping his face of tears after moving to Franklin so he could kiss his son's forehead. Kai figured he hadn't done that since Franklin was six. "Good Lord, let's change the subject before we get any more morose."

When she got a moment alone she wanted to call her mothers. The time spent with the Palmers had made her miss her conversations with them, and if she did a good enough job here, perhaps Franklin and Vivien would someday feel the same if they were away from their parents. The rest of the night was pleasant as they talked in the less formal den, but that ended when the doorbell rang.

If the Palmers had physical defenses like armor or protective shields, they would've come up when the maid walked Steve into the room. "Vivien, you're back," Steve said, and Kai picked up on the accusatory tone. "I expected to hear from you when you returned. You still owe me that dinner we talked about."

"Did something happen at the office we need to know about?" Franklin said, rolling his chair in front of Vivien.

"No," Steve said, as if adding anything else required too much effort.

"If there's nothing new, then we'll all talk tomorrow," Winston said as he stood pointing to the door. "If you don't mind, it's a night for family, not business."

It was interesting to watch how Steve's anger changed his appearance, and Kai got ready to intervene if he did something with his clenched fists. "What about…never mind," Steve said, as if figuring out how whiny he sounded. "I'll see you tomorrow," he said to Vivien.

"Not if I see you first," Vivien said, and Kai laughed, making Steve's shoulders hitch up.

"Are you planning to be in the office tomorrow?" Winston asked Vivien. "Business goes on no matter what, but I doubt we'll make any progress on the new leases."

"I might be late, but I'll be there, and with any luck I'll get Kai to join us to see if you two are hiding any other secret projects from us." Vivien seemed to stop herself as she reached for her. "Thanks for having us over tonight. I really enjoyed it."

"Could I borrow Kai for a moment before you go?" Winston asked.

Winston held up a glass from the bar and she shook her head. Hard liquor straight up had never been her thing, but she did share a drink occasionally with her mother Hadley, who enjoyed a cognac every so often. Winston seemed to have that in common with her, as he sat with his snifter and closed his eyes while taking his first sip.

"What can I do for you, sir?"

"With everything going on, I thought we should talk about what comes next and how you fit in." He took another sip but she stayed quiet. "Your job is on hiatus for the moment, but I didn't want you to think your position is in jeopardy. Why don't you come in tomorrow and work with Vivien and Franklin. It might be good to have perspective from the field for once."

"Are you sure? Usually corner-office folks think the rabble belongs in the field for a reason," she said and smiled.

"My daughter has rabble running through her veins, so she comes by it naturally. I'm sure you've figured out by now that she doesn't see me in the best light, as they say, but I understand her more than she thinks. I really enjoyed my days on the water with responsibility for only the metal under my feet, so I can see why Vivien loves it so much."

"From the few days I was on Triton I could tell she's very good at her job. Everyone on the rig made a point of telling me that much and more. They like her, and more importantly, they respect her."

He nodded, and his smile she assumed was from pride. "We've battled for years, so I'm not asking you to take sides, but I think Vivien needs someone to lean on and confide in who's not Franklin."

"You're not asking me to report back to you, are you?" she asked, raising her right eyebrow. "I'll gladly help you and Vivien, but I'm no Steve."

"What's that supposed to mean?"

She stood and poured him a little more cognac. "That you already have a kiss-ass in your life—you don't need two."

"You barely know Steve, and that's the picture you see?"

She laughed and nodded. "How many other employees stop by to see how you are? And how many other people who work for you talk to your children as if they were either simpleminded or pieces of property?" She pointed at him before holding up her index finger. "I imagine that's a short list of one."

"You're here, aren't you?"

"At Vivien's invitation, Mr. Palmer, and that's the only reason. When she does the same with Steve, I'll buy your argument."

"I doubt that'll ever happen."

"Then I'll see you tomorrow, but not to kiss your ass."

CHAPTER TWENTY-FOUR

A nything you need to tell me?" Vivien asked when Kai closed the passenger-side door. "I know what trips to that study usually entail."

"He asked if I'd come in tomorrow with you until production starts up again and I'm thrown out of there back to Triton."

"And you agreed?"

Kai smiled and nodded. "I figure it's good for a lunch date, at least."

She was glad when Vivien laughed and didn't press for any more details. Winston Palmer still had a way to go, and she didn't want to derail the progress they'd made. When they arrived at Vivien's, they headed to the master bedroom, where they took their time undressing each other and got into bed without much conversation. She felt Vivien's growing feelings for her in the way she touched her.

Their lovemaking this time was slow but still passionate, and she enjoyed the way Vivien pressed against her and went to sleep. Kai wasn't a sexual novice, but this was the first time she'd spent the entire night with someone. Once Vivien's breathing evened out she linked their shells and deepened the sleep she was enjoying so she could get up without Vivien sensing it.

Both her mothers appeared on the screen when she accessed their most secure line, and she smiled to try to relax the tension on their faces. "Sorry this has taken so long, but everyone got kicked off the rig. How are you guys?"

"We're fine," Hadley said, her expression not changing much. "Where exactly are you, and more importantly, where's your team?"

"Isla and Talia are bringing the *Salacia* back in, but we've been in touch. From their report, more military is sailing into the area."

"You forgot the where-are-you question?" Galen said with a smile that Kai knew preceded some teasing.

"I'm staying with Vivien until the *Salacia*'s in port," she said, hoping the conversation about that would end there, but that was incredibly unlikely.

"Kai, you're an adult, so no lectures from either of us when it comes to how you're handling this," Hadley said as Galen leaned against her, seeming content to let Hadley take care of this aspect of their talk. "But can I ask you a question?"

"Mom, if you have something to say, just say it." She spoke evenly since she knew exactly what the question would be and it didn't upset her.

"Do you think Vivien and her family will benefit by abandonment when all this is over?"

"It'll make me sound immature in your eyes, I'm sure, but I haven't thought that far ahead." She glanced down at her hands, but not for long, since she wanted to own up to her choices. "You have my word I won't compromise either Vivien or what's expected of me when my time here is up."

"Sweetheart," Galen said to Hadley, "could you excuse us a moment?"

"Sure, but send for me before you go," Hadley said to her.

Galen waited for the door to close before she said anything, and for once she lost her smile. However, it wasn't replaced by anger or anything remotely close to it. "How are you, really, and don't give me the stoic-warrior routine. This is your mother asking."

"I'm fine in a sense and totally lost in another, if you want the whole truth."

"Talk to me, Kai—I'm here to listen." Galen lifted her hand like she often did when they had to speak through screens.

"After spending some time with Vivien, I thought the best thing I could do for her was to show her how wonderful she is and how it wasn't wrong to pursue her passions. When I got the chance with her father, I tried to mend that void between them by showing him what a treasure his children are." Saying it all out loud made her eyes glassy because her mom Hadley was right. There was no good ending here.

"But by doing that, you figured out how wonderful Vivien is, didn't you?"

"She's the perfect woman for someone like me, except for one cruel twist of fate," she said, cursing herself for not realizing how deep she was in before having to admit it not only to her mother, but her queen.

"It's okay to be honest, my love. She's perfect for *you*, not someone like you, in ways you never owned up to with Oba. Am I right?" Galen's tone was gentle but held a note of sadness.

"Leaving opened my mind to the truth of who Oba and I have to be going forward, which I'm sure will thrill you and her."

"But it opened your heart to other possibilities that leave you in kind of the same place," Galen said and sighed. "I've always told you to follow your heart, but this time I'm afraid for you to do that because it might lead you away from us."

"Don't ever fear that. I'm many things, but a mythical prophecy in the flesh isn't one of them. Tonight I learned something you always preached to me, and it was a lesson that maybe I would've been better off never finding the answer to."

"Tell me."

"My shell has found its match, but it's one made by my own hand so I can't rejoice in that because I can't have her. I'll come back and complete every aspect of my duty, but what you and Mama have won't be possible for me." A few of her tears fell, and she saw that her mom was in the same state. "The throne and children will have to be enough. Is that fair to the woman who'll marry me?"

"Kai, I love you enough to change the rules, but you know Vivien can't give you heirs, so you realize what that will mean to your reign. No heirs to follow you means your years on the throne will revolve most likely around chaos and confusion."

"I totally screwed this up, didn't I?"

"Nothing done by a good heart can be totally bad, tadpole," Hadley said from the door, her hand around her shell. She'd probably come back because of Galen's distress. "I'm sure you'll come up with a solution. If not, we'll think of something together. If everything else fails you can change her mind about what she wants with a small mental push away from you. Kind of like a reset."

She had done the same thing to Winston when he was on the rig, but his thoughts were centered on Vivien and Steve's wedding. She told her mothers about it and could only wonder what the look they shared was about.

"Was it hard to change his mind-set?" Hadley asked.

"I need more practice, but I did get through to him. Why would any one of our people plant that thought?"

"Kai, any manipulation like that needs royal approval, so we can't answer that," Hadley said.

"Mom, I have clearance, remember?"

"We can't answer that because neither of us approved that order," Galen said. "We use that skill sparingly in the human realm and never for something that ridiculous. What interest would we have in who marries who?"

"Only this time it's the marriage of someone who happens to own a large rig with a large number of communication pods attached to it," she said, her back coming off the chair. "Could we have stumbled into something by accident only because we were trying to fix some old wrong?"

"Who exactly is Winston Palmer's dream son-in-law?" Galen asked.

"Steve Hawksworth," she said, trying to remember if there was something interesting about the man. "He's an asshole with an ego that would choke both Ram and Ivan."

"He sounds charming, but find out more about him," Hadley said. "Better yet, I'll have Talia and Isla follow up from a neutral spot. You stick to Vivien and the Palmers for now and be careful."

"And the rest?"

"Tadpole, I'm sure your mama gave you some good advice, so I'll add my bit." Hadley put her arm around Galen and kissed her temple. "I refuse to believe that a child we conceived through the bond we share will spend her life alone—the goddess isn't that cruel. Have faith in who you are and what you have to offer someone, and that'll be rewarded."

"Thanks, Mom," she said and held her hand up to Galen. "I know you worry, Mama, but I'll be fine. I'll call more often too to share information."

"If it's something urgent we'll call the cell phone we gave you," Galen said.

"Thanks for everything—I love you both very much."

Vivien opened her eyes the next morning and wanted to laugh she was so happy to be in Kai's arms. It was still dark outside, but she'd slept so well she was ready to start her day, though she was also content to watch Kai sleep.

"What's going through that imaginative brain of yours?" Kai said softly as her hand headed south.

"Whatever it was has been replaced with one question—are you a morning person?"

"In what context?" Kai asked, and Vivien's ears grew hot. She knew Triton inside and out, but sex wasn't her strongest talent.

"I thought a jog in the park."

"Sure, but I have to take care of something first."

The joke badly misfired if Kai was leaving and expected real exercise. "Okay, can I help with anything?"

"I'm counting on it, but first can I help you with this?" Kai moved her hand down and put her fingers between her legs. One touch and she needed more. "You're not the only one awake."

"I can't help what my overactive imagination comes up with when you're this close to me." She moved her hips, gliding her hard clitoris over Kai's fingers. It electrified every cell in her body, but she wanted more.

"Tell me," Kai said as if reading her mind again. "It's okay to ask."

"If you're ready, can we do it like yesterday—together, I mean. I want to come with you." The heat in her ears got worse, but Kai only smiled and rolled her onto her back so she could move over her.

Kai took her time kissing her and whispering how beautiful she was and how much she wanted her. It was so good and yet so strange in that she swore the shell around her neck had come alive and wanted Kai as much as she did. Sometimes in the past she'd thought it helped her hear what Franklin was thinking, but this was something completely different.

It was like she could see and hear what was inside of Kai's heart and mind, and all Kai wanted was her. She could sense not only the passion building in both of them, but also what Kai felt for her, and her very being wanted it all. Kai was her mate, and all that mattered was connecting with her and letting her in where she'd never allowed anyone.

"Are you okay?" Kai asked before kissing along her neck.

"Yes...I need you." She spread her legs and it was absurd, but she could swear her body and sex were opening and only Kai could fill her.

When Kai situated herself over her and pressed her sex to hers, she dug her fingertips into Kai's back. In that instance they were one, and the rightness of it made her jerk her hips up into Kai, but after that Kai set their pace and she gladly followed her lead. All that mattered now was to give Kai the same pleasure she was receiving.

"Don't stop," she said as she clung to Kai, needing the closeness. It might've started slow and gentle, but now it was all about the culmination of her need and passion. She needed Kai to give her the orgasm she craved.

Kai lifted her upper body a little for what she guessed was better leverage, and she enjoyed the grunts that Kai couldn't seem to help but make. She looped her legs around Kai's body and welcomed the orgasm she needed as much as air.

The end made her want to spend the rest of the day in bed memorizing every inch of Kai's body as well as everything she loved in life so she'd stay. Vivien was so overwhelmed she couldn't say anything as Kai held her. The way Kai pressed her lips to her forehead made her hopeful for their future. How much better would this be when they really knew each other?

"You're incredibly inspiring to my imagination," Kai said, which made her laugh.

"I could say the same thing, and after that, being in the office with you should be torturous." Kai rolled off her and held her head up so she could look at her. "Now I almost, and I'm putting the emphasis on almost, feel sorry for Steve."

"The only way Steve trades places with you is by holding a gun to my head. You've got nothing to worry about." She turned to face

Kai and welcomed Kai's leg between her own. "You aren't worried about that, are you?"

"I'd worry more about me keeping my hands off you while we're at work than anything to do with Steve."

They talked a little more before heading down for coffee, and by the time they were ready to go, Vivien prayed the clock would move as fast as it had that morning. She didn't know what her father had in mind, but she was setting Kai up in her office. She was also taking Kai up on her offer to lunch, but she was asking Franklin along too. As much as she enjoyed Kai's company, their relationship wouldn't go anywhere if she didn't understand her bond with her brother.

"Will this do until I can go shopping for stuff other than shorts and Dickies?" Kai asked as they headed out.

The navy slacks and white shirt would help Kai blend in with the people on the top floor, and she'd gone to so much effort that Vivien had thrown on a skirt and top she hadn't worn in almost a year to appease her mother at some function they'd attended. "You look fantastic," she said as she held out her hand to Kai.

"Thank you, but I doubt you'll be safe for long since your ass is a work of art in that skirt." Kai smiled, she assumed at her blush, as she held her door for her. "One way of getting me to behave is to invite Franklin to lunch with us, if he's available."

The offer made her almost suspicious, but it was ridiculous to think that Kai had the ability to read her mind. "Franklin loves being treated to anything, so don't say it if you don't mean it."

"I rarely offer anything if I don't mean it. Besides, he's important to you, and you're someone I want to get to know better."

"Careful," she said, not sure what to add to that.

"I am, and more importantly, I will be with you," Kai said, then kissed her. "If you think I'll pass inspection, invite Marsha too. She seems important to you as well."

"Thank you." She pressed her hand against Kai's cheek.

"For what?"

"For seeing in me what I thought was invisible to everyone else."

CHAPTER TWENTY-FIVE

Y ou can't still have nothing," Steve said through clenched teeth to Tanice. He'd spent two weeks watching Vivien and Franklin act like Kai Merlin was the answer to everything wrong with their lives. To make things worse, Winston had started inviting her to their executive staff meetings.

"I can make something up if you want me to, but she's everything her resume says she is. You can do whatever you want, but if you want my advice, don't try to set her up. Mr. Palmer seems to like her, so if he finds out, it'll backfire on you." Tanice walked behind him and put her hands on his shoulders. "You're so close."

"Get back to your desk and take your advice with you." He shrugged her off and waited for her to leave before picking up the phone. "Can I see you in my office?" When he hung up, he had five minutes tops to come up with something, so it startled him when Kai seemed to fill his doorway sooner than he'd expected.

"What can I do for you, Mr. Hawksworth?"

He glanced at his screen and noticed two of the wells off the Mississippi coast had been given the green light to start again. "We need you to head to Condor One and Two to check the structures before we start pumping again. The coast guard says the situation is fine, but I don't trust that advice."

"When do you need me?"

"I'll have a chopper waiting within the hour." He leaned back, glad this was going to be easy.

"Where are you going?" Franklin asked, a stack of folders on his lap.

"A little diving for the team, but I don't mind," Kai said, then laughed when Franklin moved past her and dumped his load on Steve's desk. "Some blue water will beat the hell out of that." She pointed to the stack.

"Stop by my office before you go," Franklin said and closed the door when Kai left. "I believe at last count we have in the vicinity of fifty-six thousand employees."

"Should I pay attention because there'll be a test later?" Steve laughed at Franklin's inadequacy.

"All those people, and you pick Kai to dive two of our smallest operations?"

"That's her job, Frankie," he said, throwing his hands up. "Or am I the only one who remembers that? Besides, she jumped at the chance. Maybe you and your sister aren't as fascinating as you think."

He laughed when Franklin left without calling him on the insult. It was time to chance a few things to get back on track. The door opening again with Winston coming for a visit was a first.

"You sent Merlin out to the Condor sites?"

The way Winston's fists rested on his hips made him hesitate. "She volunteered when I told her about it."

"Then I'm sure you wouldn't mind doing the same with our Mexican assets," Winston said, holding up a sheet of paper. "Here's the list, and I expect progress reports."

"Wait," he said, not needing a printed list to know how long the damn thing was. He'd be out of the office a solid month if the weather was perfect that long. "What about all our pending contracts?"

"Franklin has all that covered, so don't forget your sunscreen."

"Winston, the board's not going to like you exiling me to the Gulf while everything's up in the air like this." He moved closer with his hands outstretched, palms up.

"I'll take my chances." Winston slammed the paper against his chest. "And if that was a veiled threat, don't push me. You do, and I'll fuck you over so bad your mother won't recognize you. Are we clear?"

He nodded automatically, somewhat shocked at the outburst. Winston had never spoken to him like this, and he quickly reviewed mentally where he could've gone wrong. The trip to Triton had started a change, and the only new factor was Kai Merlin, so it was paramount he bring her down before the damage became fatal.

"I asked if you understand me?" Winston stared at him.

"Yes, sir," he said, crumpling the sheet in one fist. "I understand perfectly."

Kai was going to pay for the humiliation one way or another.

"Have we narrowed the list?" Hadley asked the council members with the highest level of clearance. Natal had been added to the list, but Hadley had directed her question at Laud Mandina, the head of the royal guards.

"Yes, Your Majesty. Considering the information found, on the date it was found, we're able to narrow the possibilities to forty-six individuals. It seems like a lot, but you have to consider the size of the queen's staff." Laud put her hands up when she took a deep breath, getting ready to express how unacceptable that was. Hadley had recommended this woman to Galen, and they both trusted her with Galen's safety, since she and Laud had known each other for years and graduated together, but at the moment they didn't have the luxury of blind faith in anyone. "I realize that number is too high so we tried to narrow it in other ways."

"Don't skip any steps, but that list is too long to be feasible," she said as she tapped the table with the fleshy side of her fist. "If they divulged this information to some unknown entity, Galen's in danger. We can plan for every contingency, but it's hard to defend yourself against a surprise attack, especially if it's someone with access to her. If something happens to my wife—"

"Hadley, I know," Laud said gently. "The queen isn't only my sovereign. She's my friend. I know how devastating to everyone it would be if something happened to her. That possibility is immeasurable when it comes to you."

"So where do we start?"

"I'd like to meet with you alone before we discuss that."

Everyone rose when she waved her hand, except her mother Brook and Galen's mother Sibyl. "They aren't going and I'm not asking them to, so let's hear it."

Laud pressed a button on the table and five faces appeared. "When you found the boxes, they provided a good starting point." Laud split the screen and brought up Galen's itinerary. "Her highness's schedule is both set and fluid, so there's always the possibility of change if something comes up that needs her attention. The day you ran the information these were all the incorrect entries, and these four," she pointed to them with a laser, "were the most recent changes. Because the staff is privy to the information, the forty-six on the original list would've had the incorrect information. These five, though, are the only ones with family who've raised doubts or open complaints to her majesty's rule."

"How close a family?" Sibyl asked.

"Of the five, the closest family tie is Bella Riverstone." The system showed only Bella's photo and information for now. "She's been on the queen's staff since her graduation from the academy four years ago. Her mother died about three years ago, and soon after that her birth mother remarried Francesca Yelter."

"Are you talking about the ass who preaches the destruction of all human life on the planet, that Francesca Yelter?" Hadley asked.

"The one and only. Her birth mother Wilma served on the queen mother's staff during her reign and briefly worked for the queen until her second marriage," Laud said.

"Isn't part of Yelter's problem the ruling family itself?" Brook asked.

"Yes, ma'am. I've read her literature extensively, and it mentions the Oberons quite often. She and her followers believe the ruling family has strayed too far from the strength and leadership of the Oberons."

"How in the hell did someone like that end up on Galen's staff?" Hadley asked.

"Because Bella can't be blamed for who her mother falls in love with. I've met Bella on numerous occasions so I don't have any cause to doubt her," Galen said as she picked up one of Francesca's educational brochures as she walked in.

"This makes sense though," Hadley said as she pulled a chair for Galen. "Bella might not have directly shared the information, but if she brought anything home or this fanatic broke into our system, we've got a problem."

"One of many. What I'd like to know is where all these communication pods came from," Brook asked, and Galen nodded. "I haven't been able to work that out. Even if they were from the original batch, these account for almost their entire inventory."

"Not to mention there isn't that much genga on the planet. That stuff corroded so fast the archive has the only serious amount," Sibyl said.

"We can dance around the truth all we want, but the only possibility that makes sense is that our system somehow missed the shipment coming in from outer space," Hadley said.

"Actually I've thought about how that could've happened and how we could have missed it," Laud said, and Galen lifted her hand slightly for her to continue. "If the pods came in all at once, we wouldn't have been the only ones to notice, but if they came in small batches and not regularly, they would've just showed up on radar as an anomaly like a meteor crashing."

"That's totally possible, but you'd still need someone to attach them in the various locations," Hadley said as she glanced at the map with all the pods they'd found so far. "If they came in batches, then no one would notice the absence of someone like Francesca and her followers as much if they were out placing them. We need to find out for sure, and we need to know if her stepdaughter had anything to do with this."

"I've already placed surveillance," Laud said.

"At the first sign she's involved, bring Bella in, but keep it quiet," Hadley said, taking Galen's hand when she held it out. "If Francesca whips up her disciples, haul her in and I'll show her a few things about my family and what happens to anyone who threatens them."

"Behave, all of you," Galen said. "I knew exactly who Bella's family was when she came to work for me. Laud, do your job, but don't be too heavy-handed, and let me know how it goes."

The room emptied and Hadley moved to her knees in front of Galen. "I'll do whatever you ask, but be careful letting people off too easily. Someone did this, and we need to find out why."

"I intend to let everyone do what they're trained to do, but we're all entitled to our opinion. It's the main premise this great society was founded on. Not everyone is going to love me, Mama told me that a very long time ago, and she was right, as usual." Galen ran the tips of her fingers along her jawline, and as comforting as it was, she shivered from the sudden cold.

It was her fear of losing times like this that had dropped the temperature in the room. "I can't lose you or Kai, my love," she said, her throat closing at the sudden onslaught of fear and emotion. "I couldn't go on if something like that happens."

"I'm safe with you." Galen put her arms around her and ran her hands up and down her back in comfort. "Until this is over, I'll cancel all unnecessary meetings and let Laud deal with the staff. If we do that, though, we have to make an announcement of some kind."

"As much as I want to isolate you, if you do that, it'll drive whoever's responsible into a deep crab hole. We need to flush them out, so get used to me traveling with you from now on." She stayed in Galen's arms a little longer before helping her stand. "Sorry I freaked out there for a moment."

"I never want you to have masks to hide your true self from me, so don't apologize." Galen kissed her eyelids, then pressed her cheek to the top of her head. "Do whatever it takes to get this done," she whispered. "I'll have no one take what's rightfully ours, especially what belongs to Kai."

"I'll gladly do your bidding, my Queen."

CHAPTER TWENTY-SIX

Y ou should volunteer for more stuff more often," Vivien said as she stood behind Kai on the *Salacia.*

"Believe me, I'm thrilled to be out here with you, but this was more of a ram job than me volunteering for anything." She laughed, really happy with Vivien and the salt water hitting her skin. Her mothers were right in that to get away from the water for too long definitely muted something essential in her soul. "But you, me, and the water are something I don't mind being pushed into."

"It could be worse," Vivien said as she kissed her shoulder. "You could be Steve." She laughed for a long while. "He should be really tanned by the time he gets back."

"We're going to work on our tan lines too," she said, smiling at Vivien when she moved to the front of her.

She was planning to enjoy herself, but after talking with her parents again before taking off without her team, she'd agreed to have the protection unit move along with them under the water. The unit would keep enough distance between them to stay out of Vivien's sight, but close enough to neutralize any threat. She knew Edil was personally heading up the security detail and had welcomed her presence as a way to help her get back in her mother Hadley's good graces. She knew from experience that wasn't always the easiest thing in the world to accomplish.

"We could do that." Vivien ran her hands up her arms to the back of her neck. "Think we have time to check out the area you mapped out?"

"The rig dive should be easy, so sure." She set their course and tied the wheel off so they could sit and eat. They'd be at least another three hours, but Winston had personally told her to take her time and invite Vivien. His matchmaking skills needed work, but getting Vivien to agree had taken none.

After lunch they both enjoyed light conversation and a lot of silence. And when they arrived at the rig, she convinced Vivien to stay aboard and study the rover's findings. Underwater she headed away from the rig footings to the beacon Edil was putting out to mark their meeting spot.

Kai saw three swimmers ahead of her so she raised her hand to greet them, not concerned that she didn't recognize any of them. She questioned their identity for only a second, but figured her mother had sent the best team available. Atlantis was large in scope and in residents so it was impossible to know them all, but whoever this was lifted some sort of weapon and aimed it in her direction. The two women who flanked the shooter seemed to be guarding the aggressor, so Kai swam down and to the right.

She cursed as she picked up speed, but the three didn't have trouble keeping up. The idiot carried what basically was a spear gun, but if she'd poisoned the tip she'd die just as effectively as if it were a triton.

Edil appeared to the right of her and signaled her to the left. Just as she moved, her leg exploded in pain and she looked down to see at least six inches of the shaft sticking out of her thigh. The water around her crackled with the pulses coming from the tritons her protectors fired. Hopefully they were set to stun, but from the blood cloud behind her, that was doubtful.

"Your Highness, we need to move you to the ship," Edil said as her team swam to whoever was now dead in the water. She had a communication square strapped to her throat so Kai heard her as clearly as if she'd spoken the words out loud.

"Take the tip," she mouthed. "Vivien Palmer," she said and pointed up.

"We'll test it, but if we find anything we're coming to get you aboard for medical help." Edil snapped the tip off and placed it in a bag one of her team held open. "I'm going to report this, so you might have to pull out no matter what the results are."

Kai turned and started back to her vessel, and once they were close she motioned for one of the command units the woman next to Edil had buckled to her chest. She opened a line only her mothers were privy to and tapped out a message before clearing the device and handing it back. "Guards every fifty feet, fifty yards out." Edil gave her a thumbs-up and moved back, but Kai could see the hesitation in her movements.

The blood from her leg was flowing freely, but she didn't feel any tingling or numbness, just pain, so she wasn't worried yet. She tried to stay calm, but when she surfaced, Vivien was anything but. "What the hell?" Vivien yelled.

"Lower the ladder." She pointed to the release button. "Someone shot me." It was in so many ways surreal. Nothing like this had remotely come into her mind when she'd planned every facet of this assignment. Her overprotective mothers were about to skewer Edil, but she'd worry about that after putting Vivien at ease. Their time together like this was growing short.

"Who?" Vivien grabbed everything she could, but she'd have to make it aboard herself. "Did you see anyone, anything?"

"Viv, I need you to take a deep breath, okay," she said when Vivien started crying. "The first-aid kit is over my bunk—let's start there." She needed to get to her command unit that was cleverly disguised as an iPad and get in touch with her parents for a conversation. Being attacked by some of their own people meant there might be some plan in place that would go all the way back to the capital.

"Sit," Vivien said, the kit pressed to her chest.

"Come here first." She held her hand up. When Vivien sat next to her, she kissed her as she moved her hand to the base of Vivien's neck. It didn't take long for Vivien to fall limply against her, so she carefully laid her down. When Vivien was secure she sent a signal, so the team guarding the boat came aboard and tended to her wound.

"Who was that?" she asked Edil while the unit medic took the spear out.

"We're still trying to make positive identifications, but they're no one tied to the military group we have in the area."

"Good to know," she said, grimacing as the shaft came out. "Bring my comm unit up, please." Once her leg was bandaged, she dismissed everyone back to the water and called for her mothers. They looked worried so she quickly explained what had happened. "You need to beef up the security in the palace."

"Laud has that covered and I've limited my public appearances," Galen said before taking a deep breath. "But we need to talk about your coming back. What happened could've been so much worse. We were lucky, but we can't give them another shot at you."

"I don't want to run, so double the guards if you want." She noticed the change in her mother Hadley's face. Hadley's anger was about to bubble out of her mouth in the form of orders, she was sure. "You didn't raise me to hide behind the palace walls, and if I do, that'll be my legacy no matter what else comes from my reign."

"Someone tried to kill you, Kai," Hadley said, her teeth and fists clenched. "Do you think this woman was aiming for your leg? If you're dead, your legacy will be all your mother, your people, and I will have left."

"I'm not planning to die," she said, placing her hand on her chest. "I'm planning to flush these idiots out and blast them from existence. There was an easier path to the truth, but Edil and her soldiers killed them all. Dead women aren't of use to us, but it took more than three people to place all those pods. The shooter today was low in the line of command, even if she has a military background. The suits they were wearing aren't our standard issue and didn't stop the blast of Edil's triton from a chest shot."

"You can stay for now, but a unit will be with you at all times. Try to shake loose to try something on your own and you're back here," Galen said. "Do we understand each other?"

"Yes, Majesty, perfectly." She bowed and saluted, since Galen's statement hadn't been motherly advice but a command. "I'll report daily unless we find something." She knew she had to see this through, but nothing she'd said softened Hadley's expression. "Mom, would you do something differently?"

"No, but maybe we're not meant to solve every problem."

"Vivien's with me. Would you leave Mama somewhere with no defense?"

"My worry for you doesn't mean you're doing anything wrong. I'm proud that you're the kind of leader who won't back down, so may the goddess watch over you and keep you both safe."

"Thanks, Mom, and you have my word I won't enter any fight without backup."

"Stay true to who you are, my love, and that will see you through," Galen said as both she and Hadley made the hand sign for love.

The screen went dark, and for the first time in her life, the water that was her home and a place she thrived in held dark secrets that meant her harm. She keyed in Edil's line and was relieved the spear was clean. All she had to figure out was why someone had shot it at her.

Vivien looked out through clear water, and her mouth stretched in a smile when she saw the school of clownfish swim by in a riot of color. She was amazed at how long she'd been under without a tank, but not as shocked to find Frankie swimming alongside her. He kicked his legs and seemed to laugh, releasing a stream of bubbles.

Franklin never went in the water, but now he seemed as at ease in it as she'd always been. She swam over to him and took his hand so they could explore this beautiful place together, but suddenly a large cloud of blood formed and the temperature dropped.

She started to panic as the water filled with large predator sharks and then—her eyes opened and she was in Kai's arms. The dream had lasted as long as it usually did, but there were so many differences. Frankie had never been there, and she'd never woken up before the sharks tore into the girl.

"Hey, you okay?" Kai asked, pressing her hand to her cheek.

"Bad dream I haven't had in a long time." It struck her fast that Kai was hurt and she'd been helping her but hadn't finished. "Why didn't you wake me?" She stared at the white bandage on Kai's leg.

"You were tired after we got back from the hospital so I didn't want to disturb you. It's been a weird day so it's okay to zonk out for a while."

"Wait." She scrubbed her hands over her face and blinked furiously. "We went to the hospital? I don't remember any of that."

"It wasn't that memorable, but I'm sure our meeting with the coast guard will be more so. In all the years I've been diving no one has ever aimed anything at me, much less shot me." Kai stretched out more, and she moved to make them both comfortable.

"We need to call my dad," she said, and continuing with her day of surprises, she found she really needed to talk to her father. "I don't remember any other boats around us, and I doubt anyone on the rig was waiting to hurt you."

"I was clear underwater too until I felt the spear."

Having Kai's fingers run along her back was putting her to sleep again, but she needed to get so much done. "I have to get up."

"Your dad can wait until they're finished." Kai pointed to the cutter coming toward them. "Maybe they can figure out what all this is about."

"Maybe," she said softly. A thought surfaced that they might be after Kai, but why?

The coast-guard guys took their statements and said no one had reported any other suspicious activities, but they were putting divers in the water to see if the intruders were after anything specific. As they watched them go down, she reached for her phone.

Winston was quiet as she told him what had happened, and when she finished, he still didn't say anything. "Dad, are you there?" she finally asked.

"Are you two planning to come back? If you do, I want you both to come stay with us."

"Thanks for the offer, but I'm not sure Kai will be up for that." In a matter of weeks her life had changed so much she barely recognized herself. "We'll be fine at my place."

"Viv, our place is more secure. All this stuff we've found and all that's happened makes me afraid for you and Franklin. Please don't fight me on this."

"I'll call you when we get back," she said as she watched Kai start to raise anchor. "Can you call Frankie for me?"

"Will do, and be safe."

"If you tell me what needs to be done, I'll do it," she said to Kai. She really wanted to be back in her room alone with Kai.

"Let me get everything ready since it'll be faster. Then you can set our course back. Everything okay with your dad?"

"I…" The words ran through her head like a ticker tape, but she wasn't sure how Kai would take it if she added *love you* to complete the phrase. It frightened her that it might be possible to scare Kai away.

"Don't think so much, okay?" Kai said with a smile. She never looked away from her, and that gave her some courage but not enough. "You're safe with me."

"I know, and you make me want things, but we don't have time for me to list them all." She laughed when Kai nodded, and she wanted the next step to be telling her family about them. "Daddy wants us to stay at the house until we know what all this is."

"Sure, if that's what you want." The sails went up, and she hung on as the *Salacia* started to move. This was one of the most perfect moments of her life.

The trip back was smooth and the same two women who'd helped them off were there to take care of Kai's boat when they docked. She'd intended to ask about their Palmer work shirts but forgot about it when Kai held her hand out to her. They didn't talk much as she drove them to her parents' place and was surprised to see the front filled with cars.

"I think we missed an invitation," Kai said when she parked.

"I recognize one car for sure, but it doesn't make sense."

"Who?" Kai said, grimacing a little when she stood up.

"That's Steve's image enhancer over there." She pointed to the Corvette. "I'm sure someone, somewhere is impressed."

Kai laughed, but she couldn't join in. Something was wrong. Franklin came out, and from his expression she was right.

"I'm here for you both," Kai said, and her reassurance lessened Vivien's fear.

Chapter Twenty-seven

A s of today, Winston, we're voting to remove you," one of the board members said as Steve tapped his fingers against his knees. His original plan was taking too long so he'd revised it after Winston exiled him to Mexico. "For now you'll retain your post in name only, but by unanimous vote we're putting Steve in charge of the day-to-day operations until we can find a permanent replacement. Hopefully you won't do anything to start a run on the stock."

"Can you at least explain what you're doing? I've worked hard to get us here, and you're going to just screw me over." Winston pointed at the guy, and even though they were feet apart, the guy backed up. "Do you honestly think I'm going to roll over and thank you for this?"

"Considering this will end up in court, give us your reasoning," Franklin said as he reentered. Steve stared at the ceiling with a smirk, and Winston had never wanted to hit someone as much as he did right then. He stared at Steve, but he wouldn't make eye contact, and Winston was almost afraid to glance at his son. He'd almost sacrificed his family for this asshole.

"Your father has made substantial unauthorized purchases, which could've been overlooked, but there are other human-resources issues that couldn't. Since that has to do with employee information, it's privileged." The man who seemed to have been elected the spokesman moved closer to Steve's father and board member Jonathon. "It's your prerogative to drag this into the courts, but you need to know the board's vote was unanimous."

Winston thought back to his last conversation with Kai before she left, and the one with Vivien. For months he'd been locked in a competition he didn't have the brains to figure out he was a part of, so Steve and his family had played this masterfully. Kai hadn't seen who had attacked her, but from Steve's expression he wouldn't doubt he had something to do with that as well, since he'd been the one who sent her to that spot.

He'd been an asshole all right, and Kai had been right about Steve and the faith he'd put in him. It was too late, though, so now he was an asshole with only a forty-percent share of the company that bore his family's name.

"I'll call a stockholder meeting as soon as possible," he said.

"Winston," Steve's father Jonathon said before their spokesman got the chance. "The people in this room represent thirty percent of all available stock." You and your family have another forty, so think about it before you do something that costs us a lot of money. The truth is, for you to even suggest it means we're right in removing you. It's time to start thinking of the company and not your ego."

"As one of the majority stockholders, it's our right to call a meeting," Franklin said. "Not only can we do that, but we can also call for a vote of the board."

"Do you honestly think the rest of the twenty percent will side with you? Steve asked. "Why not stop embarrassing yourself while you and your family have the opportunity."

"Call it, or we'll take the steps to get it done," Franklin said, making Winston take a deep breath.

His son was a strong man who had gotten to this point without a lot of input from him. A pain that was more of an ache ran across his chest, and he knew it was from shame and not any medical problem. "It'll take a week to send notices, and our bylaws say we must allow another week after that. My staff will send the notices and set the time," Winston said, and two of the board members made the motion and seconded it, and he guessed as a last sign of loyalty it was passed. He pointed to the door when his was the only dissenting vote to put Steve in charge.

"Try to understand it wasn't personal," Jonathon said.

"Get the fuck out of my house," he said, slamming the door once Jonathon made it over the threshold. "Son," he said to Franklin as he leaned against the door with one hand. "I don't deserve your forgiveness, but I'm asking anyway. If we win this vote you should take my place."

"You're my father, so I should say forgiveness isn't necessary, but thanks for saying that. If we're honest with each other, it'd be okay to admit I'm not the son you wanted or expected, and we can move on from there with you back in the big chair." Franklin took his hand. "It'd be great if you remembered you're my dad once we win."

"Someone told me that exact thing just recently, so I think I've got it." He kissed the top of Franklin's head and hugged him. "And you're wrong. You're exactly the son I wanted. It's not your fault I haven't been the father you deserve."

"Sir, you need to call anyone you know in the coast guard and tell them to drag their feet," Kai said. She was alone in Winston's study at his request again, and Vivien and the rest of the family were out in the gardens catching up. "You have to try to keep the assets out of Steve and the board's hands until you're reinstated.

"I don't have that kind of power, even if I'd like to think I do."

"I know from experience you can be persuasive when you want to be." The numbing agent was starting to wear off so she propped her leg up. "Did the lockdown keep you from being able to communicate between the rigs?"

"We can if there was anyone to talk to. Did you need to reach someone?"

"Stupid question, so forget I asked."

"I don't believe you ask too many of those, but enough of that for now. How's the leg?"

"Starting to hurt, but I'll be okay. Let's get back to the others—I don't want to monopolize your time." She touched the shell at her throat and tried to reach into Winston's mind once more, then embedded a thought for his heart. "I believe they've missed you long enough," she said when he opened his eyes and nodded.

Both Palmer children seemed to brighten with their parents' attention, but they all retired when Vivien insisted Kai needed to lie down. Their bags were in what appeared to be Vivien's old bedroom, and Vivien laughed when she cocked an eyebrow in question.

"My mom directed the staff, so go with it and take your clothes off."

She did as Vivien asked and came close to humming when Vivien lay naked beside her. She forgot the idea that had come to her with Winston as Vivien kissed down her body. Through their link, she could sense how Vivien felt about her, and she opened up to the love Vivien was offering.

The rest of the night kept her mind off her leg, and when she slept she purposely joined Vivien's dreams to keep her safe and at peace there as well. To find Franklin swimming beside Vivien made her realize how strong the bond and the link between them was.

In the morning she awoke alone but heard Vivien retching close by, so she jumped up to find her. "You okay?" She held Vivien's hair out of the way and wiped her face with a cool facecloth.

"I think the chicken last night did me in." Vivien moaned as her stomach heaved again. "Jesus, I hate doing that," Vivien said when she heaved again. "Not exactly sexy."

"You never know. I might be vomit-freaky." She wiped Vivien's face before handing her a glass of water to rinse her mouth out. "You're a much better patient than I'd be."

"You're too nice," Vivien said, falling against her chest still moaning. "Want to stay home with me today?"

"If you don't mind me running a quick errand, I'll be happy to spend the day running my fingers through your hair." She put her arms around Vivien and stood up so she could cradle her and carry her back to bed.

"My mom used to do that a long time ago," Vivien said, her eyes glassy with tears. "Do you really have to go?"

"Etta's got something for me, and she's leaving for a few months, but I'll skip it if you're sick." Vivien snuggled against her when she lay down.

"Has she ever told you where she goes on her extended vacations?"

"Research is always her answer when I ask, so I stopped asking. I like to think she goes to visit a great love." She ran her hand in a circular motion up and down Vivien's back.

"You're a romantic at heart," Vivien said softly, her hand wrapped in Kai's T-shirt. "How lucky does that make me?"

"Lucky enough to get a nurse for the day, so can I start by getting you something?"

"I'd rather nap than eat, so go visit Etta at Tulane and see if you can get her to give up her plans. If she got you another lead on your hunt, maybe we can go back out once all this cools down."

She pressed her cheek to Vivien's forehead, glad it was cool. Her immune system was much stronger than that of any human, but she saw no reason to take chances. If this was perhaps more than a virus, she'd figure out a way to intervene. "Etta can wait, and there's always a courier service if it's important."

"You're sweet, but all you'll be doing here is watching me sleep. Go and pick up a croissant from the place I first saw you. Maybe by the time you return I won't feel like roadkill."

"Right now just concentrate on going back to sleep and dream about non-nauseating things," she said as she kissed the side of Vivien's head.

She took a deep breath when Vivien placed her hand over her shell, so she cleared her mind and concentrated on bringing Vivien peace. She would induce the same deep sleep she had before, but she wanted to get Vivien there as calmly as she could. Today Vivien seemed to need the easiest path possible in every aspect of life.

The house was quiet as she moved to the front door, and outside only Vivien's truck was in the drive. She bypassed it, opting to walk despite the heat and taking the time to talk to Isla and Talia. Everything was still quiet while they stayed on the *Salacia* close to shore in case the vessel was needed for anything.

"How's your leg?" Talia asked.

"It's there, and I can walk with no problem. The traitor hit me but missed bone. Any word on who that was?"

Isla sighed, signaling she was aggravated. "The capital is not being cooperative with information, at least with us, but you might have better luck. All we know is Edil has the Gulf on hyperdrive when it comes to patrol."

"She's probably afraid Hadley will have her drawn and quartered if one more thing is either found or something else happens to you," Talia said, and they all laughed. They'd all been there, so they could relate to Edil's nervous-cat mentality.

"I've got an idea about that and probably should've called you in for my meeting with Etta this morning." She crossed St. Charles Avenue to stay on the sunny side, but also to make sure she wasn't being followed. Maybe her head guard wasn't the only paranoid one in the bunch. "Why don't you come in and meet her and give her an escort back to the capital? If my plan works, I want to try it as soon as we can implement it."

"No hints?" Isla asked.

"Aside from Etta, you two will be the first to know."

"Good fortune then, Highness," Isla said, and Talia agreed.

"Good fortune to us all, sisters," she said, but didn't think the woman walking at the same pace but across the street agreed with her wish.

"Do you have a team in place?" Galen asked from the throne room, trying her best not to lose her temper. "It's a simple question so I'd appreciate it if you'd stop talking in circles."

Sol Oberon tapped his fingers together and smiled at her through the monitor. The first twenty minutes of their conversation had centered around how fortunate she was that he'd taken the time to talk to her at all. Everything that followed had been gibberish to avoid answering anything directly.

"Watch your tone, Princess. We are separated by space, but I'm still your king."

"My title is Queen Galen, heir of Nessa, first queen of Atlantis. Your realm, rule, or law has no sway here, and we'll fight to prove that fact."

He laughed and finally put his hands down when she didn't join him. "According to the true throne of Atlantis, we've given no such quarter, so you have no say in what happens here or in any territory under our rule." He leaned forward and raised his voice. "If that's all, go back to whatever takes up your day and stop wasting our time."

"That man is an ass," Hadley said when the screen went dark.

"Words that have been repeated by every queen since Nessa, I'm sure." She stood and flexed her hands as she moved her head from side to side, trying to relax. "Are you sure they can't pinpoint where we are?"

"Very few citizens in Atlantis have our true coordinates, since every system responds to what everyone believes to be our location. If it came to war, those systems would be changed and any attack would happen leagues from here, where the only casualties would be fish." Hadley took her hand and walked to the large window that overlooked the city. "It's a safeguard very few even realize exist, which makes me think your ancestors were geniuses."

"You were right about Francesca Yelter. She was the one who shot Kai, and the women with her were part of the movement to take control of the entire planet." She'd forbidden Laud from removing Bella from her staff until she'd talked to Hadley, but she'd already had something in mind as to how to handle this situation.

"The morgue confirmed it?"

"About an hour ago, so don't pout," she said as she sat on the grass and watched the lights of vessels through the corridors of buildings and homes. "I had Laud place discreet surveillance on both Wilma Yelter and Bella. In my heart I hope Francesca was in all this alone with a few lunatics, but if she wasn't, I have to be prepared to act."

"Is there a question in there? No matter what, I'm here at your side, and I'll never allow anyone to hurt you as long as I have fight left in me." Hadley laid her head in her lap and smiled up at her. "You shouldn't feel guilty about punishing those who conspire to break our laws."

"That's true. I could have forgiven treason against the throne after an adequate punishment, but they tried to kill our child. I try not to think what would've happened if that bitch had as good an aim as you or Kai." She took a deep breath to settle her heart rate. "I'd have ordered a trial for the entire lot of those people who followed

Francesca. And if the council can prove they knew about the attack on Kai and helped her in any way, I'm going to order them killed and will gladly do it myself if that's their vote."

"And if that includes Bella and Wilma? That they were willing participants, I mean."

"What would you do?" She placed her hand on Hadley's forehead and thanked the goddess again for the unwavering strength she saw in Hadley's gaze.

"I'd kill them all and would be blessed if my queen gives me the privilege of wielding the triton." Hadley sat up and pointed outside. "My love, you have to realize that the people out there love you and they love Kai. They see your faults, but they trust your leadership and your ability to keep them safe. Why this Yelter woman or anyone else would think giving the Oberons an in will change their lives for the better is too stupid to waste time on."

"That's my decision if they helped plan the attack on Kai, and I hope it doesn't cast me as a monster, but I can't allow Sol to become any more brazen. He'll take this throne only by killing me."

"That'll only happen if every Atlantean woman died protecting you, and I don't foresee that."

She smiled and kissed Hadley's chin. "What do you foresee?"

"Your reign will last another thousand years."

The words were part of the official royal toasts. Any queen's reign would last another thousand years because of their heirs, so it was a blessing for all their royals. "Thank you, and my prayer is to share that eternity with you."

CHAPTER TWENTY-EIGHT

The woman stopped when Kai slowed to check the traffic before she crossed the street. Obviously following someone wasn't one of this woman's talents, or she was actually part of the security detail Laud had sent. It wouldn't do any good to complain about the latter, but if this wasn't part of that scenario, the security around her would triple. She stared right at the woman as she got close, prepared to act if need be.

Her shadow made only brief eye contact and stayed quiet as she walked toward Etta's building. Kai wasn't about to lead her to her old friend so she entered a building halfway there. She didn't hurry until she made it through the door and ran for the stairs. The door slammed behind her, but it didn't concern her as she waited to the left of the opening. The woman was actually laughing when she opened the door, obviously at her expense for being so predictable, but she quickly stopped when Kai wrapped her arm around her neck and squeezed. She struggled for only a moment before becoming dead weight, so Kai put her down carefully and removed the backpack and her wallet. The pack held only a camera and the wallet only cash. It was what someone carried when there was even a remote chance of discovery.

"I'm sure this is one of those purchased phones, but let's give it a shot," Kai said as she removed the cell from the woman's front pocket. Thankfully it wasn't pass-code protected so she dialed the only number in memory.

"Where the hell are you?" a man gruffly asked.

"Following, like you asked," she whispered. "Why?" she asked, trying to figure out who this was.

"Get back here. I told you we don't need anything else on that front. I need you here to keep the fuckers on the board occupied. Don't flake out on me now that we're so close."

This had to be Steve, but why in the hell would he need her followed? "No problem. She's too close for me to talk anyway."

"Where are you?" Steve asked and laughed. If she had to guess, he was still obsessed with Vivien and obviously anyone who got in the way of that.

"Got to go." She hung up and snapped the cheap phone in half. She went through the photos in the camera, not liking the number of shots of Vivien, her family, and her. Before she left, she positioned the woman so she could take her picture to show the Palmers later. "Hope you have aspirin handy," she said as she let the woman go and she slumped over. "Your headache will wake you up in about an hour."

Etta downloaded the picture after Kai made sure the woman was working alone. "You don't recognize her?" Etta asked.

"Her face is vaguely familiar, but no. Maybe the team will get a lead with that." She pointed to the computer screen. "That's not why I'm here though. Did you get what I asked for?"

Etta opened her laptop and brought up a world map that had a red dot wherever the strange boxes had been found. So far they'd appeared only on oil rigs, military ships, and other vessels with high clearance. Kai started typing in a command-strategy sequence and waited for the results.

"Do you have anything interesting? Vivien will want to know why I'm here since I'm staying with her and her family." She smiled when Etta immediately handed her a rolled-up map. "She also wants to know if you've got a young lover you run off to see every summer."

"I'm working on it, but it's just my parents for now. I live surrounded by water here, but it's nice to go home. Your mother, and grandmother, and I have a lot of cataloging to do."

The computer emitted a small ping so they both looked. "Don't worry. I won't keep you long."

"Your Highness, I'll do whatever you require to help you," Etta said, lowering her head.

"I know, but your mothers are waiting and I want you to go. Right now I only want to see how viable my theory is." The dots were connected by a series of lines that overlapped more frequently in four different locations worldwide. From what she could tell, they seemed to concentrate around oil platforms but all of them in deep water. "Could you secure the door?"

She typed another strategy scenario and watched what the capital's main computer system's prediction would be. All the lines and dots disappeared toward the end. "Mom," she said to Hadley when she opened a link.

"How's the leg?" Hadley asked, and Kai noticed her grandmothers Brook and Mari had joined in.

"Stings a little but I'm good. I wanted to check in and give you some updates." She started with the woman in the stairwell.

"You've never seen her?" Brook asked.

"Was she a citizen?" Mari asked.

"No and no, and she works for Steve Hawksworth, so I kind of see her motives. What I really called about are the boxes."

"We've got people working on it," Hadley said, watching their system tie the boxes together and coming up with the four locations Kai had pinpointed. "We've had the same results, but placing a signal with the amount of strength it's going to take to annihilate them will take time."

"I've got an idea about that and wanted your input before I make a fool of myself in front of the council."

"Let's hear it, tadpole," Mari said, the others nodding.

She explained what had come to her the night before and ran the simulations for them. No one had an explanation yet as to where the boxes had come from or who had placed them, but destroying them would also destroy their usefulness. They'd have to find another way to trace them.

"We've got a lead on who, but not why yet," Hadley said, running the scenario again. "Laud and the others came up with the same thing but don't have the specifics needed. Will what you're proposing withstand the strength of the beam? We've never mixed our technology with that of the humans like this before."

"I might cook it, but can we try this tomorrow if you agree?"

"I'll have teams in place by tonight."

"Thanks, Mom."

All three of her family members bowed. "Thank you, Highness. You've been a good student, and now you've proved beyond doubt that you've learned well. I'd be proud to follow you into any fight," Hadley said.

"Let's hope this keeps us off the battlefield."

"Well spoken," Mari and Brook said almost together.

Vivien opened her eyes slowly, hoping the room wasn't spinning like it had been when she first woke up. She very seldom got sick so the morning's bout of vomiting was definitely memorable. Like earlier, though, she didn't move, enjoying the feel of Kai next to her. The desire to touch Kai and be touched was there even if her stomach issues hadn't completely vanished.

"You're back early," she said, turning slightly and molding her body to Kai's.

"I missed you so I asked Etta for the condensed version. She didn't mind, since she could leave early to visit her parents."

"So no great love affair?" she asked, laughing. "That's a shame. She doesn't realize what she's missing."

"How are you feeling, my little romantic fool?" Kai tightened her hold and brought her closer so she was practically on top of her.

"I'm much better. Thank you for taking care of me." She gently ran her fingers along Kai's eyebrows, and suddenly her eyes filled with tears, blurring her vision. Her face was hot from a blush, she was sure, but she couldn't help the onslaught of emotion. She had never been this completely happy.

Kai surprised her by not asking why she was crying and simply held her. It was like a reassurance that she could express whatever she was feeling and still be safe in Kai's arms. She'd been content with her life, happy when she was with Frankie and free from judgment or ridicule, but nothing like this.

"You want to try to eat anything?" Kai asked after thirty minutes.

"I guess we need to go in to the office today, even though I'd rather gouge my eyes out. I still can't believe that weasel got the board to go along with him." She kissed Kai's shoulder before getting up. "That won't stand," Kai said, joining her in the bathroom. "I'm sure things will return to normal as soon as the general stock-meeting vote takes place."

"I wish I could be so sure." Standing in the shower with Kai was like a shot of adrenaline to her system that seemed to stabilize the queasiness in her stomach. They didn't talk much after that, but she enjoyed having Kai nearby as they got ready.

Kai held her hand until they got to the elevators and smiled when the doors closed with only them in the car. "Remember who you are and what's rightfully yours. The rest is annoying background noise," Kai said when they reached the top floor.

Winston was in his office with his feet propped up, listening to Frankie give him some kind of report, but Frankie stopped when they walked in. "Sorry we're late. I wasn't feeling well this morning," Vivien said.

Kai closed her eyes momentarily when the tension in the room seemed to close in around her. The Palmers weren't upset with each other, but they were still reeling from the shock. She sat between Vivien and Frankie, needing the nearness of all of them to sway their thoughts to what she had to do.

"All set on the stock-holder meeting?" she asked, concentrating on her shell. She smiled when the siblings lifted their hands to touch their own, as if they couldn't help the motion.

"Frankie can give you both the date, but it's set. Hope those fuckers know it's a two-way street once it's convened. The stockholders can vote the board out too," Winston said. He started rubbing his temples after he spoke. "Kai, I hate to ask, but could you make a quick trip out to Triton and see if everything's okay?"

Vivien's expression was unreadable at first, but she eventually nodded. "That's a good idea, so we can have an update for the meeting."

"I won't mind at all, sir. Anything you need, just ask. You deserve better than you've gotten." The manipulation of their thoughts was necessary because she didn't want company out on the water, so she was glad Vivien didn't object. "Let's see how close I can get." Vivien followed her out and pointed to her office. "Remember where you're staying when you get back."

She put her arms around Vivien and kissed the top of her head. The bond between them was growing and strengthening, which would make it excruciatingly painful when she severed it. "I'd lose sight of who I am before I forget you. I won't be long."

Vivien moaned when they kissed, and she didn't let go when the door opened behind them. "Steve's going to be devastated, but you've got much nicer hair," Frankie said with a wide smile.

"The rest of her is as spectacular," Vivien said, so she took the opportunity to leave.

"I'll give you a chance to talk about me," she said, then kissed Vivien again and shook Franklin's hand on the way out. "Keep an eye on her for me."

"Sure, but I don't mind sharing the job," Franklin said.

"What job is that?" Steve asked as Franklin's shoulders hitched at the sound of his voice. "Never mind. Before too long you won't have any job here to worry about, but I'll make sure the board saddles you with the bill for all your great progressive ideas."

"If you're trying to scare me, dig a little deeper," she said, staring intently at him. Something about him was off, but she couldn't quite grasp what that was, though she recognized the woman who stood behind him. "How's your head, Miss…?"

"Tanice Themis," Tanice said but wouldn't make eye contact. "I'm Mr. Hawksworth's assistant."

"You two know each other?" Vivien asked.

"Not really, no," she said, laughing. "Miss Themis just looks like someone who has a splitting headache. See you soon."

In the elevator she made a call to Edil and ordered some of her people ashore to watch over Vivien and her family. "Make sure they're not spotted, and if you have anyone to spare I need Steve Hawksworth and his assistant followed. For some reason I get the impression we'll find some of our answers with these two."

"As you wish, Highness," Edil said, and she could sense some hesitation. "Etta did as you asked this morning and contacted your parents about what happened."

"How many are you sending?" She'd been right in that her freedom was about to be curtailed.

"Your guards are waiting aboard the *Salacia*, but if you return to shore, Consort Hadley requested four guards at all times."

"Relax, Edil," she said, blowing out a long breath. "I rarely kill the messenger, and I'll see you in a few hours."

"Can I have that in writing about not killing the messenger?" Edil asked, laughing.

"Sure, but if you want me to sign it in blood, don't say I didn't warn you about the bloody nose you'll have to provide."

❖

"What did that bitch mean about your head?" Steve asked, pinning Tanis against the closed door of his office. She didn't move when he wrapped his hand around her throat, her eyes closing as if to hide something from him. "What aren't you telling me?" He tightened his grip.

"I waited outside the Palmer place today to see what their next move would be, but Merlin came out alone. It was odd so I followed her."

"Taking your time won't save you."

"She spotted me and disarmed me. When I came to, my camera was gone and my phone was in pieces."

"You fucking little idiot." The whisper from earlier wasn't Tanice. "Did you call me from wherever you were this morning?" He had to be sure.

"No."

He had control of the company so he didn't really need Vivien or Kai, or anyone else that once stood in his way, but loose ends had a way of wrapping around your neck if left alone and forgotten. His orders had been to get the job done as quietly as possible so as to not raise any alarms in the business and military worlds, and this development had the potential to derail that. "Get out of my sight."

He sat at his desk and tried to calm his anger before he called in. "We may have a problem," he said, once verification had been made.

"Problems so soon after reporting such good news? It makes me wonder if you were the right choice. Your sister might've been further along by now."

"You can solve my problem with a kill shot," he said, snapping a pen in half. His hand was covered in ink but it didn't matter. "After that you can replace me, but you've been successful because of me."

"Leaders have no need to gloat or self-promote. Finish what needs to be done, or you'll lose more than my faith in you. When will you be operational?"

"In four days you'll have what you need."

"Then eliminate your problems and wait for my order to launch."

"Yes, sir," he said, but the line was dead. "I won't go so quietly, old man."

CHAPTER TWENTY-NINE

Kai anchored well away from Triton and set the security measures on board before diving into the inky water. She and Talia had fished in case someone was watching while Isla joined Edil's people to prepare. Their radar showed plenty of coast guard and military ships still in the area, but that didn't bother her.

Once the sun completely set she flicked off all their lights and swam to meet their team. The water against her skin felt good, as did her leg when she pressed the others for speed. Before too long the massive legs of Triton came into view, a large metal ornament lit up like a strange Christmas decoration completely out of place.

"We're a go on your mark, Highness," Edil said as she stopped beside her.

Kai opened a line with her mothers, knowing their top military personnel were listening in. "Are all the units in position?"

"The team leaders are waiting on your signal," Hadley said.

"May the goddess watch over you and bring victory to Atlantis," Galen said, followed by a cheer from those listening in as well as those in the water with her.

"Go ahead and put out the lights, Edil," she said, referring to Triton. "If you encounter any hostiles, try to take them alive, but eliminate them if you have no choice."

The coast-guard cutters patrolled close to their position, but everything went still when Edil started the device she'd brought along. It killed all power, no matter if it was electrical or gas, within a five-mile radius. On a night with low cloud cover and a half-moon, it was all the cover they needed. The only things still operational aside from their own equipment were the boxes and comm unit attached and close to Triton.

Kai was out of the water after Isla and Talia but didn't wait for them to make the long climb to the rig's command center. Once they were on deck she waited to see if they had company, but the rig seemed deserted. "Edil, take two with you and get the radio and satellite working."

"I don't mind placing the webbing if you'd like to handle the radio," Edil said.

"Get going before those boats put divers in the water." She wasn't in the mood to be coddled, and Edil must've understood that when she quickly started moving.

The webbing Edil referred to was easy to place since it was shot out of a specialized triton, making quick work of covering the deck when the rest of the unit spread out. They didn't use this method often since they rarely needed to eliminate human technology, but in some instances it was necessary to keep their locations secret. The result only added to the mystique of the world's devil's triangles like the famous Bermuda Triangle.

"We're ready in the water, Highness," someone reported from below.

"Edil, you ready?" she asked.

"The frequency is ready, Highness. We were able to access the ships' radios as well, so that should cut our time down."

"Everyone ready?" she asked, needing to know if all the other units were in position to deploy. It was the only way to cover the entire planet at once.

"Kai, count us down," Galen said.

"Ready." She moved to the edge to look overboard. "Three, two, one—engage."

The dark lit up with an intense blue light that resembled electricity, with the webbing allowing it to finger out for miles. Eventually the lines would meet, and any technology underwater on the same frequency as the foreign boxes would be destroyed. The phenomena of it would baffle anyone on the water, but it was the fastest way to eliminate the problem.

Kai had also tweaked the program so there would be an added bonus, but now she concentrated on the growing pool of green in the water. "We're good here," she reported as the sound of a bubble popping came from the distance. The comm unit was gone, the pieces sinking fast.

"Good job, Highness," one of the commanders said. "We have affirmatives from every location that the water's clear of spyware."

"Send out patrols to the home offices of every location that had the boxes attached to their equipment," she said, ignoring for now the loud voices coming from the military ships. "The power surge was programed to back feed to any equipment gathering the information the boxes contained."

"Detain anyone responsible for what you find," Galen said, and Kai understood her meaning perfectly. It'd be a tough decision, but they had to eliminate anyone who had conspired against the throne.

"Yes, Highness, we'll make it so," she said before switching her comm unit off. "Let's hit the water," she said when someone assured her the webbing had completely burned away. "It's time to head back in to see what has landed in our net."

Sunrise was a few hours off when Kai arrived back at the Palmer house, and she sat on her bike and enjoyed the silence around her. It seemed this city slept only for these few hours before another day truly began. She opened her eyes when the front door did.

"Are you avoiding me?" Vivien asked.

"More like I'm thinking about you," she said, dropping her helmet on the seat and moving to touch Vivien. "I was looking forward to this." She put her hand behind Vivien's neck and kissed her. The sight of her had warmed her shell and awakened her soul.

The sensation scared her. This wasn't supposed to happen but the reality was clear. She'd fallen in love with Vivien, and Oba's warnings echoed loudly in her head. What had been her cocky response to Oba's worried question? That nothing would keep her from her duty? But that was before this woman. She couldn't have ever imagined the pull of Vivien's allure, but this morning it was even more than that. Something important had changed, and she couldn't figure it out.

"We need to get upstairs," Vivien said, her foot anchored behind Kai's leg. "Now."

She hoped none of the Palmers were early risers as she picked Vivien up and carried her to the bed they shared. When she laid Vivien down, Vivien spread her legs and reached down and spread herself open as if presenting her with a gift. Vivien was wet and ready and moaned loud enough to wake the entire house when she put her mouth on her. It was as if in that one act the force of Vivien's shell reached into her chest and closed its fist around her heart.

"Mine." The word exploded in her mind and she didn't fight it.

Vivien intertwined her fingers with hers as she thrust her hips against her mouth. The way Vivien tasted was different, sweeter, and it made her suck harder. She kept pace until Vivien went rigid before jerking a few more times, as if reaching her peak but refusing to climb down.

"I'm not sure why you came back so soon, but thank you," Vivien said as she wiped her mouth with the nightgown she'd just removed. "That sure as hell beats the hot dreams I was having about you."

Kai stripped before she lay down. "I came back because something weird happened," she said, having to report what had occurred from a human point of view. Hiding something witnessed by so many would raise too many red flags.

"Honey," Vivien said, rolling over to lie pressed along the length of her, "start that sentence next time with, I missed you." She laughed, so Kai smiled at the teasing reprimand. "Makes me think I'm an afterthought."

"I believe I mentioned that earlier downstairs," she said, not moving as Vivien ran her hand up the inside of her thigh. "It's just that what I saw was really strange. Your father needs to hear this."

"Does he need to hear it right this second?" Vivien moved her hand again, pressing her fingers against her now-hard clit. "If you want my opinion, there are so many other things we could be talking about."

"I'm beginning to see what you mean," she said as the muscles of her abdomen flexed almost involuntarily when Vivien pressed harder.

When Vivien moved to kneel between her legs, she stopped thinking and centered her attention on Vivien's touch. It was so sensual and intimate that Kai closed her eyes and waited for Vivien to move at her own pace, since it seemed to be important to her.

"Open your eyes," she heard Vivien say, but when she did Vivien appeared startled. It was then that she realized Vivien had made the request in her thoughts. "What the hell?"

"What?" she asked as calmly as she could. Explaining the complete secrets of the shell would end with her having to tell her every secret that wasn't exactly hers to share. But by goddess she wanted to. This would be so much easier if Vivien knew.

"Sorry," Vivien said, but her concentration was broken and her hands stilled. "Please tell me I'm not going crazy," Vivien said in her mind.

"Are you okay?" She moved to hold Vivien since an answer was impossible. "Do you feel sick again?"

"No. I shouldn't have stopped," Vivien said, appearing upset with herself. "That's selfish, considering how you make me feel."

"You were throwing up yesterday so forget about it. A little waiting is good for the soul," she said and smiled. "Come on and I'll tell you a story," she said, lying back.

Vivien sat up when she first described the blue light. Her story was that she witnessed it all from the deck of her boat, but she did mention she'd lost power. "Whatever happened, it lit up Triton and the water around it like it was connected to an electrical socket."

"Was it the coast guard?"

"From the screaming I heard, I doubt it. I've never seen anything like it, so I'm not ashamed to say it was interesting."

Vivien shook her head and groaned. "You're going to hate me, but we've got to get up. We really need to tell my father. If anything happened to that rig he's going to have a stroke."

"I'm willing to take a rain check, so let's go shower."

After they got dressed Vivien sent her down to her father's study while she went to wake everyone up. Winston appeared to be in pain when she repeated her story.

They were all in the office not long after that, having stopped in front of Steve's office since his door was charred and hanging from only one hinge.

"Frankie, get security up here," Winston said. "Tell them to bring the tapes since yesterday afternoon. I don't want to be blamed for torching this guy's office. If I'm chancing anything, I'd rather torch him."

They waited for the security people to show up, but Kai was itching to go in. The only explanation for the damage was in the office somewhere, and she had to find it before Steve had a chance to destroy the trail. Her trap had been sprung, and that he couldn't hide.

"The only thing on the tapes is a sudden flash, Mr. Palmer," the older of the security guards said. "It was a quick blue flash that didn't really look like a fire. There's hardly anyone up here at that hour, so we weren't looking."

"If it was a fire, should we go in to make sure everything is completely out?" she asked.

Winston followed her in after asking Vivien and the others to wait outside. She scanned every surface, finally seeing the top drawer of his desk. The damage seemed to radiate out from there. She took a pen from the desk and tried to pry it open. Inside, the phone appeared normal but still held some of the power source they'd released last night. It would be hot for another week, like any other device similar to it around the world. Having that kind of time would give Kai's people the chance to find them.

"His phone did all this?" Winston asked, peering over her shoulder.

"If this is what happens when you're late on your bill, I'll have to make sure my account is current," she said, relieved when Winston joined her in laughing. "Let's get out of here and wait for the fire department to make sure there's no danger."

She followed the Palmers towards Winston's office, excusing herself at the last minute to head to the restroom. "Isla, contact Edil and see who's watching Hawksworth. When they get a chance, pick him up and lock him down. If Edil put someone on his assistant, pick her up too."

"That's not going to raise any alarms?"

"He had a comm unit that blew up his office last night with the back feed. That raises more alarms for us than anyone who'll miss this jackass." She spoke softly, then stopped when the door opened. She hung up when she heard someone retching in the next stall. "Viv, is that you?"

"I'm not sure what's—" Vivien heaved again, but Kai was behind her holding her up. "This has to be grossing you out by now," Vivien said as she accepted the wad of tissue she pressed into her hand.

"Don't worry about me, and you're going home with Frankie. Make sure someone calls for a doctor's appointment." She helped Vivien to her feet and carefully wiped her face, kissing her forehead when she was done. "I'm going to stay and help your dad out, but call me when you get a time, and I'll go to the doctor with you."

"Thank you." Vivien leaned against her as if exhausted. "I want to stay, but I feel like a truck hit me."

"Go rest, and I'll be back with your dad in a while."

It didn't take the fire department long after their arrival to completely shut down the building, and it didn't surprise her since this had to be foreign to them. None of Atlantis's power sources resembled the electric currents and combustion engines the topside world ran on, so the immense current they'd sent through the webbing had to be scary if you'd never seen it.

"We need to find that bastard," Winston said as they headed home. "The company didn't need this on top of the feds closing down the Gulf. Now the office is off limits too."

"Might give you some leverage with the stockholders, sir."

"Maybe, but I want you to stick around no matter what. You're good for Vivien, and even if she thinks *I'm* a bastard, I like seeing her happy." He gripped the wheel and didn't look at her.

"No worries, sir, and I wouldn't worry about losing anything except maybe the Hawksworth family from your life." Everything appeared normal when they pulled through the gates, but she was vigilant until Steve and whoever was working for him were in restraints. "And Vivien is safe with me."

"I have no choice but to believe you."

CHAPTER THIRTY

W hat the hell is happening?" Steve screamed at the security guard blocking his way into the building. "Under whose order can you keep me out?"

"We have an unknown contaminant in an office on the top floor, so until I know what it is, no one goes in," an older man in a fireman's uniform said.

"Which office?" he asked, a ball of cold settling in his stomach.

"The middle one on the right side of the building."

He turned and pointed to Tanice back in the car. "Give me your phone," he demanded once they were inside.

His "father" picked up on the third ring. "What do you know?" Jonathon sighed but didn't say anything. "I said, what do you know?"

"From what we can tell, last night every communication device we placed was destroyed. Whoever detonated the surge figured out a way to back feed it into every comm unit we have. Our command center and the ships' controls are completely fried. We're stuck here with no link back to the palace."

Steve stripped his tie off and pulled over the first chance he got so he could punch the steering wheel a few times. "I haven't spent the last five years in that stinking place to lose out now. How did you allow something like this to happen?"

"Your Highness," Jonathon said in a tone that was close to pleading, "we've lost contact with those loyal to our cause, but it was before last night's incident. Their orders were to report in no matter the reason, so we have to assume they're dead."

"What other orders did you give them?" The reality that he was stranded here was starting to become a nightmare, but his title brought back his anger. It was time to shed the persona of Steve Hawksworth and start acting like the man his father had raised.

Prince Pontos Oberon, son of Sol and Rhea Oberon, would never allow the stain of defeat at the hands of an inferior race of women to be written into the history books. Even if they were related by blood, he'd erase their existence from this planet.

"Asher," he said, using Jonathon's real name, "think about what mistakes you've made that let these idiots be discovered. If they're dead it was on orders from either Galen or Hadley."

Asher Pailter had been Pontos's protector since he was six, so it had made sense that he'd assume the role of his father so his presence wouldn't be questioned. "It wasn't until a few days ago that Francesca informed us that the princess was in this area so they intended to try to take her out. That's the last we heard from her or her group, sire. Remember, we were under your orders to receive communications only from them and not return any unless it was imperative."

"So you're blaming me?" Pontos pushed his hands against the wheel, pressing his back against the seat.

"No, sire, but I believe she kept it to herself to prove she was worthy of your trust. Her failure, though, might have uncovered the rest who have shown favor to you and the king. And she died before she revealed who the princess is."

Pontos closed his eyes as the reality of the situation hit him like a human bullet to his chest. He should've figured it out that first night when that tall bitch put her hand on the fish tank. Very few of the rulers after Nessa's father actually knew the identity of Nessa's heirs until they actually ascended to the throne, each more defiant than the rest.

Kai had to be Galen's child, and she'd been close enough to him so many times that it would've been easy to eliminate her if he'd been thinking clearly. He still had some advantage since the Oberons never revealed their children either until it was necessary. They had no idea who he really was or his mission.

"Gather everyone who's close and tell them to meet at the barracks. I'll be there in an hour."

"As you wish, sire," Asher said.

"Francesca might've failed but I certainly will not."

The trip to the doctor was quick, and Vivien was resting with the medication the doctor had prescribed when his prognosis had been a simple stomach virus. As she slept, Kai had talked to Edil and Laud about security since Steve and Tanice had effectively disappeared.

Of all her calls, the one to her mother Hadley had been the most difficult, since she was beyond angry that she'd missed such a lapse in their security. "Mom, we've always had dissenters. That's part of our history. I'm concerned they helped an outsider into our world, but we've got a lead on where to start looking. Stop beating yourself up."

"It's a bit more complicated than that," Hadley said gruffly. "Today, Wilma Yelter and her daughter Bella disappeared as well, after shaking the people I put on them. We've looked, so if they're still here, someone is hiding them."

"And the others with Francesca's group?" she asked, rubbing Vivien's back when she mumbled in her sleep.

"Most of them are detained, along with the families of the women killed with Francesca. They're all proclaiming their innocence, and only the threat of treason against your mother shut them up about those fairy tales, so we should get the whole story soon. They're smart enough to know the penalty for treason, which makes for more cooperative prisoners."

"Is Mama okay?"

"She's upset, and I can't convince her this has nothing to do with her reign."

"No. The Oberons have been planning and scheming since Nessa sat on the throne and possessed the golden triton." She stilled her hand and sensed what was coming next. "I have to go back, don't I?"

"Kai, it has nothing to do with your abilities or our faith in you. This situation, though, makes it impossible to truly protect you. There are too many unknowns for Laud and the others to contend with."

"When?" she asked, her chest achy from the thought of leaving Vivien.

"We'll give you tonight, tadpole. Your mother and I are proud of the job you've done bringing that family back together. Vivien has more to count on now than just her brother."

"Thanks." The device went silent so she lay there and watched Vivien sleep. She wanted to promise herself that she'd return, but to prolong what had to be would be cruel to both of them. "I'll never forget you, and you'll forever own a part of my heart," she said softly.

Vivien didn't move or wake, so she held her and waited for her to open her eyes on her own, getting up for only a moment to prepare for what came next. It didn't take long before Vivien's breathing pattern changed and her embrace tightened. Neither of them said anything so it was nice not to break the silence, which only angered her when she heard her phone ring. A limited number of people had the number, so it had to be important.

"Come out or I'm going to blow the house."

She recognized the voice even if she'd heard it only once on the phone. "Calm down," she said as she got to her feet and went to the window. Steve stood in the center of the courtyard surrounded by a group of warriors in the crimson uniforms of their home planet. "These people have nothing of importance to you."

"Don't give orders, Princess, and move." Steve nodded to one of the men, who hit Vivien's truck with a bright-red beam and it burst into flames. "Get out here."

"What's he doing?" Vivien asked, standing by Kai's side and staring outside.

"Viv, I need you to get to the back door but don't go outside," she said, but Vivien didn't take her eyes off the group in the yard. "Vivien, you need to get down there and be ready to move."

"We can all leave together since Steve's obviously lost his mind."

"You need to go," she said, more sternly than she meant, but if he concentrated all those beams on the house they'd all die together.

"Don't go," Vivien said, her tears about to fall.

"Keep yourself and your family safe—promise me," she said, and almost cried herself when Vivien turned to leave. "Are you in position?" she asked Isla, who stood at the corner of the house for cover. "Yes, and a couple of Edil's people are waiting out back. They cleared a path out the back garden, so don't worry. Be careful, Highness. This guy is full of hate and he knows who you are, but from the looks of it we have most of his men in one place."

Now outside, she took her triton out of her packed bag and drew a deep breath, thinking of Oba. Maybe her course wouldn't change because of Vivien after all. Her path might end on land right here, but she refused to go down without a fight.

"I see you're no different in battle than you were at Palmer," she said as she tightened her grip on the triton. "You need plenty of backup no matter where you are."

"You think I need anyone to help me kill you?" Steve twirled the metal pole in his hands and started to slowly circle. "My father told me this would be easy, but I don't think he realized how simple-minded your mother is."

"Your father?" She didn't step toward him but only turned to keep him in front of her. Her attention wavered only slightly as she saw her people coming over the wall, and Steve's men were clueless since they were waiting to see him destroy her.

"King Sol Oberon." He ran at her and seemed to be trying to knock her down with his momentum. "I'm going to gift him with your head, and my reward will be seeing your mother's face when I tell her as I take over the city."

She stood and felt the strain in her thighs as he pushed down on her triton with his weapon, but she wasn't worried about going down. The power she could hear vibrating through the weapon made her hyperaware to keep him from pointing the end at her. She kept her triton up and waited for a sign that he was about to add more pressure, and when he flexed the muscles in his arms she kicked him in the knee.

Steve stumbled but managed to knock her in the chest with the nonlethal side of his weapon. The men with him moved closer to them when he dropped to his knees as she kicked him again. "I guess you need help killing a woman," she taunted him.

"Back off," Steve screamed as he got back to his feet, but he was limping.

Hurting an opponent was always good, but from her training she also knew it made them more dangerous. He blocked her next kick and swung up with his weapon when she was committed and connected with her shoulder. It tore her shirt, but her suit protected her from the crackle of power. She was glad she'd taken the time to put it on while Vivien slept.

She recovered and met his blows as they knocked weapon to weapon. The sparring reminded her of the sessions she'd had with her mother Hadley when she was younger. Hadley's size and strength had intimidated her at first, but she'd learned quickly that she could defeat both with speed and by keeping her head in the game. The expression of triumph on his face almost made her laugh as one of her undercuts knocked the triton out of her hand.

"Prepare to—" He stopped gloating abruptly when she knocked his head back in rapid succession with her fist; she hit him so hard she felt the impact all the way up her arm to her shoulder. By the fifth blow her fists were bloody, and she reached down for her triton when he shook his head as if to clear it.

Her head rattled in pain as she lowered it for an instant and he came down with his fist. Steve wasn't as tall as she was, but he was powerful—strong. Her minuscule break in attention had taken her back a few steps. She tightened her grip on the triton and turned fast enough that his next punch glanced off her shoulder. She had time then to move out of his range and clear her head enough to continue.

"It's time for you and the rest of the *women* your mother thinks she rules to bow to their true ruler." The red beam shot from the end of his weapon and made a hole in the Palmers' driveway.

She trusted her aim and shot a quick pulse that knocked it out of his hand, and as it bounced away from him, his men brought their weapons up and started to point them at her. Talia and Isla moved first, aiming for the heads of the men positioned to strike against her. Steve turned and seemed shocked that half of his warriors lay dead right behind him.

He screamed and ran at her with the dagger he'd unsheathed from his back, which he swung in a wide arch, slicing into her cheek.

She had no choice but to drop her triton, which was useless with him this close. Her protectors weren't of any help now since the rest of Steve's men had engaged them.

"I've worked too long to lose to you, bitch," he said as he knocked her to the ground and straddled her hips. He gripped the dagger with both hands and used his position to push it down toward her throat.

She strained in an effort to keep it from coming down any farther, but he had the advantage so her mind frantically worked to come up with a counter before the bastard pinned her head to the ground. Just then Vivien screamed her name from the corner of the house. The split-second distraction was all she needed as she pushed against Steve so the tip came down on her chest, allowing her to punch him directly in the nose.

Kai momentarily closed her eyes to keep the spray of blood from Steve's nose from blinding her. It was one of those wounds that made you instinctively cover the area with your hands, and Steve was no different, despite his opinion of superior birth.

She rolled, knocking him off her, and moved to retrieve her triton. Isla's yell of warning came as she began to stand up, and she immediately turned to put her back toward the house since all the hostiles were in the driveway. Even though Steve was injured and still bleeding, he easily caught the weapon Tanice had thrown him, and this time he didn't hesitate to fire. She had no time to fire off a shot so she did the only thing she could think to survive. The blast to her chest came instantly as she acted.

Then there was only darkness.

Chapter Thirty-one

No," Vivien screamed, echoed by Tanice's similar anguish. The two adversaries lay dead so the tie didn't seem fair. Steve had the weapon Kai had thrown like a javelin sticking out of his throat, and Kai had a large burn mark that encompassed her entire chest. "Let me go," she said to the strange woman who held her back.

"Please, Miss Palmer, it's not safe." Those were the last words Vivien heard.

Edil gently laid her down like she had Franklin, while her backup took care of the parents. An induced sleep would at least keep them out of harm's way, so she ran to join the fight against the few men left around Tanice. Isla and Talia were on their knees leaning over Kai, and their expression of sadness made her choke back the tears.

"Put down your weapons or you'll die where you stand," she said loudly, killing one of them to make her point when he tried to fire on her. The act did nothing to calm her anger, but it did take the fight out of them.

"Edil, you know where to take them," Isla said, not moving from Kai's side. "We'll carry the princess home."

Edil's unit bound the prisoners with their best restraints, then sedated them once they were loaded in their vehicles. The others drove Steve's car away from the house and made the best repairs they could to clean up any sign of their fight. Steve's men would be transported to one of their bases under the arctic tundra, where their most talented interrogators were located.

"Do you want me to try to erase this from their memories?" she asked Talia about the Palmers.

"Leave them to us and go. You and your warriors did a good job today. You should be proud of yourself and them."

"Thank you, but I still feel like we failed," she said as she glanced at Kai.

"That's not what we'll report to our queen, so go, and we'll take care of the rest," Talia said, putting her hand on Edil's shoulder and squeezing. "I'm serious about the pride you should take away from this."

Edil nodded and turned to join her group. When the vehicles pulled away, Talia's heart rate went down since they didn't have any human authorities to deal with to complicate the situation. "Did you make contact with Laud?" she asked Isla.

"It's all taken care of, and the known resistance members are all in custody except for Wilma and Bella, but Laud said they were close to finding them. The rest, I'm sure, will come once those idiots go through questioning, but let's finish up here before we have to face the queen and her consort."

They worked together to gently wrap Kai up for transport and take the Palmers inside. When they came to in an induced state, Talia gave them a choice as to what to believe since she didn't think it possible to wipe Kai and what had happened completely from their minds without impairing their complete mental health. She wasn't that talented. Some people, though, had trouble believing things so out of their norm, so at times they needed another explanation to help them hang on to their safe reality.

The *Salacia* was moored at the shipyard, but they waited until the place was fairly deserted to leave, wanting the cover of night to make it to the Gulf. It wasn't from fear but so they could submerge without too many witnesses if they were followed.

"Do you think we'll ever come back here?" Isla asked as she put out a call to Ivan and Ram. It was time to go home.

"Kai has left enough of a mark here that I think we will. The work is important so it has to continue." Talia put her arm around Isla's waist and held her. Sometimes only the closeness of a friend you loved could conquer pain.

"We'll make sure it does, no matter what."

Chapter Thirty-two

Vivien sat between her father and Frankie three weeks later and waited for the final vote of the stockholders. It took every ounce of will in her to get out of bed, since the nagging stomach issues and Kai's absence had weighed heavily on her. Her family hadn't talked about it, and Frankie had been unusually quiet about the whole thing, but she knew what she'd witnessed. Nothing or no one would ever convince her otherwise.

"We are as upset as anyone with the disappearance of the Hawksworth family, but we were right in the actions we took as a board," Shawn Reagan, the acting head of the board, said in answer to a question from the audience.

The woman at the microphone looked like someone she'd met, but Vivien couldn't place from where. "What concern required the removal of Mr. Palmer from the helm of the company?"

Shawn explained the programs that had to do with the environment and nothing to do with oil production, as well as leaving Steve out of some of the major decisions made after they'd been shut down. The rest of the board nodded as he spoke, but the woman showed no sign of emotion one way or another.

"So you don't believe the two-billion-dollar contract with the state of Louisiana to grow both the fish farms and land-expander programs good for the company?" the woman said with heat. "Or that you placed all your trust in a man who's disappeared along with his family, deserting the company when we desperately need leadership?"

"What contract?" Shawn asked, looking back at the board and then Vivien's family as if someone would feed him the answer.

"I'm here representing clients who own fifteen percent of the common stock, and I make a motion to place Mr. Winston Palmer back to his original position." The motion was immediately seconded and passed with a strong majority. "I also make a motion to have another vote once new, better-qualified people are found to replace the entire board. We can consider a new tally of names in a month's time."

"Wait a minute," Shawn said as some of the board members stood.

"No. You wait until my motion has been addressed." Like the first, it was immediately ratified.

Vivien thought how right her father had been and how helpful this woman had been in giving him what he wanted. It was almost as if she'd been privy to the conversation they'd had about it when Kai had been present. The memory twisted the knife that seemed to have lodged in her heart.

Once the meeting was adjourned, the way her father laughed cut through some of her pain. "Hopefully he'll stay the same now that he has the big chair back," Frankie said with a smile that appeared melancholy. "It's been nice to have him finally be simply Dad."

"I think it'll be okay." She took Frankie's hand to anchor herself in something familiar. "Do you know the woman asking the questions?"

"The speaker card she filled out said Oba Priest, but I've never met her. Thank God, she and the people she represents sided with us."

"That was lucky," she said as she stared at the woman, who was retreating from the room. "I'm glad, though, since there's still plenty to do in our name, especially since it'll be more than just taking crude out of the ground," she said, remembering what Kai had said on the subject when she and Frankie had considered quitting.

If she couldn't have love, she'd work on their legacy.

Oba walked out of the massive Palmer building on Laud's arm. Queen Galen had insisted she go to not only vote their stock, but to see how the Palmers were doing. They had both agreed something was unfinished, especially when it came to Vivien Palmer.

"Are you ready to return, Priestess?" Laud said, scanning the area as they moved to the car. "Her majesty was adamant you take your time, but we're ready to sail if there's nothing else."

"I need you to get me back to the capital as soon as possible, thank you."

The driver took them to the city south of New Orleans and dropped them at the top of the levee with only the wide river on the other side. They waited until they were alone before walking to the water's edge and swimming out to the large military transport Laud had insisted on.

She meditated on the trip back, concentrating on how wrong she'd been when she'd talked to Kai right before she left on her mission. She'd been so far off she was prepared to offer Galen her resignation after they returned.

"My Queen," she said as she dropped to her knees when she made it to the throne room. Galen still appeared thinner and paler after everything that had happened, and she took the blame for her distress. "I beg your forgiveness."

"For what?" Galen asked.

"I interpreted what the orb showed me one way, convinced that's what would come about, but I was wrong for not expanding what could have been." She stayed on her knees even after Galen had signaled for her to rise.

"Will this mistake have brought back my child?" Galen's obvious fatigue seemed to come from sadness. Oba was surprised Hadley wasn't at Galen's side, which had been the norm, even more so now.

"Highness, will you walk with me and I'll answer your question?"

She reached for Galen's hand, glad the queen didn't shun the offer. They strolled through the wide corridors to the private section of the palace. The door to Kai's room was open, and she saw Hadley sitting in front of the large windows with a book, but her attention seemed to be on the view outside. The sun had set, so the only light in the room was the lamp over Hadley's head.

"Hey," Galen said, and Hadley sprang to her feet and turned around. "Oba's back."

"How'd it go?" The question was almost a whisper tinged with pain, and it made Oba close her eyes. That Kai was here at all was reason to give thanks, but it was painful to see Kai hurt.

The day Kai came home unresponsive, Oba had never seen Galen and Hadley so distraught. From that moment neither of them had been too far away from their child. It had taken a week for Kai to open her eyes, but they were all thankful Kai had followed her training and put on her uniform under her street clothes that last day in New Orleans.

The blast Steve had gotten off before Kai killed him had come close to crushing her chest, but the suit had done its job and she was still alive. It would take the medical team another week before Kai was completely healed, but she'd stubbornly refused the pain-management procedures.

"The board makeup is due for another vote in a month, and Mr. Palmer is in charge again. The percentage of stock the realm holds in trust was enough to sway those people in attendance."

Kai looked at Oba, who sat on the end of the bed, finding none of the familiar feelings she'd had for so long. She steeled herself to not show pain, but she needed to take a deep breath. "And Vivien?" she asked. That question hurt more than her broken bones.

"The vision of your battle seems to dominate her thoughts, and she has no outlet for the pain," Oba said, and Kai was grateful for the truth. "She also questions herself when it comes to those memories and finds the truth of it all hard to accept."

"We received a transmission from Sol, and he seemed to be fishing," Galen said. Kai doubted she was purposely trying to change the subject for no reason. "He didn't come out and say it, but I believe Steve really was his son. However, we don't know yet if we got all the people who made the voyage with him. Until we do, I plan to keep security around Vivien, since Steve made her and her family targets for retaliation."

"What did he want with Palmer Oil?" she asked.

"To take it over as a stepping stone to other oil companies. Disrupting the flow of oil was the easiest way to create worldwide chaos, making it easy for an invading force to gain victory," Hadley said. "That's what we know so far, after a few sessions with Tanice Themis."

"We need to put more people on Vivien Palmer," Oba said, her tears silently tracking down her face.

"Why?" she said and sat up despite the pain. Then Oba told her, and she fell back just like she'd been shot with another blast to the heart.

❖

"You don't have to talk about it if you don't want to, but at least tell me I'm not crazy." Vivien curled up on the deck her grandparents had built to accommodate Frankie's chair. The trip to their childhood haunt had been his idea, and their parents had totally agreed.

"Viv," he said, reaching for her hand, "just like that day here, I know what I saw and you're not crazy. I do, though, know how you felt about her, so I didn't say anything because I didn't want to add to what you were going through. I'm sorry if that hurt you more." He shook his head and held her hand tighter. "Maybe I also thought I was a little nuts. I have no reference for what I was looking at."

He was right, but it didn't change what they'd witnessed. "You have to promise not to freak out, but I have to tell you something." All that flew from her mind when she peered out over the water. Two large fins broke the surface and circled slowly. Her childhood nightmare came rushing back, only this time she wasn't afraid.

"Don't get too close," Frankie yelled when she stood and walked to the waterline.

She covered her mouth to hold back the sob when the rest of her memory played out. "Oh, my God."

There was a break in the wave, and there Kai stood, waist deep, and seemed to hesitate. "I'm sorry," she said.

The sharks didn't matter as she moved into Kai's arms as fast as she could manage it without falling on her face. "Thank God you're not dead," she said as she ran her hands along Kai's chest and face. "Why did you stay away? Damn you, did you have any idea what this was doing to me?"

"I know, and I have so much to tell you, but I ask your forgiveness for so many things." Kai cupped her face in her hands and her world righted.

"It was you that day, wasn't it?" The blue wetsuit was the same but a little different in that more symbols were attached to the sleeves. "You know what I'm talking about."

"I do, and yes," Kai said and held her close when the sharks swam up and bumped her side. They were massive great whites but Vivien didn't panic, so perhaps she *was* going crazy. "These are Ivan and Ram, and they're sorry too for scaring you all those years ago," Kai said, then clicked her tongue and immediately the two backed away. "Go play but be good."

"Please don't leave me." She clung to Kai, knowing in her gut that if Kai turned around and dove in, she'd be gone for good. She couldn't guess what Kai was, but she was different in a special way.

"We need to talk, but you have to understand who I am before you ask me to stay with you." Kai led her to the deck and let her hands go so she could squat next to Frankie's chair. "Hello, Franklin." Kai took his hands. "Do you remember me?"

"It's you, isn't it? We never forgot you," he said, and Vivien choked back her emotions when Frankie started crying.

"It's me, and this was my gift to you." Kai reached in his T-shirt and took hold of his shell. "Close your eyes," Kai said as he did the same, and whatever happened next made Frankie cry harder. "Do you remember that?"

"Yes, and if it was you—just thank you is all I can say."

"I tried making up for my mistakes when I came back, but I fell considerably short in erasing all the pain I caused. Because of what happened, I've been granted permission to give you a gift that might make a dent in my debt." Kai let go of his shell and took his other hand. "Do you trust me even if you have no reason to?"

"Yes," Frankie said as he leaned toward Kai and nodded as if Kai had asked him a question.

Kai stood and held her hand out to Vivien, and when she accepted it, Kai kissed her and put a thought into Vivien's mind. She gazed at Vivien to see if she understood and smiled at Vivien's expression of wonder. Her wounds were thankfully healed enough with their medical experts' procedures that sped up the timeline, but she still braced herself as she lifted Franklin from his chair.

"Don't be afraid," she said as she walked to the water's edge with Vivien right beside her. He stiffened when she entered the water, but the appearance of Isla and Talia seemed to take his mind off his nerves.

Talia injected something into his neck and he went limp in her arms, making it easy for Isla to put a respirator over his face. They took him from her and bowed slightly as they headed for deeper water.

"Will he be okay? I trust you, but he's terrified of the water," Vivien said as she leaned against her and took her hand.

"You have my word, but this time is for us. Are you ready?"

"I've been waiting for you since I was a little girl on this beach."

The room Vivien and Franklin shared as children had been remodeled after they'd inherited the house and changed it to make it easier for Frankie to move around. Vivien had taken out the twin beds and replaced them with an antique sleigh bed that now faced the window. At night she still enjoyed listening to the surf and dreaming about the life she wanted.

"Are you okay?" she asked Kai, thinking it was a dream seeing her standing by the windows. "Whatever Steve did to you looked dangerous."

"Steve will never be a problem to you and your family, but we'll get to that. Are *you* okay? How are you feeling?" Kai asked, but her eyes had dropped to her midsection.

"You know, don't you?" The answer to the greatest mystery she'd ever faced alone was right there in front of her.

"That you're pregnant? Yes, and I hope you're not too upset about that reality."

"I've always been sure that I didn't want children, but this baby, it's yours, isn't it?" It was a crazy question, but it had to be true because Kai had been the only one. To believe anything else was too disturbing for something she was truly happy about.

"When I came to work for your father I never imagined falling in love with his daughter, especially since she was a woman I'd met before as a child." Kai explained the significance of the shells. "To my people they're a conduit to so many things, especially when they find their life mate. My heart soared when I realized that's who you are to me, but the sharing shouldn't have worked."

"Your people? The sharing, what does that mean?" Vivien asked, willingly following when Kai moved to the bed. "Where exactly are you from?"

"You have to keep an open mind, but I'm from Atlantis."

"I'm guessing you don't mean the resort in the islands, do you?" Kai shook her head. "The lost city of Atlantis, really?"

"It's right where it's been for thousands of years, so it's not lost to us. The spot near Greece that was written about was probably the last humans we worked closely with, and its destruction came about when they used powers they had very little knowledge about." She sighed at the thought of so many deaths.

"It was too long ago for it to have been your fault, sweetheart," Vivien said, and Kai laughed at how easily she'd read her mind.

This was a glimpse of what her mothers must experience. "No, but it's sobering to think about. Ever since that event we've gone to the depths to protect our secrets, a job made interesting by people like you," she said, tapping the tip of Vivien's nose.

"How did you get here?" Vivien asked, and Kai was grateful for the questions. It beat having to calm down a hysterical Vivien, which she wouldn't have blamed her for being. So as concisely as she could, she gave Vivien a history lesson on their civilization, starting with Queen Nessa, and their ongoing battle with their home planet. "I knew there was something bizarre about that bastard Steve."

"It's one reason my mothers allowed me to return, aside from your current condition. When I revealed myself to you and Franklin when we were children, my mothers weren't thrilled, but my error was the basis for stumbling onto the boxes on Triton and discovering Steve's plot."

"Can you stay with me?" Vivien asked, lying back and pulling her down with her. "I don't want to go through this alone."

"First, you have to know I love you," she said, taking time to savor their first real kiss since their reunion. "That first day we made love, the shells made a connection that started the sharing, and when the conditions are right, it creates life. You have to know that it wouldn't have happened if, in my heart, I didn't totally believe you are the woman who owns my soul. This child of ours is a wonder that I can't wait to share with you."

"I love you too," Vivien said as she wrapped her arms around her neck. "From that first day we went swimming, I thought you were perfect for me. I never thought that would be possible for me."

"Thank you," she said, and her shell along with the rest of her grew warm. "I want to be with you, to formalize our bond, but you have to understand the sacrifice that might require of you."

"What sacrifice?" Vivien finally sounded wary.

"I'm not simply a citizen of Atlantis—I'm the heir to its throne. My mother Galen is the reigning queen. I cannot abandon my people and leave the realm in chaos. To join with me requires simply that— for you to join me. Just like the shells combined to make the baby that grows within you, the shells knew before us that we belong together."

"I want that more than anything, but can I come back to see Frankie, or will he and my family be forbidden to know where I've gone?"

"I'd never deny you seeing Franklin, my love." She kissed Vivien again and placed her hand over her lower abdomen. "Besides, I have a lot invested in this part of the world, including Palmer Oil, so we'll return regularly."

"You're the mystery stockholder who voted for my father?"

"He deserved a second chance, and eventually you'll see that a lot of his behavior wasn't in his control." She moved her hand lower, and Vivien's legs spread slightly apart.

"We have a lifetime of talk, but right now I need to feel you."

Kai stood long enough to remove her uniform and helped Vivien out of her swimsuit. When their skin touched she thought it was too good to be true, but Oba had explained it best. The old prophecy was right in that she chose differently than the path she'd been expected to take and it would change their world forever. Her heirs would have a place in both the human world and their own. The balance would, in her opinion, make them great rulers when it was their turn.

"I love you, Vivien Palmer, and I will for the rest of time," she said as she started to touch Vivien, only this time she opened her heart and mind to her. When Vivien gazed at her in wonder, Kai knew her life would never be perfect in anything but this. Vivien was hers, and she would give her the strength to face whatever came next.

❖

At sunrise a month later, Kai led Vivien back to the water and held her as different shades of pink colored the morning sky. She pointed to the ripples in the dead-calm water and released Vivien so she could fully enjoy what was coming.

"Where are you going?" Vivien asked when she took a step back. Kai pointed to the water again, then waved.

"Viv," Franklin said.

Vivien stood motionless as she stared at Frankie, and the wonder on her face would be a sight Kai would cherish always. "Even when you were in that chair I knew you'd be this tall," Vivien said softly.

Franklin stood in water to his knees, and Kai could tell he was a little shell-shocked that the legs he'd been born with along with his lower spine had been replaced with perfectly healthy parts that had been grown in their labs just for him. The healing process would take a few more weeks, but she knew the doctors liked movement as a way for all the nerves and muscle to bond to their new host.

He hugged Vivien first but didn't leave her out. Like the day Kai had returned, he cried as he put his arms around her. "I can never repay you for this, but I can simply ask if I have anything in my power to give you."

"Just one thing, learn to swim," she said, patting him on the back. "Your niece will want to share the water with you." She reached down and found another shell and handed it to him. "Feel free to keep the shell I gifted you with before, but you must swear to never remove this one." Like before, she rubbed her hands together and spoke the ancient words with a slight addition. The lines she carved on the new stone were vastly different because they contained the marking from the old and the new necessary ones.

"Will this change my relationship with Vivien?" he said, accepting her new gift.

"The old lines are there, but the new ones will block the memory of your chair from anyone who knows you. The technology that fixed you doesn't exist anywhere on the planet, so it will keep your secrets safe. It'll also block your mind from everyone except Vivien and me." She placed it around his neck, leaving the old one for him to decide what to do with. "Now make your distant memory a reality."

He laughed as he ran down the beach with Vivien chasing him. Kai looked forward to what the future held and, more importantly, what her past had gifted her with. That day Oba had said it was part of her destiny to come out of the water, and now it was time to enjoy what that chance meeting would bring to her life.

Down the beach, Vivien stopped and turned to look back with her hand out. Kai ran and caught up, needing Vivien close. Together they'd find a way to make a happy life.

"I love you," she said as Vivien placed her hand over her heart.

"I love you, and thank you for finding me," Vivien said, resting her cheek against her chest as if needing the closeness. "I was right when I told my father a woman ruled the waters, and now I belong to her."

"One day you'll rule with me, and the secrets that lie beneath the waves will belong to you as wholly as my heart and love do."

About the Author

Ali Vali is originally from Cuba and has frequently used many of her family's traditions and language in her stories. Having her father read adventure stories and poetry before bed as a child infused her with a love of reading, which is even stronger today. In 2000, Ali decided to embark on a new path and started writing.

Ali lives in the suburbs of New Orleans with her partner of thirty-one years, and finds that residing in such an historically rich area provides plenty of material to draw from in creating her novels and short stories. Mixing imagination with different life experiences makes it easier to create the slew of characters that are engaging to the reader on many levels.

Books Available from Bold Strokes Books

A Reluctant Enterprise by Gun Brooke. When two women grow up learning nothing but distrust, unworthiness, and abandonment, it's no wonder they are apprehensive and fearful when an overwhelming love just won't be denied. (978-1-62639-500-8)

Above the Law by Carsen Taite. Love is the last thing on Agent Dale Nelson's mind, but reporter Lindsey Ryan's investigation could change the way she sees everything—her career, her past, and her future. (978-1-62639-558-9)

Actual Stop by Kara A. McLeod. When Special Agent Ryan O'Connor's present collides abruptly with her past, shots are fired, and the course of her life is irrevocably altered. (978-1-62639-675-3)

Embracing the Dawn by Jeannie Levig. When ex-con Jinx Tanner and business executive E. J. Bastien awaken after a one-night stand to find their lives inextricably entangled, love has its work cut out for it. (978-1-62639-576-3)

Jane's World by Paige Braddock. Jane's PayBuddy account gets hacked and she inadvertently purchases a mail order bride from the Eastern Block. (978-1-62639-494-0)

Love's Redemption by Donna K. Ford. For ex-convict Rhea Daniels and ex-priest Morgan Scott, redemption lies in the thin line between right and wrong. (978-1-62639-673-9)

The Shewstone by Jane Fletcher. The prophetic Shewstone is in Eawynn's care, but unfortunately for her, Matt is coming to steal it. (978-1-62639-554-1)

A Touch of Temptation by Julie Blair. Recent law school graduate Kate Dawson's ordained path to the perfect life gets thrown off course when handsome butch top Chris Brent initiates her to sexual pleasure. (978-1-62639-488-9)

Beneath the Waves by Ali Vali. Kai Merlin and Vivien Palmer love the water and the secrets trapped in the depths, but if Kai gives in to her feelings, it might come at a cost to her entire realm. (978-1-62639-609-8)

Girls on Campus edited by Sandy Lowe and Stacia Seaman. College: four years when rules are made to be broken. This collection is required reading for anyone looking to earn an A in sex ed. (978-1-62639-733-0)

Heart of the Pack by Jenny Frame. Human Selena Miller falls for the domineering Caden Wolfgang, but will their love survive Selena learning the Wolfgangs are werewolves? (978-1-62639-566-4)

Miss Match by Fiona Riley. Matchmaker Samantha Monteiro makes the impossible possible for everyone but herself. Is mysterious dancer Lucinda Moss her own perfect match? (978-1-62639-574-9)

Paladins of the Storm Lord by Barbara Ann Wright. Lieutenant Cordelia Ross must choose between duty and honor when a man with godlike powers forces her soldiers to provoke an alien threat. (978-1-62639-604-3)

Taking a Gamble by P.J. Trebelhorn. Storage auction buyer Cassidy Holmes and postal worker Erica Jacobs want different things out of life, but taking a gamble on love might prove lucky for them both. (978-1-62639-542-8)

The Copper Egg by Catherine Friend. Archeologist Claire Adams wants to find the buried treasure in Peru. Her ex, Sochi Castillo, wants to steal it. The last thing either of them wants is to still be in love. (978-1-62639-613-5)

The Iron Phoenix by Rebecca Harwell. Seventeen-year-old Nadya must master her unusual powers to stop a killer, prevent civil war, and rescue the girl she loves, while storms ravage her island city. (978-1-62639-744-6)

A Reunion to Remember by TJ Thomas. Reunited after a decade, Jo Adams and Rhonda Black must navigate a significant age difference, family dynamics, and their own desires and fears to explore an opportunity for love. (978-1-62639-534-3)

Built to Last by Aurora Rey. When Professor Olivia Bennett hires contractor Joss Bauer to restore her dilapidated farmhouse, she learns her heart, as much as her house, is in need of a renovation. (978-1-62639-552-7)

Capsized by Julie Cannon. What happens when a woman turns your life completely upside down? (978-1-62639-479-7)

Girls With Guns by Ali Vali, Carsen Taite, and Michelle Grubb. Three stories by three talented crime writers—Carsen Taite, Ali Vali, and Michelle Grubb—each packing her own special brand of heat. (978-1-62639-585-5)

Heartscapes by MJ Williamz. Will Odette ever recover her memory or is Jesse condemned to remember their love alone? (978-1-62639-532-9)

Murder on the Rocks by Clara Nipper. Detective Jill Rogers lives with two things on her mind: sex and murder. While an ice storm cripples Tulsa, two things stand in Jill's way: her lover and the DA. (978-1-62639-600-5)

Necromantia by Sheri Lewis Wohl. When seeing dead people is more than a movie tagline. (978-1-62639-611-1)

Salvation by I. Beacham. Claire's long-term partner now hates her, for all the wrong reasons, and she sees no future until she meets Regan, who challenges her to face the truth and find love. (978-1-62639-548-0)

Trigger by Jessica Webb. Dr. Kate Morrison races to discover how to defuse human bombs while learning to trust her increasingly strong feelings for the lead investigator, Sergeant Andy Wyles. (978-1-62639-669-2)

24/7 by Yolanda Wallace. When the trip of a lifetime becomes a pitched battle between life and death, will anyone survive? (978-1-62639-6-197)

A Return to Arms by Sheree Greer. When a police shooting makes national headlines, activists Folami and Toya struggle to balance their relationship and political allegiances, a struggle intensified after a fiery young artist enters their lives. (978-1-62639-6-814)

After the Fire by Emily Smith. Paramedic Connor Haus is convinced her time for love has come and gone, but when firefighter Logan Curtis comes into town, she learns it may not be too late after all. (978-1-62639-6-524)

Dian's Ghost by Justine Saracen. The road to genocide is paved with good intentions. (978-1-62639-5-947)

Fortunate Sum by M. Ullrich. Financial advisor Catherine Carter lives a calculated life, but after a collision with spunky Imogene Harris (her latest client) and unsolicited predictions, Catherine finds herself facing an unexpected variable: Love. (978-1-62639-5-305)

Soul to Keep by Rebekah Weatherspoon. What *won't* a vampire do for love… (978-1-62639-6-166)

When I Knew You by KE Payne. Eight letters, three friends, two lovers, one secret. Can the past ever be forgiven? (978-1-62639-5-626)

Wild Shores by Radclyffe. Can two women on opposite sides of an oil spill find a way to save both a wildlife sanctuary and their hearts? (978-1-62639-6-456)

Love on Tap by Karis Walsh. Beer and romance are brewing for Tace Lomond when archaeologist Berit Katsaros comes into her life. (987-1-62639-564-0)

Love on the Red Rocks by Lisa Moreau. An unexpected romance at a lesbian resort forces Malley to face her greatest fears where she must choose between playing it safe or taking a chance at true happiness. (987-1-62639-660-9)

Tracker and the Spy by D. Jackson Leigh. There are lessons for all when Captain Tanisha is assigned untried pyro Kyle and a lovesick dragon horse for a mission to track the leader of a dangerous cult. (987-1-62639-448-3)

Whirlwind Romance by Kris Bryant. Will chasing the girl break Tristan's heart or give her something she's never had before? (987-1-62639-581-7)

Whiskey Sunrise by Missouri Vaun. Culture and religion collide when Lovey Porter, daughter of a local Baptist minister, falls for the handsome thrill-seeking moonshine runner, Royal Duval. (987-1-62639-519-0)

Dyre: By Moon's Light by Rachel E. Bailey. A young werewolf, Des, guards the aging leader of all the Packs: the Dyre. Stable employment—nice work, if you can get it…at least until silver bullets start to fly. (978-1-62639-6-623)

Fragile Wings by Rebecca S. Buck. In Roaring Twenties London, can Evelyn Hopkins find love with Jos Singleton or will the scars of the Great War crush her dreams? (978-1-62639-5-466)

Live and Love Again by Jan Gayle. Jessica Whitney could be Sarah Jarret's second chance at love, but their differences and Sarah's grief continue to come between their budding relationship. (978-1-62639-5-176)

Starstruck by Lesley Davis. Actress Cassidy Hayes and writer Aiden Darrow find out the hard way not all life-threatening drama is confined to the TV screen or the pages of a manuscript. (978-1-62639-5-237)